Also by Stuart Stevens

The Last Season

*The Big Enchilada: Campaign Adventures with the Cockeyed
Optimists from Texas Who Won the Biggest Prize in Politics*

Feeding Frenzy: Across Europe in Search of the Perfect Meal

Scorched Earth: A Political Love Story

Malaria Dreams: An African Adventure

*Night Train to Turkistan: Modern Adventures Along
China's Ancient Silk Road*

The Innocent Have Nothing to Fear

The Innocent Have

★ ★ ★

Nothing to Fear

STUART STEVENS

Alfred A. Knopf New York 2016

THIS IS A BORZOI BOOK PUBLISHED BY ALFRED A. KNOPF

Copyright © 2016 by Stuart Stevens

Library of Congress Cataloging-in-Publication Data
Names: Stevens, Stuart, author.
Title: The innocent have nothing to fear : a novel / Stuart Stevens.
Description: First edition. | New York : Alfred A. Knopf, 2016.
Identifiers: LCCN 2015049144 | ISBN 9780451493194 (hardcover) |
ISBN 9780451493200 (ebook)
Subjects: LCSH: Political fiction. | BISAC: FICTION / Humorous. |
FICTION / Political. | FICTION / Satire.
Classification: LCC PS3569.T4532 I56 2016 | DDC 813/.54—dc23
LC record available at http://lccn.loc.gov/2015049144

Jacket design by Oliver Munday

Manufactured in the United States of America
First Edition

For Bill Janklow,
one of the great ones who always made me laugh

A week is a long time in politics.

—SIR HAROLD WILSON

The Innocent Have Nothing to Fear

Prologue

IT WAS HOT IN THE BROADCAST TRUCK. The climate control system that would have kept the electronics at an even sixty-five degrees should have been replaced months ago, but dollars were tight at the network, like everywhere, and it had fallen on the in-house mechanics to keep it going. Which might have worked—they were great mechanics—if they hadn't been on a work slowdown to protest the wage decreases that the network was trying to negotiate. With ad revenues down almost forty percent, everybody was taking a beating, even the on-air, big-name talent.

Dan Huang, the senior video operator, pressed the large red RECORD button on the digital Sony deck before the president entered the Oval Office. The crew was still fussing with the lights and the exact camera angle, but Huang didn't want to take any chances. When Nixon had resigned, the tape operator had bootlegged ten minutes of footage of Nixon ranting about how Kissinger had plotted against him before his resignation speech and had made a cool $100,000, or so everyone said, selling it to Kissinger world to keep it quiet. Dan Huang's $38-an-hour salary plus benefits had shrunk to $25 and a whole lot fewer benefits in the eighteen months since the world went crazy, and he liked the sound of $100,000. He was sure the market would come back, and with the Dow at around 9,500, a bargain wasn't hard to come by. Huang particularly liked the looks of Micro-Com, one of dozens of companies that had sprung up after the government finally broke up Google. A thirty-one-year-old Vietnamese guy, whose father was a distant cousin of Huang's, owned it. Most importantly, the kid was American born, so even with the most extreme anti-immigration measures floating around, he was safe. Not even Governor Armstrong George of Colorado, the fire-breather who was talking about running in a primary against the president, had plans to send back the children of naturalized citizens. Not yet, anyway.

"Can you believe that crap?" Eddie Sanchez nudged Dan and pointed out through the small porthole in the production truck toward Pennsylvania Avenue. They were parked across from the Corcoran Museum, just to the side of the White House. Through the large security fence, often compared to the one that Armstrong George wanted to build along the U.S.-Mexican border, they could see a glimpse of Lafayette Park, which was teeming with demonstrators. It had been like this almost every day since the surprise right-wing coup in China had seized control of the Shanghai, Shenzhen, and Hong Kong stock exchanges. That was like a 100-on-the-Richter-scale undersea earthquake creating a tsunami that washed across the international economic system.

The U.S. did better than most countries until the Chinese government called in the billions the U.S. owed China. That sent the market down another twenty percent, and some in Congress started to demand that the U.S. retaliate in any and every way possible, from slapping a fifty percent tariff on everything made

in China to military action. The president did what he could,
holding events with Silicon Valley tech workers whose jobs would
be lost if iPhones shot up in price. He called up the crazies in the
Republican Party who were talking about military action against
China's crazies. When *The Wall Street Journal* uncovered that
his vice president had sold stocks based on information from
intelligence briefings, the president demanded his resignation.
"No special deals," he thundered. Then he reached out to the
governor of Vermont, Hilda Smith, a squeaky-clean Republican of the old school, definitely not one of the crazies, for his
new vice president. But none of it really helped. The markets
kept going down, unemployment up, and it was all one perfect
nightmare.

"*Sí, señor,*" said Dan Huang, chuckling. "Stick with me. I'll
vouch for your work permit."

"Work permit, my ass," Sanchez muttered. "My daddy came
over from Havana in '61. That's like the goddamn *Mayflower*."

"*Sí, señor,*" Huang repeated.

"Fuck you," Sanchez said, without anger. The two spent a lot
of time together in the small truck.

"Hey," Huang said. "El Big Guy."

On their monitor they saw the president of the United States
entering the Oval Office with his longtime chief political consultant, a woman named Emily Lazar.

"What are you down for?" Sanchez asked.

"Reelect," Huang answered. "Good odds."

There was an office pool on what the president was going to
announce. The odds were three and a half to one that he resigned,
one to three that he announced for reelection.

"Reelect? Are you out of your mind?"

"Sí, señor."

"Fuck you. Look at that fat ass."

Inside the Oval Office, the president was arguing with Emily Lazar about where he was going to sit. He wanted to give the address from the edge of the desk. When he had first run for Congress, a million years ago, he had shot all his spots on the edge of a desk, looking straight at the camera. That was when he was a young real estate developer with a salesman's charm. And more than a hundred pounds lighter. In the one thousand four days he'd been in office, the president had gained a hundred and three pounds, an average of three-quarters of a pound per week. Someone had figured out that if he kept up this rate, he'd be pushing four-seventy-five at the start of his second term.

The president had once been a strikingly handsome man who radiated an intense energy of perpetual motion. He had been elected with a promise that he would "end the anguish caused by low wages and stagnant incomes." Now the once-vital figure had slowed to a ponderous waddle.

At the moment, it was up to Emily Lazar to explain to him that sitting behind the desk would result in a more pleasing angle. "This is great stuff," Dan Huang chuckled, turning up the volume of the microphones. They could hear the consultant, a woman in her early fifties, whispering to the network pool producer.

"He looks like Moby goddamn Dick washed up on that desk," she said, looking into the monitor that showed the president perched on the edge.

"Hey, he wants to do it in boxers, we'll shoot it." Jimmy Kovacks was sixty-four and had shot more than a half-dozen presidents.

"Can't you do something with the lighting?" Emily Lazar pleaded. "Bring down the key, maybe?" She was from North Carolina and had a pleasing drawl. It contrasted with her look, which was New York designer all the way. She was a formidable sight: almost six feet tall and always in a skirt that showed miles of legs. At UNC she had played basketball.

"Emily," Kovacks growled, "you got to be kidding me. Tell you what—we could kill all the lights and shoot it in the dark. That would help. But mass that size still glows."

"You're a big help." She sighed.

"I'm not in the help business. *You're* in the help business. I'm in the news business."

"You guys, you just love this, don't you? Country falling apart, but it's a hell of a story." She said it without rancor. They knew each other well.

"Yeah," Kovacks agreed, "I particularly liked it when my shares in the profit-sharing plan fell seventy-six percent. That was a hell of a story. I hated the idea of retiring anyway."

"We going to run through this or what?" the president asked. He had been quietly staring into a blank space, like a survivor of a long and brutal battle.

"Mr. President," Emily said, moving across the Oval Office, all legs and heels, "I'm thinking it would look more presidential if you sat behind the desk."

"You used to hate that. You said I looked like an insurance salesman."

"This is different," she cooed, leaning over to straighten his tie. Everyone knew they had been sleeping together for years.

"Why is it different?" he asked, but there was no fight in his voice. He stood up in front of the desk, facing the camera in a full-body shot.

"Jesus, Mary, and Joseph." Eddie Sanchez whistled in the control van. "He's bigger than this truck."

It was a full-on body shot, an angle that was rarely seen these days, as the White House did everything it could to hide the president behind condominium-sized podiums. The president turned and waddled to the high-backed chair behind his desk. His suit was wrinkled and there were dark spots of sweat on his massive back.

"Flop sweat," Dan Huang noted. "Sweated right through his suit."

"And you still like reelect? This guy is a train wreck."

"I liked the odds," Huang said, wondering if he had made the wrong bet. This fellow did look pretty bad. "Hey," he said. "Say he doesn't run, you want some action on Armstrong George against the ice queen vice president?"

"Are you kidding me? Armstrong George will goddamn kill that woman. Hilda Smith? An appointed vice president from Vermont? She's gonna beat the fire-breather of the Rockies? Hell, I'll take that action, you bet."

"Just kidding," Huang assured him, backing away quickly. Sanchez was probably right. What kind of chance would Hilda Smith have against a guy like Governor Armstrong George?

"Look at that slob," Sanchez hooted, tapping on the monitor. "He swallowed the air hose. He's going to explode."

They both laughed. They knew that Jimmy Kovacks was trying to make the president look as bad as possible. He held him personally responsible for ruining his plans to take early retirement and move lock, stock, and barrel to his place in the Poconos. Now his pension plan was in the tank and his house in Queens was worth less than what he had paid for it thirty years earlier. If you could even find anybody who wanted to buy it. With all the anti-immigration fever sweeping the country, Queens, which had more Hispanics and Asians than what Armstrong George called "real Americans," was losing population every week. The only government agency that had its budget tripled even during the worst of the financial collapse was Immigration and Naturalization. And as if their green-uniformed sweeps weren't bad enough, there was the threat of the roving "Americans for America" gangs that liked to descend on neighborhoods, making what they called "citizens' arrests."

"My fellow Americans," the president began, "these are difficult days in our nation's history. Never before have we needed leadership as we do today. That's why I have decided that I must ask for your continued support. I intend to run for reelection as president of the United States—"

"Yes!" Huang shouted. "Thank you, baby!"

The president stopped his rehearsal and looked down mournfully at the speech draft in front of him. He slowly put it into a drawer and focused on the draft he knew he had to give.

"You ready?" Emily Lazar asked gently. "We have time for one run-through."

He nodded and began the speech where he had broken off. "It is clear that our country needs new leadership like rarely before in our nation's history. Therefore, I have determined not to seek or accept the nomination of my party for president of the United States. I will not run for reelection in the upcoming election."

"Son of a bitch," Huang muttered, wiping sweat off his forehead. It must have been ninety-five degrees inside the control truck.

"I have done my best in a difficult time," the president said.

"What about my stock!" Sanchez shouted at the monitor. "You fat moron! I was vested at seventy-eight! It's six now! Six!"

Chapter
★
One

IT WAS THE HEAT EVERYONE NOTICED FIRST when they got off the plane. Then it was the smell of garbage.

Welcome to my hometown. America's favorite party town.

Broke, full of garbage, half the city on strike, twenty-nine percent unemployment, the highest murder rate in the civilized world (if the adjective fits), a leader in kidney disease and strange tropical maladies normally found in the slums of Mumbai, a town so corrupt that even a casino went bankrupt before it opened because the politicians were so greedy they couldn't wait to steal it all.

Welcome to New Orleans.

Mayor Simmons had promised that if the Republican National Convention came to New Orleans, he'd scrub the city like his mama's kitchen. Even though he was a Democrat, he understood what the convention money would mean for a very broke city. Everybody on the Site Selection Committee had said they were very impressed, but of course they weren't thinking about silly things like cleanliness and sanitation when they picked New Orleans. Hell no. At a time when half the country was convinced that the nation was in a depression and the other half was hoping it was only the worst recession in fifty years, with a president so shell-shocked he wasn't running for reelection and a disgraced vice president forced to resign, the honorable men and women of the Republican Party Site Selection Committee knew they had to keep their focus on the important elements of a successful convention: a massive and ready supply of sex and alcohol and a local culture that made it damn near imperative that you take advantage of both at every opportunity.

New Orleans was a city still in crisis after Katrina and the Crash, and the Republicans on the selection committee could claim with a straight face that they were picking the city as a show of support in the "great city's difficult days." Never mind that was true of just about every city in America these days, but with New Orleans you could also pretend it was such a fascinating place—so quaint, so Old World, such a cultural jambalaya, wasn't it? When the Site Selection Committee came to New Orleans and the mayor greeted them at Louis Armstrong Airport with the Second Line Jazz Band and took them straight to Antoine's and a private room, where they marveled at the waiters who could remember every order and never write down a word, well, the deal was just about done. Everybody had "Huîtres en coquille à la Rockefeller"—Oysters Rockefeller, a dish the restaurant had created in 1899 and named not because John D. Rockefeller liked the dish but because he was rich and so was the sauce.

Then they wandered out on St. Louis Street and quickly found their way to Bourbon Street, and by sunrise there was little doubt that the Republicans were coming to New Orleans. To show solidarity with the great American city that had suffered so much. Of course.

The Site Selection Committee had visited in December when the city was just cool enough not to smell, but now it stunk like a big pot of gumbo that had been rotting in the heat for several weeks. It had been over a hundred degrees every day for more than a month with ninety percent humidity, the hottest summer in a century. Didn't Democrats warn us about global warming? This was a climate invented to make garbage smell in a hurry, and the stench brought tears to your eyes. A fierce run on scented candles had driven prices up and more incense had been sold in the city since Ravi Shankar played a three-day concert in 1968 at the Warehouse.

As if to deliberately torture Republicans for their troubled history with labor unions, the whole city seemed to be on strike: the cabdrivers, the teachers, even the cops were threatening to walk out. Everybody saw the Republican convention as their big chance to cash in, to embarrass the city into coughing up more pay to avoid ruining a moment of glory.

But that only worked if you could embarrass the city, and so far, God bless him, Mayor Tom Simmons, the first white mayor of New Orleans in over two decades, gave a very good impression of not giving one good goddamn what anybody thought. What I loved about the guy was that he understood his market. He knew he didn't get elected to bring the city together; he wasn't the guy who was going to get everybody to join hands and sing "Kumbaya" out by Lake Pontchartrain at sunset. Hell no. He was elected to play the tough guy, the enforcer who was brought in to bring a little order to a place where cops were hiring themselves out as hit men in their off-hours. Nobody thought he was nice when they voted for him, and by God he hadn't let anybody down yet.

Simmons had become my personal hero when he was a state legislator and introduced a bill requiring every woman in New Orleans to carry a gun. This truly was a different kind of Democrat. The proposed legislation had followed a spate of particularly brutal carjackings of women at red lights. The bill hadn't passed, of course, but a compromise piece of legislation made it perfectly legal for any citizen to use deadly force against a carjacker. Within the first forty-eight hours, a twenty-one-year-old secretary blew the face off of one carjacker, and an eighty-one-year-old man shot another in the ass as the poor fellow tried to flee down Rampart Street after he saw Grandpa had a sawed-off shotgun under a huge muffuletta from Mandina's on the passenger seat. The elderly man was considered a local hero until two weeks later, when he walked into his stockbroker's office and put two twelve-gauge slugs into his young broker for not getting him out of Apple before the Crash. But then a lot of brokers were getting shot right after the Crash.

When it looked like the Site Selection Committee was leaning toward picking New Orleans, I'd done everything I could to squash the idea. Nobody could figure out why I was against it, and a lot of people thought I was just being modest. After all, I was a local hometown boy made good, the son of a famous civil rights journalist, which had double currency in the Republican Party, which was desperate for some credibility on that front. I'd be returning home in at least quasi-triumph, the guy who had saved Vice President Hilda Smith's campaign, brought her back from near death in New Hampshire to a few delegates shy of winning the nomination. I was helping beat back Governor Armstrong George and the barbarians at the gate, and everybody agreed my Pulitzer-winning father, Powell Callahan, would have been so proud. If only he hadn't drunk himself to death. No, they didn't say that. But I did, that and a whole lot more. New Orleans was the last place on earth I wanted to come back to. Yes, it was my hometown. People knew me there, had known me all my life. And that, of course, is why it terrified me so much.

It was thirty-six hours before the convention opened. A real convention, like the one everybody had been dying for since Al Smith won it on the thirty-sixth ballot in 1928 and Ford snatched it from Reagan in 1976. That was what a convention was supposed to be—a deliberative body, by God, not a made-for-television spectacle.

I hated it.

Any campaign manager would. It was a horrifying idea to roll into a convention and not have the entire process rigged gavel to gavel. This was simply unheard of. Leaving a decision as important as selecting a party's nominee to the collection of hungover party hacks, weirdo activists, political groupies, and small-timers who comprised the delegates at any convention was an affront to the very concept of modern politics, a process designed to ensure that a powerful few would manipulate a disinterested many. That's how the system worked; everybody knew that. This was America, for heaven's sake, where no one was particularly interested in parties—the political type, anyway—and everybody knew it didn't really matter who won. That was the genius of the American political system.

But this time, it did matter. The country was in crisis. The Republican Party had watched a president, nominated just four years earlier in a hail of glory and promise, melt like an ice cream cone on a New Orleans sidewalk. Now the party faced what was being called the most fundamentally different choice in its history: Governor Armstrong George or Vice President Hilda Smith. In politics we always like to call each election the most important in generations. This time, it might actually be true.

Faced with this crisis, the delegates and alternates and assorted hangers-on of the Republican convention were handling their responsibility in the time-honored fashion of conventions past: they took to the bars and clubs and partied like death-row inmates paroled for one night.

But who was I to complain? It was thirty-six hours before the convention opened and I was up onstage with a bunch of Indians stoned out of their minds. Not Native Americans, but the Mardi Gras Indians, one of those New Orleans bands that never broke big nationally but were local gods. The Indians were singing "Voodoo Sex," and Tyrone Robichoux, the lead, was leaning into me, sweating like a warm waterfall. He had a blank look in his eyes and I assumed that he was high on heroin. He usually was. Great headline: "J. D. CALLAHAN, CAMPAIGN MANAGER FOR VICE PRESIDENT HILDA SMITH, BUSTED FOR DRUGS AT CONVENTION." Now that would be just splendid. "Following his much-publicized personal difficulties surrounding the breakup of his relationship with prominent television journalist Sandra Juarez, J. D. Callahan added to his woes by being caught with the Mardi Gras Indians in a drug bust." Yes, that would be just perfect. I'd have to claim that I did it as part of a community-outreach campaign tactic, like "Building a bridge to the addicted community." It might work. This was, after all, New Orleans, where the town's resident cultural hero was a not-very-reformed heroin addict named Aaron Neville, who, when asked about his heroin addiction, remarked, "It works for me." And God knows the Indians were a diverse bunch. They probably had French, Spanish, African American, even a little Asian bouncing around in their drug-addled veins. And, yes, some Native American blood as well, the Chickasaw tribe most predominantly.

Appearing with the Indians at Tip's the night before the convention opened hadn't been my idea. Blame it on Ginny Tran, press secretary extraordinaire at twenty-seven. "It'll be so cool," she'd insisted. "The vice president's campaign manager onstage at Tipitina's. You were almost a rock star once, it'll be fabulous. Show that we're confident right before the convention. And anyway, you should get out. You look like crap." So I'd left our war room down at the Windsor Court Hotel and committed to doing something enjoyable for a couple of hours. It had been so long, I'd forgotten what it was like.

Ginny was lying, of course. At least that part about me being almost a rock star. I'm sure she wasn't lying that I looked like crap. I'd grown up in New Orleans and been a journeyman guitar player in a not-so-bad blues/funk band, my major distinction being that I was the only white guy in the group. What was really embarrassing—at least it would have been if anybody had known it—was that I'd made it into the band with the help of my father, Powell Callahan, one of the last white civil rights heroes, or so everyone seemed to believe. Powell Callahan knew everybody in town. The lead singer in the band was the son of a lawyer, once a civil rights lawyer, now a corporate hotshot just off Canal Street, an old friend of my father's from the "movement days." J. D. Callahan, the only guitarist who networked his way into a black/funk band. It was silly. They dumped me after a year.

Of course, I knew that a photo op with the Indians onstage at Tip's wasn't going to get us a single delegate, but I had gone along with it. Why not? It wouldn't hurt, and if it made me look a little hip and cool and confident, that was just great. God knows I sure didn't feel like any of those things. I hadn't slept worth a damn in months, I had a woman candidate who was on the verge of becoming unglued at any moment, a force of nature called Armstrong George about to devour us like a hungry wolf, and, to top it all off, they had to go and have the damn convention in my hometown. For Christ's sake, was God spending all of His time trying to screw with me, or just most of it?

On the other hand, if a woman named Sandra Juarez just happened to see me with the Indians up onstage looking like I had my act together in a big-time way, that was just fine by me. It had been a little over eighteen months since my very public meltdown, which had coincided with Sandra Juarez and me breaking up. No, that wasn't accurate: my very public meltdown that resulted from Sandra Juarez dumping me. I'd like to think I was over it, focused on the future, all those things you are supposed to do. But I still thought about her more than I liked to admit. Mostly I thought about how humiliated I had been after splitting in such a spectacularly public way, which had been my fault. But also I thought about—and this is what I really hated to admit—

how much I had loved being with her, living together for that year and a half.

Sandra was one of the few really good print reporters who had made the transition from covering politics for *The Wall Street Journal* to working for television. She was first-generation Mexican-Cuban American, an unusual mix. Her Cuban mother was a doctor and her Mexican father was an auto dealer. It wasn't exactly the hardscrabble immigrant story, but still, when she looked in the camera and said, "As a first-generation Mexican-Cuban American, I understand . . . ," few people stopped to point out that she had gone to Groton and then Harvard. We had met when Sandra was covering the Florida governor's race. She had already moved from the Orlando market to CNN but was back in her home state covering the race. We met in the spin room after the first debate; a less romantic, tawdrier place for a first encounter would be hard to imagine. My candidate was a Cuban American woman running against a wealthy North Florida businessman, and I made the mistake of trying to play the Cuban-and-female card with Sandra. It didn't go well.

"Don't you think Florida would benefit from having a Cuban American female as governor?" I asked.

She smiled very nicely and then took my head off: "So the best case you can make for your candidate is what she achieved before she was born? That is probably the most pathetic defense I've ever heard." Then she walked off. I did the only reasonable thing in this circumstance: I chased her and groveled. Not because she was beautiful and smart but because it was in my client's best interest. I told her I was an idiot and she was right and then spilled out all the policy reasons Roberta Bello was the best choice. She listened to all of it with a blank face, then said, "Thanks, not bad," and left. Her post-debate coverage was okay, not great. I sent her an email telling her I thought it was fantastic and to get in touch if I could help with anything else. Nothing works with any kind of reporters like flattery, since mostly they just get the crap beat out of them, but she ignored it.

A week after Roberta won, I was at CNN doing an on-air hit about the elections. I'd won every race I'd worked on that cycle and was feeling fairly bulletproof. It was the standard setup, where you show up for five minutes or so and try to sound smart, which for five minutes is usually not that hard. I ran into Sandra in the greenroom and she asked me if I was going to work for Roberta's administration, or for any of the other clients I'd elected. "God no. I don't do government. I hate government."

"Great," she said. "So no conflicts. Want to get a drink?" We spent every night together for the next 418 days, at least the nights when I wasn't traveling for clients or she wasn't out on the road. Until I was standing in the Piggly Wiggly grocery store in Baton Rouge, Louisiana, and saw the *National Enquirer* front-page story about her and That Actor Whose Name Shall Not Be Mentioned. It's one thing to get dumped by your girlfriend. It's another thing to get dumped by your girlfriend for a famous actor and hear about it standing in line at the Piggly Wiggly. I bought the *National Enquirer,* and when the nice lady behind the counter saw the photo, she said, "Lucky girl," and then I left before I killed her and was the next candidate for the death penalty in Louisiana, a place that doesn't need Armstrong George's New Bill of Rights to get the job done.

God, it was awful. And two days later I was dumb enough

not to cancel a scheduled slot on *Meet the Press* and ended up in a screaming match with some Democratic moron—a screaming match on *Meet the* goddamn *Press,* for crying out loud—and walked off the set, all live on national television. That was followed by an entire political cycle in which every candidate in America would have preferred to be photographed in a shirtless embrace with Vladimir Putin than hire me to run their campaigns. So yes, if playing part of a set with the Mardi Gras Indians the night before the Republican convention might make me look a little cool, or at least less pathetic, than the figure storming off *Meet the Press,* I was definitely willing to give it a go. In the back of my head I had a fantasy that Sandra would be sitting lonely in a hotel room and happen to tune in to some video clip of me and the Indians.

Right.

But the big moment, the magic one, would come if we could just get a half-dozen more delegates and pull Hilda Smith back from the dead. Then, at least for a few days, I'd be a genius. For a few days, I could forget about the horror show of Sandra. And on the side, I could finish cutting my deal to have my own political show. That was the plan: make this my last campaign and get famous as a pundit. After months of work, it was all lined up, if I could just pull off this come-from-behind miracle. All I had to do was beat back the forces of darkness and vanquish Armstrong George. Even if we lost to Democratic senator Tommy Aldrich in the general election, at least I would be hailed for doing what no one expected—saving Hilda Smith. The show was going on the new Amazon Channel, and since I'd gone to them with the idea, all neatly packaged, I'd been able to keep partial ownership of the show. That meant quasi-serious dollars if the show worked and we found an audience. The deal was already signed, but they had an out clause if Hilda lost the nomination.

But we wouldn't lose. I wouldn't let us lose.

The dance floor of Tip's was a mass of soaking-wet humanity bouncing up and down to the irresistible funk of the Indians. Except for Lisa Henderson, who stood on the side with a cool, detached look, too attractive to be a wallflower but definitely not of this crowd. She was dressed in the same dark suit she had been wearing all day and she looked like a corporate lawyer, which was what she had been before she was chief of staff to Hilda Smith, first as governor of Vermont and now as vice president. She had been a law student of Professor Smith's, and there when Hilda made her first run for the state house of representatives. And she had been by her side when she was sworn in as vice president, picked by the president after his first vice president became the first veep to resign since Spiro Agnew. Lisa hated me, and I didn't blame her a bit. She had been Smith's campaign manager until they came in third in Iowa and I'd made my move, knocking on the candidate's door in New Hampshire and convincing her she would lose if she didn't throw over her best friend and campaign manager. She was just terrified enough to do it, and when we won New Hampshire, I was back.

It was probably a very bad thing I had done, knocking on Hilda Smith's door. She was exhausted and beaten down in a way you only felt when your chance to become president of the United States was slipping away, but that was how I'd wanted her. Vulnerable. She said she'd give me a half hour, and that was all it took. Me and Eddie Basha—the best field operative in

America, in my book—had laid out exactly what she should do to win the New Hampshire primary. We had a simple strategy; it was amazing that Smith hadn't tried it before. For months Armstrong George had put her on the defensive and she'd responded by trying to prove she could match him in toughness without going down the crazy train of his wacky New Bill of Rights or the bundle of "anti-terror" legislation he was supporting called "Protect the Homeland." It had been and always would be a losing game. Those who wanted what Armstrong George was selling would never be satisfied with Hilda Smith being a more polite version of George. For once I could tell a client what she wanted to hear and still give the right political advice: she needed to stand and fight Armstrong George.

There was one more debate in New Hampshire before the primary, at WMUR, the posh TV station built with the fortunes spent on presidential dreams. "No matter what the first question is," I said to the vice president, while her husband looked quietly on, "you should say, 'I'll answer that in a minute. But first I have something to say to my opponent. Governor George, you are a disgrace. You have played to the worst instincts of our politics and tried to bully your way to the Oval Office. Tonight it stops. New Hampshire is better than Armstrong George. America is better than Armstrong George. Now I'll answer that question.' "

Hilda Smith had looked at me like a dying patient wondering if she'd been promised a miracle cure. "You think it will really work?" she asked.

"I don't know," I said. "I think it will. But if it doesn't, wouldn't you rather die with dignity?"

That was it. She hired Eddie and me on the spot. By that evening, every news outlet in America was carrying the story that Lisa Henderson had been dumped and J. D. Callahan, the controversial campaign strategist, had been tapped to take over Hilda Smith's campaign. And damned if it didn't turn things around in New Hampshire and a bunch of states that followed. Eddie still gives me a hard time about that line: "Wouldn't you rather die with dignity?" But hey, I thought it was pretty good.

It had been humiliating for Lisa, and I was a guy who had come to understand a thing or two about humiliation. That she had moved back into her position as chief of staff to Vice President Hilda Smith was hardly consoling. The paths to greater glory were rarely paved with chiefs of staff to vice presidents. Lisa Henderson had cried the night we won New Hampshire. Three hundred and twenty votes, but it was a win. I've often asked myself if she was crying because we had won, or crying because we hadn't lost and she knew I'd been proved right. And now we were only a handful of delegates short. If we won and Hilda Smith went on to become president, I didn't know if Lisa would forgive me or just hate me more.

From the stage, I could see the tall Secret Service agent whispering in Lisa Henderson's ear. The agent's name was Ernie Hawkins and I knew him well. He was a fanatical triathlete and liked to ask my advice on bicycle equipment and technique. Like most serious bike racers, I was convinced that triathletes were a bunch of idiots when it came to bikes, an opinion I didn't hesitate to share with him. Ernie was off duty and had come to Tipitina's to hear the Mardi Gras Indians and pick up women. That wouldn't be hard for him. Women loved Ernie—a certain kind of woman, at least. The kind who liked a guy who knew several exotic ways to kill people and had enough firepower lying around his apartment in Alexandria, Virginia, to start a small war.

Lisa Henderson scowled as Ernie whispered in her ear. Typical Lisa. Every other woman in New Orleans would be smiling like crazy if Ernie was that close but not Lisa. It was a subject of some speculation among staffers in the vice president's office that she had a secret life as a dominatrix. I hoped like hell it was true. Anything to make her seem more human. A guy could like a dominatrix. But liking Lisa, that was harder.

Then Ginny Tran appeared at the edge of the stage, looking rattled. I'd worked with Ginny since those first days in New Hampshire and couldn't remember ever seeing her look like this, even when every political expert in America thought we were running an expensive funeral and not a campaign. Something had to be bad wrong. Christ. I wondered if maybe Hilda had finally blown up at a reporter asking the same questions over and over. It wasn't easy being just a few delegates shy of winning a nomination, and the idea that you might lose to an idiot like Armstrong George didn't help. In the years I'd spent working with candidates, the one overwhelming lesson I'd learned was that even the best still had moments of terrible vulnerability. And waiting for a bunch of whack-job delegates to decide your fate was a pretty good definition of vulnerability.

None of the Indians noticed me sliding offstage, but they were so much into their own drug-enhanced world, they probably wouldn't have known it if their feet caught on fire. Which actually was one of their favorite closing-number tricks, something they did with the help of New Orleans's expansive fireworks industry. Ginny pulled me into the cramped wings. For a half second I wondered how she got backstage. At the convention, where everybody was crazed about security and prestige, access was everything. For a brief few days, who had what passes to what areas was more important than how much you made or how many years you had played in the NFL. CEOs were known to offer five thousand dollars cash to junior staffers for the passes hanging around their necks. But that's how it was in the bubble of the convention.

"We've got a problem." Ginny started right in. She was shouting over the sound of the Indians.

"Houston, a problem?" It was an inside campaign joke. Right after our tracking showed us coming in second to Armstrong George in New Hampshire with only four days to go, second being as bad as fourth after coming in third in Iowa, I'd had a late-night screening at our Manchester headquarters of *Apollo 13*. We were all giddy and exhausted, laughing and crying all the way through the movie, and came out with a screw-the-world game face that helped turn it around those last four days. That and Hilda Smith's kick-ass debate performance when she had finally shamed Armstrong George into going on the defensive. It showed us what Hilda Smith might be able to do, and the debate was like a light shining down a path to lead us out of the maze. That was also the night, right after *Apollo 13,* that Ginny and I slept together for the first time. It had all been her doing, too, which made it all the better. "I knew I wanted you before the campaign was over," she'd said that night, standing in the snow outside the Quality Inn that we all called the Low Quality End, "and since this campaign might be over in three days, I'd better get with it."

"Well, you're a goddamn optimist," I'd shot back, but didn't hesitate for a second. Going back to my first campaign, I'd lived by a rule of staying away from any campaign relationships, even the late-night, one-night campaign kind of sex that everybody went for at some point. But Ginny was beautiful and smart and twenty-six, and this was New Hampshire, for Christ's sake, and it looked like my comeback campaign was about to end before it really started. And the truth was, I hadn't slept with a woman since I'd been dumped by Sandra.

"A bomb went off," Ginny shouted over the Mardi Gras Indians. "In the French Quarter."

Ernie Hawkins ushered us past the cordon of flashing lights and what looked like half of the New Orleans Police Department. On the way down, Ernie told us what he knew: some kind of explosive device had detonated down in the Quarter. But instead of being filled with shrapnel, it had been filled with dye. Red dye.

"Dye?" I asked. It made no sense, and I was wondering if maybe I had some kind of hallucinogenic contact high from the Indians.

"Dye," Eddie said. "Like somebody was trying to play a joke. One woman was injured and is at the hospital. Nothing serious, but she was right next to it."

Drunken delegates still roamed the Quarter in a light, misting rain. Despite the moisture, it was almost a hundred degrees at three twenty in the morning. The television remotes were just setting up. The reporters giving stand-ups looked either exhausted or half-drunk, turned out of bed or bar. But who could blame them? No one was expecting a piece of juicy news like this to come down in the middle of the night.

"Saigon isn't this fucking humid," Ginny moaned as we followed Ernie's towering presence toward the entrance of Pat O'Brien's. "How did you live here?"

"It's not the humidity, it's the stupidity." That had been the unofficial slogan of my high school crowd in Metairie.

"No wonder you got the hell out of this place," she said, taking my hand lightly so I could tow her through the crowd.

"Darlin', you don't know the half of it," I quipped, but I was thinking about her hand, wondering if she was trying to send me some kind of signal. Which was very unlike Ginny. She usually delivered signals by more direct means, like, "What do you think, you want to have sex or what?"

"Hey, J.D., you behind this bullshit?" The question came from a tall man with a big shock of blond hair. He was wearing a trench coat and a blue blazer, holding a microphone.

"Jesus Christ, Hendricks," I said, looking him over, "you almost look like a real reporter."

"Ain't it grand, laddie?" Paul Hendricks lapsed into an Irish brogue. He was from Boston and liked to play the working-class kid from Southie. "So the rumor is"—he leaned down to whisper, his bright blue eyes flashing—"that you set this off trying to scare Armstrong George delegates to death."

"You are so pathetic, Hendricks," I answered evenly. I paused for a moment, then continued. "You know I'd never scare anybody. I'd just kill 'em."

Hendricks chuckled. "Hey," he said, "you like my look?" He

stepped back for a second, holding the lapels of his trench coat. "Feel like a real war correspondent, covering the Blitz or something cool like that."

"You look like a flasher with a free candy van in front of St. Aloysius grade school."

"I'm getting a live shot out of this, so screw you."

Paul Hendricks was one of those political operatives who had made the switch to journalism, if that's what you could call what he did. I suppose I'd have to call him a role model, which was a depressing thought. He wrote a column, hosted a weekly show on Fox, and popped up wherever a talking head was needed on politics. In a presidential year like this, in a tight race with a genuine real convention, Paul Hendricks seemed to be everywhere. We didn't really like each other, but we had that most common of political realities, a "useful" friendship. I'd leaked to him that our tracking polls showed Hilda making big moves with older voters in New Hampshire after the last debate, and when one of Eddie Basha's field reps found flyers in a GM plant parking lot near Toledo, Ohio, saying that Hilda Smith favored replacing union jobs with illegal aliens, we fed it to Hendricks and he ran with a story blaming the Armstrong George campaign for dirty tricks. I was never quite sure if one of Eddie's guys had planted the flyers, but hey, we won Toledo and we won the Ohio primary—if only by 1.8 percent.

Hendricks had carved out a nice niche for himself, but he didn't have his own show, a show that he partly owned. That was my game plan. If everything went smoothly, he would be part of my competition. I knew I could take him on the tube. Like most everyone in the media who pretended to know something about politics, Hendricks was basically a political amateur.

Sure, he had worked some races back in the day, but his commentary was like having an old player in the booth at the Super Bowl whose last contact with football was playing for a single-wing team. Me, I was the stud quarterback fresh from the pros, the guy who could sit in the booth and tell you what it was really like out there on the field, what the players grumbled to one another across the line, how it felt to score in the last second of a big game when everybody thought it was impossible. Sports was how I was going to cover politics.

"So, look," Hendricks said, turning serious, "you have any idea what the hell is going on? This make any sense to you? Delegates are going to be really freaked out."

I'd already heard from Eddie Basha that some of our delegates were talking about leaving town. Even if only a few of them jumped ship it could be a disaster. When you were down to fighting hand to hand, every delegate was precious. Any drop in our count could be seen as fatal and start a stampede of those who were only with you because they thought you would win, delegates rarely being profiles in courage.

"Jesus, you are a sick son of a bitch, Hendricks," I shot back. "How can you even think about delegate counts now?"

"Yeah," he sneered, "and you want to tell me what the hell you're doing here? You going to play detective? Give me a break. Hey, remember, the innocent have nothing to fear!" Hendricks laughed. That was the line that Armstrong George loved to use when asked if his New Bill of Rights went too far. *The innocent have nothing to fear.* He always said it with a certain smile. He was very good.

I started to say something back to Hendricks, but Ginny pushed me discreetly forward and we followed Ernie past the outer row of sawhorses and yellow tape into the cleared area where the bomb had exploded. There was red dye that looked like dirty blood and little pieces of a gym bag that had been holding the bomb. Somber-looking men in dark windbreakers labeled FBI and NOPD BOMB SQUAD milled around as if waiting for something else to happen.

"We got the locals, the Service, the FBI, the ATF," Ernie ticked off. "Just your typical law enforcement goat rope." This was what had become known since September 11, 2001, as "A Unified Response." It was the standard procedure for every big public event, from the Super Bowl to NASCAR races. And political conventions. "Well now," Ernie said, "lookie here. We've even got the son of the great man himself. Somerfield George, in the house." Ernie nodded to a scrum of reporters and Secret Service agents moving our way. At the center, a blond, absurdly handsome head had the "concerned but not panicked" look that the best politicians adopt naturally. "You going to say howdy?" Ernie joked.

That was exactly what I intended to do. I couldn't let Somerfield George be this close and not engage. It would make me look . . . weak. And if I looked weak, Hilda Smith looked weak, and there were reporters everywhere. Okay, who was I kidding? If I looked weak, I looked like a loser, and my own image was what really mattered. I made my way through the crowd, Ginny trailing. "Paging Major Shit Storm J.D.," she said in a low voice, but I knew she'd be enjoying it. She loved confrontation.

About five feet away, the big handsome head turned my way and our eyes locked. He glared at me for a split second before a smile broke out and his eyes seemed to warm. It was like watching a killer shark trained at Sea World to accept humans. He pushed through the ring of security, hand outstretched. "J.D., sad night. You holding up?"

We shook hands while photographers scrambled to get a shot. "Hell of a thing," I said, putting my hand on his shoulder in my most friendly gesture. I pulled him down just a bit and leaned in. "What I can't figure out," I whispered, "is how you guys planted this without anybody seeing you."

Most guys would have snarked back, but he just nodded, as if I'd shared my deepest condolences. "America's better than this," Somerfield said in that perfectly modulated voice that every microphone was sure to capture. "We will never let fear defeat us."

I stared at him, deeply impressed. This was really level-A bullshit, and even coming from the candidate's son, not the candidate. I respected it. Behind me, Ginny said, "Oh, go fuck yourself, you pretty-boy piece of shit." She did it perfectly, just loud enough for Somerfield, his face tightening for just a nanosecond, to hear, but not loud enough to be captured by the reporters. It was like the experienced prison inmate in the cafeteria line who leaves the victim bleeding but isn't seen by the guards. I shrugged, as if to say, "Hey, she's right, what can I do?," reached out and shook Somerfield's hand, and then turned away. I was just making my way out of the crowd when Lisa Henderson caught me from behind.

"J.D.," she whispered, "you think it's a good idea for you to be here?" Lisa Henderson had a flat, edgy voice and a knack for making every utterance sound like she was back in the courtroom as one of Hilda Smith's assistant prosecutors, grilling an uncooperative witness. It was her style to always pose awkward questions, instantly placing the other person on the defensive. It didn't matter how small the issue, it was just how she dealt with the world. "So this is a turkey and Swiss?" she would ask the poor White House intern fetching her lunch. It was very hard not to experience a moment of deep panic and wonder if somehow the sandwich had gotten mixed up with something else, say, a fresh dog turd wrapped in aluminum foil.

I'd learned to deal with Lisa Henderson by simply ignoring most of her questions and pursuing my own line of questioning. It gave our conversations an odd, disconnected quality, something like a bad Beckett play.

"Have you spoken to the vice president?" I asked.

"What did Somerfield say?" she continued.

All at once I was very, very tired. I liked to consider myself a master of chaos management, planning for every contingency, but I hadn't in my wildest dreams considered a scenario in which a bomb would go off and scare the living hell out of the entire convention. A bomb outside Pat O'Brien's?

"He's a regular Churchill and FDR. He thinks we should never let fear defeat us."

"What a pompous ass," she said.

"We have to put out a statement," I sighed. "Hilda has to be told." I hated the idea of waking her up, but there was no escaping it.

"I have a draft working," Ginny said.

"I'll inform the vice president." Lisa bristled, ignoring Ginny. She hated it when I called the *vice president* by her first name.

"The war room in half an hour, okay, then we'll go see her?" For a moment our eyes met, and I thought I saw a hint of confusion, maybe a touch of fear. I reached out and touched her elbow. "Long night." I wondered if she realized I really did feel bad about how she had been treated after I replaced her, being particularly sensitive to the realities of public humiliation. Not that it had stopped me from pursuing her demise for one second. But I was a political consultant. Political consultants weren't expected to be good people, thank God.

She smiled, or did what Lisa Henderson did that passed for a smile. "In the war room," she said.

I had dealt with variations of Lisa from my very first campaigns. She was the staffer who was totally dedicated to her boss, and she was always suspicious of a hired-gun political consultant who would move on to another campaign win or lose. On Capitol Hill these staffers tended to be more female than male, and the joke went that each of them had the perfect recipe for beef Bourguignon—for one. Like many of them, male and female, Lisa had never married. And, like a nun, she had married her job, and her job was Hilda Smith. She saw Hilda winning the presidency as something close to divine prophecy, her religion being worship at the House of Hilda Smith. She had met our boss when Hilda was teaching part-time at the University of Vermont and followed her through every step of her career. Lisa hated me because she needed me to help Hilda Smith win. I understood that, and there was nothing I could do but manage it, not fix it.

I was halfway down the block, crafting a statement in my head expressing Hilda Smith's outrage, when I heard Sandra. She was yelling at a crew to hurry up. It was a famous voice, clear and distinct, but now with an edge never heard on the air. When she was angry or drinking or not thinking or all three, you could hear the accent she had been born with, not the one she cultivated to take her from Florida to NBC in Washington.

I stopped and instinctively took a half step backward toward the comfort of the deep shadows along St. Ann. One moment I had felt exhausted and slightly numb, then my heart was pounding like after a near miss on the freeway. Ginny looked away, as if she had caught me with my pants down emerging from a bathroom. Which she had, really, I thought. *Christ, I can't just hide here in the shadows like some scared kid.* So I stepped back out into the street and headed right toward the woman hurrying in high heels followed by a small pack of straining men.

She smiled when she saw me, and, later, replaying it all in my head, that was what bothered me the most. She didn't even feel like she had to look awkward. Just a smile, a tilt of the head, maybe a little apology in the eyes, but it was dark and I might have been imagining it.

"J.D.," she blurted, slightly out of breath, "what the holy hell is going on here?"

"A bomb," I said simply, and later I hated this moment. No witty comeback, no elegant put-down, not even a bitter exchange. Just a quiet statement of the obvious. "A bomb. One person was hurt." In that lousy dead-air blanket of the New Orleans night, I thought I could smell her perfume. But that was probably impossible, what with the reek of garbage wafting over everything. Then she held out her hand. For a moment, I stared at it, stunned. Her hand? We had lived together for eighteen months, or more or less lived together. We had made love hundreds of times. We were going to shake hands?

"Christ, Sandra," was all I muttered, and then walked away, a smiling Ginny in tow. We were only a few feet away when Ginny uttered one word, which hung there in the air: "Bitch."

Chapter

★

Two

IN THE LAST TWELVE HOURS I'd been to a bomb site and a political rally, and I'd be lying if I didn't say the political rally terrified me more. A lot more.

It had been several hours before the bombing, at the big pre-convention Armstrong George rally held in Tulane University's football stadium. As college stadiums go, it wasn't so big, with seating for about thirty thousand. Hell, Alabama's Bryant-Denny Stadium held over a hundred thousand. But for a political event—a *Republican* political event—thirty thousand was a massive crowd. And it wasn't just thirty thousand bodies. It was thirty thousand screaming, maniacal Armstrong George fanatics.

Eddie Basha and I took the streetcar up St. Charles to Tulane and walked over, surrounded by the George faithful. It was dusk and we were both wearing baseball caps and George sweatshirts with cutoff sleeves and nobody gave us a second look. We passed through the high-tech bomb detectors set up outside the entrance and found a place on the ramp to the stadium. The big halogen lights lit the green field brighter than the hazy day that was fading, and in the middle of the field there was a small stage. That was it. No elaborate props or staging. Up on the Jumbotrons, videos played of Armstrong George bus tours, his slogan, "Take America Back," emblazoned on the bus.

Were this a Hilda Smith rally, we would have a band onstage and introductory speakers, probably the most popular local pol we could get and a somebody from the area who repeated a theme we were pushing that day or week: a teacher, an unemployed worker, a female entrepreneur, a veteran. I was a big believer in the Kuleshov Effect, that early-twentieth-century Russian film experiment that took the same shot of an actor and surrounded it with different images. When you see it, you think the expression of the actor is changing, while it's actually static, the point being that viewers had different reactions based on who and what went before and after. You could take the most unempathetic candidate and surround him with happy schoolkids, and unless the candidate started actually hitting the kids or screaming at them, odds were he would look warmer and voters would talk about how he really cared about kids. Same with seniors or minorities or women or . . . you name it. I once tried to explain to a candidate what the Kuleshov Effect was and they looked at me like I was insane. Later Eddie Basha told me, "Don't ever do that again. Don't tell 'em what you are doing, just do it." It was good advice.

We did it all the time with Hilda Smith, who had a natural Yankee aloofness that read cold. Which, in truth, was pretty accurate; she *was* cold by the standards of most "hug you until you can't breathe, let me cry with you for a while" politicians of the new school. But since turning to Armstrong George and calling him out in that debate in New Hampshire, she had come to represent something that was still important to a lot of people in a beat-up country—call it dignity, or decency. At an ugly time,

Armstrong George had marshaled the ugliness within us all. It was a deep, burning anger at the large forces that controlled our lives. It was probably close to the religious fervors that swept across the country in the late 1800s. Hilda Smith stood for a different kind of country, one that wasn't seething with anger. Our bet was that something about Armstrong George made you feel worse about yourself and your country. That his calling for a New Bill of Rights and a new Constitutional Convention was radical, not conservative.

But it was a close thing, and that's why we were down to fighting over a handful of delegates. As the sky darkened and the field grew brighter under the lights, the music swelled, and then suddenly there was Armstrong George, bursting from the locker room tunnel trailed by his son, Somerfield. The two looked eerily alike, both tall and sturdy, with big, square, Protestant faces that looked like they came from a WPA mural of the wheat farmers who had tamed the prairie. Which was what the Georges had done. They were not from the mountainside of Colorado but the flat plains that resembled the heartland in geography and belief. There were no fireworks or razzle-dazzle tricks as Armstrong and his son walked toward the simple stage. But the crowd went absolutely crazy, their yells and applause growing louder the closer the Georges got to the stage.

Armstrong George bounded up the steps, took the mike in one hand, and detached it from the stand—no fancy headset for him, he wanted to work the mike the old-fashioned way—and let rip. "Americans!" he cried. "This is our moment!" It was chilling. The crowd went from fever pitch to berserk. "Are you with me? Are we together? Are we . . . Americans?"

Eddie leaned in to me and whispered, "He's big on this American thing." It was more a shout than a whisper, the stadium was so loud.

"These have been dark days in America. Our beacon has been dimmed, but not extinguished. Within each of you glows the fire to reignite the torch of American genius and greatness. You are our future!"

"God help us," Eddie groaned, looking around at the crowd. "It's 1930s Nuremberg."

I waved him off. I was there to see Armstrong George. Every time I saw him, I got some different perspective. I'd snuck into a dozen of his rallies over the past six months.

"You are the Founding Fathers of Tomorrow," he said in a suddenly low, intense voice, so the crowd leaned forward. "I say to you that, like the Founding Fathers before us, now is the time we must seize the day and control our own destiny. It is time for a New Bill of Rights. It is Time for a New Beginning."

Then the shout went up from a woman in the crowd. I would have bet anything she was a plant, but it was picked up, and soon the whole stadium was chanting in unison: "America for Americans! America for Americans! America for Americans!"

Armstrong George took a step back, put his arm around his son, and waved.

"Jesus Christ." Eddie sighed. "Jesus H. Christ. We're doomed."

The rally seemed like much more than twelve hours earlier when I walked into the Windsor Court's Presidential Suite, a name that was threatening to seem very ironic. The vice president of the United States was in a robe, looking under a couch for her slipper.

"Here," Lisa Henderson said, fishing out the green slipper from under the couch.

Hilda Smith thanked her, and they exchanged a look I knew I'd never know. These two had invented each other, and it was not a stretch to say that they were in love. Not that I thought they had been slipping under the covers together on those cold Vermont nights or playing with marital aids back at the Naval Observatory in D.C., which is where they stashed the vice president. But each had been probably the most important person in the other's life for a very long time, and that was probably something close to love. As for the sex, I always preferred to believe people had more interesting sex lives than they actually did. But the truth was probably closer to the fact that neither of them had any kind of sex, and likely hadn't for a very long time.

It was possible, I suppose, that Hilda and her husband still slept together, had sex together, that is, but I had my reasons to doubt it. Not that Quentin was off sex—not hardly, as I was pretty sure he was sleeping with one of our fundraisers. She was forty-five and married to a busy doctor and I wouldn't have been surprised if Hilda encouraged the two. I watched Quentin as he came out of the bedroom wrapping a Windsor Court bathrobe around his sizable frame. He was six foot three and had played football at Dartmouth back when six foot three made you a big player. He settled down in a chair and stuck out his feet, nodding toward Lisa and me.

"There's no upside that I can figure to this thing," I started in. "Eddie is already hearing from some of our delegates who want to leave town. The crazy Armstrong George people will love it.

All their paranoid fantasies coming true." I sighed. It was really bad. "I think we just go with a vanilla statement: Violence is bad, terrorism sucks, tragedy of human life, bullshit, bullshit, bullshit."

" 'Bullshit, bullshit, bullshit'?" Lisa repeated sardonically.

I ignored her. "But I can tell you that Armstrong George will try to turn this on us. No doubt about it."

"How?" Quentin Smith asked. He had a low, gravelly voice, still laced with his southern roots.

"I know the woman who was hurt," Hilda Smith said quietly, ignoring her husband. Her blond hair was pulled back, and she reminded me not for the first time of an aging film queen. She paused, and somewhere down below on Canal Street drunken convention crowds were shouting. Did they know about the bombing yet? They would soon enough. Everyone would. It was four thirty a.m. "She's from Wisconsin but came to Iowa to campaign for me."

"Too bad she couldn't vote in Iowa," I quipped automatically, then caught myself when Quentin Smith scowled. He had been against hiring me from the beginning, even after his wife came in third in Iowa. They had known Lisa for years, he'd argued. Lisa was family. They had to stick together.

So what the hell was I doing making some smartass remark about his wife's embarrassing loss in front of the guy? "This is going to hurt us," I said, trying to get back on track. The biggest problem was what the bombing would do to the whole mood of the convention. That's what was scaring me now.

"I want to visit her tomorrow at the hospital," the vice president said.

"That's been arranged for tomorrow morning," Lisa said

crisply. She liked to say that it was her job to know Hilda Smith so well she could anticipate her needs. Occasionally, she actually did.

"I'll go with you," Quentin said. He was a doctor, though it had been years since he had actively practiced. In the last two decades he had focused on turning the little bankrupt ski resort they had purchased into a moneymaker. Now Vermont Skiing Resorts owned three midsize ski areas, and if they weren't huge moneymakers, at least they were staying afloat, even after the Crash. He said it kept him young, the skiing. And it wasn't a bad way to meet young, athletic women, as my op research guy had uncovered. It was good to know everything you could about your candidate's spouse, especially if that spouse was waiting in the wings to drop the axe on your neck if you gave him any reason to do it.

"No press," Hilda Smith said sharply. "No press advisory. Nothing. I want to sneak in and out. Understood?"

"Absolutely," Lisa said.

I didn't say a word. It could be a nice news hit, the vice president and her husband visiting the victim, but I knew now wasn't the time to argue. Every reporter in America was within a ten-block area. It would be easy to leak.

"Who did it?" the vice president asked suddenly. "And why use red dye? Just to scare people?"

Lisa jumped in. This was a question for official White House staff, not campaign hacks like myself. Never mind that Lisa was back as chief of staff just because she'd done a lousy job at campaign hackdom. She saw herself as far above my lowly station in life, what with her security clearance and her knowing where the bathrooms were around the Situation Room. That was actually better for my purposes. I didn't give a damn about government and just needed her to stay out of my way. The more she felt superior, the less likely she would need to prove I couldn't run the campaign. Or at least that's how I figured it.

"We will have a briefing by the FBI tomorrow morning at oh-eight-hundred hours," she said firmly. "But when I spoke to several of our national security people, they thought the purpose was to spread fear."

"Well, that seems pretty obvious," I said. "That briefing is at eight a.m.?" I drawled. It drove me crazy how White House staff adopted military lingo, particularly since ninety-nine percent of them wouldn't have been caught dead in uniform.

"Does the president know?" Hilda Smith asked.

For a moment, I thought she was asking if the president knew who had set off the bomb. She had a healthy appreciation of the president's decline but still held out hope that he could swoop in and help her save the nomination. I suppose it was natural—the president had believed in her and changed her life once and surely he could do it again—but to a professional like me, it was painfully naive. The president of the United States had reached that point many politicians reach when they are convinced the Fates have conspired against them: he cared about himself, and to hell with the consequences. The Oval Office had battered him into such a self-involved, shell-shocked mess that all he could think about was trying—somehow—to make sure that whoever followed him as president would make him look better.

You could argue it round or flat. If Hilda Smith won, it would prove that he still had influence, that his own vice president, a representative of what passed for the mainstream, not-crazy wing of the party, had beaten back the forces of darkness. His legacy would be redeemed as people put the unfortunate troubles—that's what he had taken to calling the Crash, "these unfortunate troubles"—behind them. Unfortunate troubles. Talk about denial. As if the greatest economic screw-up since the Great Depression was just a minor headache. Funny how when the economy is humming along, every politician rushes to take credit, and when it's in the toilet, it's no one's fault but those damn international forces beyond anyone's control. And when it was beyond the toilet and into the sewer, it was hard to find a politician of the party in power who would even admit that elected officials could do anything about the economy.

But on the other hand, if Armstrong George was the nominee and lost, it might just redeem the president by making him look more reasonable: a good man who did his best in bad times. There was always the danger that Hilda Smith would win and prove to be a much better president and make him look hapless. Then there was the chance that Armstrong George might actually win the whole thing, and nobody knew what the hell that would mean. Put it all together, and it made for a president who was paralyzed by indecision and open to being moved by the emotions of any given moment. It scared the hell out of me. He might be a broken president, but he was still the president, and inside our party there remained a certain segment who felt he had been given a raw deal and had done the honorable thing by not running for reelection. That wasn't a huge contingent, but when you were fighting over a handful of delegates, everything and anything mattered.

"The president," Lisa said, "intends to release a statement in the first news cycle."

"He won't help us," I said.

"No?" Lisa countered. "You know what the president plans to say?"

"I can make a good guess that he won't be using it as an opportunity to remind Americans of the wisdom of his vice president's position on that bundle of goodies called the Protect the Homeland package." That was a collection of bills that supporters of Armstrong George were trying to ram through Congress. None were as completely crazy as his New Bill of Rights but it was pretty nutty stuff.

"Hilda's opposition to these draconian measures is one of the reasons she stands the best chance to win the general," Quentin Smith said. He was right, too, and we had the testing to prove it. There was a sizable piece of the Republican Party that supported just about any "get tough on crime and terrorism" proposals—at least in theory—but when it came to winning big battleground states like Ohio, it was a negative for the key independent voters Republicans needed to win.

We had research that showed independents and soft Democrats thought Hilda Smith was a "different kind of Republican." This was a good thing; the problem was that we had to win the damn nomination, and the last thing we needed was a new wave of fear rumbling through the convention.

"You know what the president should do?" Quentin Smith said. "He should resign and let Hilda become president and deal with this mess. That would guarantee she keeps the White House."

"Brilliant," Lisa said instantly. "Brilliant."

I looked out the window, where the first hint of dawn was showing. The Secret Service had covered the windows with a thick bulletproof translucent cover but it still allowed light to leak in. This was a room I'd fought hard to be in—the suite of a vice president on the verge of capturing a nomination—but there were times when I felt an overwhelming desire for another life. There were surely millions of perfectly happy people out there who didn't have to deal with trying to explain to seemingly reasonable people that their plan for a presidential resignation that was basically a coup d'état was stark raving mad. I tried not to sigh.

"Moments like this are like bombs themselves," I said. "Tremendous energy is released. Our job is to figure out how to use that energy to get the vice president over the top. There's going to be hysteria. Armstrong George will be screaming for bodies to be hung from lampposts. We can't out-scream him. Hilda has to be steady and calm."

"I'm still here." Hilda Smith sighed. "You don't have to refer to me in the third person. I'm not dead yet."

I had to smile. I'd come to like this woman, somebody I didn't know at all when I walked into her hotel room in Manchester and explained to her that her only hope of saving her campaign was hiring me to take it over. I'd learned over the years that to really sell a client, you had to believe that whatever you said at that exact moment was absolutely true. There could be no doubts. Candidates were constantly subjected to the kind of abuse and humiliation that left even the tough ones feeling raw and vulnerable. They needed to believe that you could make the pain worthwhile. And I'd been able to sell Hilda Smith because I knew, absolutely knew without a doubt, that if she didn't make a drastic change she was destined to go down in flames. It was the easiest sale I'd ever made. She was desperate. I was hopeful. We were a perfect match.

Since then we'd been married to each other. An arranged marriage, very old-fashioned, between two people who didn't know each other. "You meet, have sex, get married, have children, fall in love": that's how a stunning Czech woman had described the typical Czech marriage. She was one of Václav Havel's "aides," whom I'd met when we were working to elect the best of a bad bunch in Serbia. It wasn't a bad description of what a relationship was like with a candidate. You entered each other's lives for a certain period and you became, invariably, the most important person in each other's universe. Often they came quickly to hate their dependence on you, resenting you when you were right, never letting you forget when you were wrong. You demanded to know everything about them, from the financial to the sexual. You needed to know if they'd ever had an abortion or knocked a girl up, been arrested or caught speeding, bounced a check, if their children had drug problems or their spouses slept around. All the awful, little, petty secrets we try to hide, the small humiliations and tragedies, every tiny bit of dirty laundry, all had to be revealed to this stranger.

But, of course, most candidates lied. They lied, if only by omission. They'd forgotten about that speeding ticket, that one-night stand, the time the checking account ran dry. There was always something out there that they hadn't told you. Sometimes you never found out what it was; other times it blew up on you like that bomb outside Pat O'Brien's. The late-night phone call and the words, those dreaded words: "There's something I should have told you." God, I hated that phrase.

"The president picked Hilda," Lisa insisted. "He should realize that she's his best hope to carry on his legacy." She couldn't accept that everyone didn't see Hilda Smith the way she did, that the whole world wasn't in love with her. That was one of her greatest weaknesses as a campaign manager: her inability to understand why some people didn't like, or even hated, the woman she worshipped.

"Jesus, Lisa, I'm not saying the guy doesn't have good taste."

Nobody laughed. Not even a smile, really. It was time to go.

"We'll draft a statement," I said, standing.

"This can help us," Hilda said with a sudden fierceness.

"I'm listening," I said, sitting back down.

"How many times have we said that Armstrong George represents something terribly ugly and cruel in this country? And a horrible tragedy like this bombing could really make people step back and ask themselves what is happening to us."

"Absolutely," Lisa agreed instantly. "The same way that there was a backlash against the overkill after 9/11. All the taking away of civil liberties."

I started to remind them that George W. Bush was reelected and any backlash happened more than a decade after 9/11, when everyone was feeling safer. And it was the current absence of feeling safe that was driving Armstrong George toward the White House. But I knew it was this side of Hilda Smith, call it a fervent reasonableness, that had drawn Lisa to her years ago. One night after we had won New Hampshire and done better than expected on Super Tuesday, Lisa and I had ended up in a bar alone, drinking too much. She'd told me that Hilda had looked like a star that day she first saw her speak, her blond hair dusted with snow, standing there in her husband's trench coat, borrowed when the sunny morning had suddenly turned into a snow squall. "Government can't do everything," she had said, "but we must do a better job of educating our citizenry, or the new century is sure to dawn on the declining days of our great country." Pretty heady stuff for a state rep race.

"That's our play," I agreed. "But something like this just makes a lot of people want the toughest sheriff west of the Pecos to come in and kick ass," I said, and when Lisa and Quentin Smith both glared at me, I didn't stop. "People are scared to death out there. Their terrified, racist eyes see all these little yellow and brown people taking what jobs are left, and we shouldn't kid ourselves that there is something reassuring about—"

"A thug like Armstrong George," the vice president finished.

"On a dark night, having some jackbooted thug on your side can make you feel pretty good." I tried to smile. "Remember, the innocent have nothing to fear."

"Let's go to bed," Quentin Smith said, standing. He reached for his wife, holding out his hand.

When I was at the door, I glanced back and saw the three of them watching me, waiting for me to leave, like I was the hired help who had overstayed. It was a fact of life. They loved you for saving them and hated you for needing to be saved.

One more reason I had to get out of this business. And all I needed was a handful of delegates—then Hilda would win, and I would be a moderately Famous Person with my own political show franchise. Then I could just talk about all the people who did what I used to do. Bliss.

As soon as I stepped into the hallway, I could feel something different. I was halfway to the elevator when it struck me: in the twenty minutes I had been inside with the vice president, extra Secret Service agents had been posted. Instead of the usual detail of two agents in front of the suite door and another by the elevator (entrance to the floor was controlled by passkey), there were now eight.

They were all faces I recognized. The agents liked me because I never gave them a hard time and always respected their needs. When Kim Grunfeld, our dragon lady of a media consultant, had tried to boss them around during the filming of a commercial, I had made sure I came down on their side and told Kim to either quit acting like she was a real film director or take a walk. As I was getting on the elevator, I saw that two of the guards had swiveled their Uzi submachine guns from their normal rear-sling position, where the machine guns rode in the small of their back, to the front, just under the flaps of their coats.

My daily senior staff meeting was scheduled to convene in the war room at six thirty, which was in just a couple of hours. Moving a campaign to a convention was never easy. Our regular headquarters were in Montpelier, Vermont, the smallest capital city in the country. This was partly because it was cheap but mostly to stress Hilda's definition as a non-D.C. candidate. Our offices were just down the street—one of the two main streets in town—from the statehouse where Hilda started her political career. No reporters, other than the locals who had known the vice president forever, just "dropped by" because they were in the neighborhood, and donors hated to trek to a small town in the middle of nowhere. Quaint coffee shops, a couple of great independent bookstores, and no reporters or donors. In the history of world civilization, no good had ever come from having donors hanging around a campaign headquarters. But at the convention, suddenly the entire political world surrounded us, reporters and donors everywhere. Throw in Bourbon Street, and it was easy to see a campaign totally losing focus, like a football team at a bowl game with players skipping curfew. To fight distractions, Eddie and I had decided to keep the same schedule in New Orleans that we did back in Montpelier. People bitched and complained, but that only proved us right.

I got on the elevator to ride down one floor to my room, but when the elevator stopped I didn't get off, and let the doors close, riding down to the lobby. A few delegates were milling around with drinks, looking dazed but still arguing. Everybody was arguing in New Orleans. And drinking. In the small lobby of the Windsor Court, I counted more than a dozen uniformed NOPD cops, what looked to be three or four NOPD detectives in plain clothes, and a full contingent of Secret Service. A huddle of technicians in Secret Service jumpsuits were installing metal detectors and new bomb-sniffing scanners at the main entrance to the hotel. Almost a thousand delegates and press were going to wake up inside a "secure area." I wondered if this was happening at every delegate hotel in town or just here at the Windsor Court because of the vice president. Whatever: none of it was good for us. Hilda Smith was the candidate of hope versus fear, and it sure looked like fear was winning.

Luck is no small part of both life and politics, and I had done enough campaigns to know we were lucky to even be in this race. Nine times out of ten, after an economic meltdown the party out of power should be able to waltz into the White House. But the Gods of Politics had smiled on us one spring morning when the diary of the wife of the presumptive Democratic nominee, Pennsylvania governor Doug Banka, exploded into print. It was crazy.

Banka was in his second term as governor, an Iraq War vet from Erie, Pennsylvania, who had been reelected with huge margins. He'd been elected with the help of his wife's money, which came from the Silicon Valley world. She was a Stanford-educated engineer who had moved from Apple to Google to a venture capital start-up and made a fortune along the way. Banka had met her when he was working with a private-public aid group, Vets Recovery, and was on a fundraising trip to San Francisco. They dated transcontinentally for a year and then married in Erie. Banka ran for Congress and then made a big jump to governor after two terms. Pennsylvania loves to reelect governors, and he ran up the score, racking up numbers in the conservative part of the state like no Democrat in modern history.

While we were fighting Armstrong George hand to hand from New Hampshire all the way to New Orleans, Doug Banka was cruising to easy victories in the Dem primary. He became the first to win both Iowa and New Hampshire, and after that it was pretty much all over. Once he had the nomination sewed up, Banka started attacking Armstrong George. I hated that he wasn't attacking us. Every time Banka hit George, the guy went up with Republicans who figured if the other side was hitting our guy, he had to be pretty good. Had Banka put together a sustained attack on television and digital, he would have eventually damaged George with Republicans. At a certain point, negative information adds up, even if it's coming from the anti-Christ. But Banka didn't lay the heavy wood on him, just took shots at George's plan to build a wall the full length of the border and banged him day after day on the New Bill of Rights. Armstrong George's people loved him for all those things; it was like accusing a supermodel of being thin. That was the point.

Every poll had Banka up five to eight points over both Hilda Smith and Armstrong George. Until the Gawker Bomb hit. It came on April 19, at five a.m. EST, which gave it sort of a classy Pearl Harbor "hell at dawn" touch. I was just trying to wake up and drag myself out of bed in another hotel in Ohio, where we were slogging through the last primary, when my phone lit up like one of those flashers they give you at Fuddruckers to let you know when your crappy food is ready. Within five minutes, I had over a hundred calls, my voice mail full and throwing up. "What the hell?" I was fumbling with the cheap coffeemaker when Eddie Basha burst through my door.

"You hear?" he asked.

I was standing there in gym shorts, after my usual four hours of sleep, feeling like death before coffee. Eddie was dressed in a nicely pressed shirt and tie, looking like he had won the lottery. "How the hell did you open the door?" I asked.

He held up a key. "Advance has passkeys to all the rooms," he said. "Didn't you know that?"

"Christ." I had a rush of panic, thinking of when Ginny and I had been having mad campaign sex in other hotels. "The advance guys always have keys to every room?" I asked. Why didn't I know that?

"Her diary," Eddie said. "Focus. Gawker got her diary."

The coffee sputtered that it was ready. I was really not good at this early-morning chaos without coffee.

"Eddie," I said, feeling better after the first few sips of the coffee. "What the hell are you talking about?"

He picked up the remote and turned on the television. "Watch," he said.

And we did. Sitting next to my top guy and drinking the bad coffee, I heard the breathless story that Gawker had obtained the diary of Amanda Collins, the wife of Doug Banka, and it contained "explosive details of their intimate lives."

"Good, so good," Eddie said gleefully, and for once the reality of the story lived up to the billing. For the next two weeks, Gawker strung out the juicy details of threesomes with Amanda's college roommate, "sexcations" in Thailand, "lost weekends" in Vegas. Banka refused to comment on any of the details. About a week into the drip-drip of details as Gawker teased it out, Maureen Dowd wrote in *The New York Times* that the diary read like some *Cosmo* fantasy and she doubted that any of it had really happened. That kicked off an Internet treasure hunt for articles and stories that resembled the scenes that the first lady of Pennsylvania had described. Rumor had it that she was so offended by Dowd's accusation that she wanted to hold a press conference and reassure America that, in fact, this stuff really had taken place.

We won Ohio but no one seemed to notice, the whole political world transfixed by the meltdown of Mr. and Mrs. Banka. Editorials and what passed for "Democratic Wise Voices"—these were rare in both parties—urged Banka to withdraw and throw his delegates to the second-place finisher, Senator Richards of

Rhode Island. The problem was that Richards was such a boring "White Man of Wealth and Privilege" that no one had been particularly excited about him when he ran; the idea of turning over the nomination to the guy seemed to generate an amount of enthusiasm slightly lower than you might feel at having to kiss your aunt. The concept of honorable resignation in America had never been especially popular, and since Bill Clinton had proved that hanging on was the key to success, many seemed secretly to admire Banka's stubborn refusal to cave.

Usually the party in power has their convention last, but this time the Republicans had chosen to go first and early, sort of a Hail Mary pass in hopes of setting a narrative that could force the Democrats on the defensive at their own convention. "Setting a narrative" is the kind of phrase political consultants and journalists love to toss around when they really mean "rat-fuck." The hope was that the Republicans would spend the convention attacking the Democratic nominee and making him respond when it came time for his convention. But politics has a way of working out—or not working out—like none of us pros predict. The good news was that the Dem nominee had plenty to do just dealing with his own self-inflicted attacks. The bad news was that we were in worse shape. If Hilda didn't win the nomination, odds were that Doug Banka could live-stream having sex with monkeys and still win four hundred electoral votes against Armstrong George.

So we were in New Orleans with a chance, and sometimes a chance was all you could ask for in politics. Outside the Windsor Court, the predawn moment should have felt freshly minted and tinged with promise. But the air tasted stale and nasty, like a locker room with too many bodies and lousy toilets. By the time I reached the gates of the hotel's circular courtyard, I was dripping with sweat. I walked down Canal toward the Superdome. I told myself I didn't have a destination, that I was just out to clear my head, but of course that was a lie. Canal Street was a history of the booms and busts that had racked New Orleans. At one end, by the Windsor Court, there was that huge mausoleum of a failed casino perched on the Mississippi River like an abandoned temple of a forgotten religion. A dozen or more times, gambling had been slated to save New Orleans, but a combination of greed, graft, and inertia had always killed it before it could take hold. Locals took a sick pride in the failure of gambling in New Orleans, like the city was too proud of its heritage as a sex, drinking, and music Mecca to allow itself to be transformed into just another imitation of Las Vegas. So what if it cost the city billions in lost dollars? It had been over a hundred years since New Orleans was rich, and that was just fine by everybody. We were New Orleans. We didn't need anything as crass as money.

The few times the city had flirted with affluence, it had quickly rejected the notion, like a teenager turning down fancy French food for a hot dog. Oh, to be sure, there had been the brief petrochemical booms and the flood of post–Hurricane Katrina money, but this was greeted as a cause as much for dismay as for joy, a reaction that cut across social lines. Uptown society was terrified of the impact of any new money on their caste systems of Mardi Gras balls and debutante parties. In the Quarter, everybody from the gay community to the bar owners had panicked after real estate prices spiked a few years after Katrina, when federal dollars had rained on the city like a July thunderstorm. After the Crash, there was almost a sick relief that nobody wanted to buy real estate, and the good citizens of New Orleans were relieved of the need to talk about how much somebody's house had sold for and could instead focus on drinking, sex, crime, and the New Orleans Saints as the normal topics of conversation.

The old Werlein's Music Store was on my left, on the north side of Canal, closed now but once a place where Uptown families shopped for Steinways alongside blues musicians looking for the perfect harmonica. Then for a while it had been a restaurant, but that had closed. I'd bought my first Fender Stratocaster here; my brother Paul had driven me to the store and lent me the money for the down payment. He always had a lot of cash in those days, Paul did, money stuck in his pocket at Touchdown Club luncheons from grateful alumni. And then there was the cash that sports agents slipped him, hoping to represent Paul Callahan, LSU great, when he turned pro. Only Paul never made it to the pros, sidetracked by a hotshot young DA who was determined to break up gambling and didn't think it was altogether a bad thing to get some headlines when he netted the great Paul Callahan for making big bets with bookies. Paul didn't even try to fight the charge but spent every penny he had and could borrow to prove he had never bet against LSU. That helped with the public, but he still was convicted: a felony conviction, a year in jail, suspended.

Ten years later, when the governor officially pardoned him, there had been so much serious corruption in the post-Katrina cleanup that Paul's sins seemed almost quaint. He'd been required to do a stint of public service, which turned into him going around the state to schools to tell his story. Then he coached high school football, reaching a state championship with a New Orleans team pieced together after Katrina. Talk about rehabilitation. He was damned near a folk hero, and now he was running for public service commissioner. He'd been calling me since we got to town, and I should have called him back; but there were a lot of things I should have done.

There was a string of pawnshops and jewelry stores on the west end of Canal, each covered in steel bars and alarms, a Doberman or German shepherd asleep on the floor. Pawnshops had exploded after the Crash, and so had the number of people trying to rob them. It was the same with the jewelry stores. With the Crash came a deep, almost mystic need to buy—or steal—gold and silver. In New Orleans alone, four jewelry shop owners had been murdered in the last six months. Now young Uptown couples shopped for wedding rings with the help of a jeweler wearing a 9mm in a holster, a shotgun never far from reach. You were crazy to expect help from the NOPD, which was as bankrupt as the entire city, a department so rife with corruption that it was routine to put a twenty-dollar bill behind your license when you were stopped for speeding. And for a thousand dollars, it wasn't hard to find a cop who would be happy to settle any problems you might be having by drilling a 9mm slug into the troublemaker. The Crash had brought deflation of all sorts, even for hit men.

Two blocks from the Superdome, I passed a huddle of sleeping bodies in front of the Catholic storefront mission. Five years ago there had been three homeless centers in New Orleans; now there were more than twenty, some as small as the home of a nun who had opened her doors. The mayor had wanted to close the Canal Street and French Quarter missions down before the convention to clean the streets of the homeless who congregated on the nearby sidewalks and parking lots, turned out of the centers during the day and waiting for them to reopen at dusk. But a *New York Times* reporter had gotten wind of it and done a story that forced the Republican National Committee to contribute to various homeless charities. A vet who had been homeless but managed to get back on his feet was speaking on the second night of the convention. We had wanted a single mother, but Armstrong George's people had balked, and a vet was the compromise. It was amazing what you could fight over at a convention.

Outside the Superdome, gray NOPD buses were pulling up, discharging sleepy-looking uniformed cops. They were assembling in squads, waiting for their sergeants to brief them. Even with my all-access pass it took fifteen minutes to work my way inside the Dome. I couldn't believe what I was seeing—a second cordon of security was being erected inside the already-tight security. This was a disaster. For months I'd studied the layout of the convention floor, poring over diagrams with Eddie, looking for every way to maximize our chances in a floor fight. We knew exactly how many feet it was from our command trailer to every delegation's spot on the floor. We knew which aisles were most likely to be crowded and had alternative routes mapped: if center aisle C was blocked with a floor demonstration, the fastest way to the Maine delegation was around the CBS trailer, past the visitors' locker room, through the floor to the left of the stage, and down side aisle F-6 to F-7. Approximate time of travel: four and a half minutes. One of Eddie's hotshot digital team had made us an app we could use to time exactly how long it would take to get from any point in the convention hall to another, given the current crowd conditions. It was the sort of thing that campaigns did to convince themselves they had an edge. Sometimes it was even true.

Blindfold me and I still could have moved around without a problem on the convention floor. And always, in every diagram, planning session, mock-up, and app, there was one security perimeter with the new bomb-scan devices at each door, twenty-two security stations in all. Now there would be a second interior security border, a smaller, concentric circle through which everyone would be funneled. I quickly worked the numbers: 2,472 delegates, 2,400 alternates with floor passes, 2,100 journalists, 3,000 staff, another 2,000 or so assorted families and friends, odd hangers-on, contributors. All of these people herded through two security levels. It was going to be a train wreck.

The worst thing about the added security was the inevitable feeling of paranoia it would create with the delegates. More security, more guards with guns: this was hardly an environment that helped a do-good healer like Hilda Smith. To believe in Hilda you had to be convinced that the country needed a president to appeal to our Better Angels. That was her pitch, when you really came down to it. She was hope against fear. Armstrong George was the fear candidate, and right now, watching the most intense security in the history of presidential conventions going up on the floor of the Superdome, you had to believe that fear was looking a hell of a lot better than hope.

I stepped out of the tunnel onto the convention floor. Dozens of workers were still erecting the high-definition television screens behind the stage. I felt like an athlete walking onto the empty Super Bowl field hours before the game began. It was the kind of vainglorious image that I liked—star athlete, hero. Even a gunslinger headed toward high noon was okay. Anything but a beat-up political hack who was trying to drag a wounded candidate over the line. Out on the convention floor, sleepy workers were just starting to set up chairs. I closed my eyes and pictured the scene: state chairmen screaming into iPhones, the desperate promises, the deals, the lies, the threats. All that emotion jammed into seventy-two hours. It would be brutal and wonderful, and, with a little luck, I would show the world that J. D. Callahan was back—so I could get out.

Chapter
★
Three

WE WERE HALFWAY THROUGH the six thirty a.m. senior staff meeting when Ginny walked into the war room holding an envelope. As usual, Kim Grunfeld, the media consultant I'd inherited when I took over the campaign, was yelling at somebody. This time it was Tommy Singh, who was one of the gentlest people you'd ever find in a nasty business like politics. He had the demeanor of a math professor, which is what he had been before he realized he could get rich playing with numbers for politicians.

"That is the most unholy stupid idea I have ever heard," Kim sneered. She did this well.

"Why?" Tommy said in the same soft voice he always used. Everybody considered him a genius when it came to numbers. He might have been born in India, but he could rattle off even the most obscure election returns in parts of the United States that had probably only been mapped by air.

A hush fell over the room when everyone noticed Ginny standing by the door. The reaction was typically self-important and pompous. A non-war-room-group person had entered the room! How dare she! As if we were nuclear scientists discussing classified technology instead of a bunch of tired and frustrated political operatives in a bland meeting room at a fancy hotel. The higher you go in politics, the more time you spend in these kinds of hotel rooms, the catered food as limp and exhausted as you feel, the coffee as burnt as you've been for months. It's like running away to join the circus and discovering that it's really run by Google nerds who sit in cubicles. But we always call them "war rooms" to feel more powerful. If you made it seem exclusive and important, people would die to be granted admission.

"Ginny," I said, nodding and managing a smile, trying to pretend that everything was perfectly normal, that what passed for Hilda Smith's brain trust wasn't staring at her like she had just landed in a spaceship and burst out singing Armstrong George's praises.

"Everything okay?" I asked. From the way she was glaring at me, it was clear that Ginny saw this as some kind of test I was failing. This seemed to happen regularly to me with women. Sandra said I veered radically from oblivious to clinging, without a stop for companionship. I'm sure she was right. Either I was so caught up in my own little world, which meant some goddamn campaign death struggle, or I had nothing to do but focus on her and think way too hard about how lucky I was to be the boyfriend of this famous, very hot journalist. Pathetic, really. But Ginny and I had a good time together, more or less. It was a campaign and we were having sex, but it hadn't really been that strange kind of campaign sex that made you wish you hadn't had sex as soon as you did.

Ginny looked like she might hit me. "Here," was all she said, thrusting an envelope into my hand. "I hate you," she mouthed silently, and turned on her heel.

"See ya, Ginny," Dick Shenkoph mumbled as she reached the

door. She turned and winked at Shenkoph, who, as always, was dressed in a rumpled black suit that looked slept in. He blushed, an odd sight on his sagging seventy-something-year-old face.

No one said anything for a long moment after Ginny left, waiting for me to explain. Everyone in the room was wondering, *What in God's name is in that envelope?* So was I, but I wouldn't give them the satisfaction, and picked up where we had been when Ginny walked in.

"You don't like Tommy's idea, Kim?" I asked Kim.

"What?" she grumbled, trying to focus. Kim Grunfeld was only thirty-one or so but already had bags under her eyes. Her mother, a congresswoman from Manhattan's Upper West Side, was a walking advertisement for cosmetic surgery, with one of those faces that looked like it had melted under a too-hot sun. Kim had grown up in the family business, and the business was politics. Nationally her mother was known as a crazy-left Democrat of the sort a family trust fund helps develop. No one in Congress really liked her. She was self-important and self-involved, a bore even to her own true believers. But to those out there who didn't have to deal with her, she was a great champion of the left with a narrow but intense following across the country. Her father was an advertising exec who had been at various times the head of most of the big Madison Avenue agencies. One late night on a campaign bus coming back from shooting Hilda on a rainy day in Ohio, Kim had told me, "What you have to understand is that my mom is the nice one in the family." I thought it was the saddest thing I'd ever heard. She had become a Republican out of family rebellion, an instinct I found all too understandable.

Tommy didn't wait for her to get worked up again. "Why is

this not a good idea? This bombing is a defining moment whether we want it or not. We must poll to gauge our reaction."

"I'm all for polling, you know," Dick Shenkoph mumbled, and a few people chuckled. Shenkoph had been a major pollster a decade ago, until he was caught cooking numbers in a Texas governor's race. Instead of completing full samples of six hundred calls for weekly polls, Shenkoph had his company make only sixty or so calls and then "weighted" the numbers, extrapolating the results that would have resulted if he had made the full six hundred calls. But he was charging, of course, as if he were making all the calls. When his client discovered what was going on, Shenkoph defended himself by asserting that however he came up with the numbers, they were right on the money, which was a hell of a lot more than you could say for a lot of pollsters. The governor, a self-made millionaire, was not a stupid man. He kept Shenkoph as his pollster and strategist until he won, then waited a week and had his campaign manager announce to the world that they had just discovered this grievous fraud and demanded a full refund on all polling. The lawsuit that followed had driven Shenkoph into bankruptcy. The assistant campaign manager on that campaign had been a young hotshot—me.

"But I hate to think," I barked, "what kind of holy shit would come down on our heads if one of our brothers in the media found out we were in the field the morning after this bombing trying to figure out how the hell the vice president should respond. Let me go out on a limb here, guys: I think we ought to be against it."

"No, but really, Tommy," Kim cut in, "if your poll showed that maybe we should come out in support of more terrorist bombing, I'd love to make a spot about it." She turned away in disgust and lit an unfiltered Camel. Only Shenkoph and she smoked. And Camels? They were still legal?

"Kim," Tommy said in the same logical voice, "I am sure, given your track record in other campaigns, that you would do precisely that."

"Goddamn it!" She was half out of her chair in an instant. "I've won more races—"

"It is a matter of nuance I am speaking of," Tommy continued, unfazed. "The wording. The precise language of our response." He held out his hands like a teacher reduced to proving simple theorems to children. "This is what is critical and this is what a poll could assist us in formulating."

I shook my head. This was a bad idea. The last thing we needed was a nasty story about how we were so unsure how to respond to the bombing that we needed to poll. And the truth was that in all likelihood, Hilda Smith was going to say whatever she wanted to say, regardless of what we told her to.

"Let's move on," I said.

Eddie stood up and passed around sheets of paper to the seven people in the room. "We have heard from a half-dozen delegates that they are leaving town. We may be able to turn some of those around or it may get worse. These are bios on the alternate delegates who will replace anyone who leaves."

"What about George delegates leaving?" Kim asked. We all looked at her and then she shook her head. "Yeah, right. They're dying for this fight. They'll probably have alternates already riding horses into town. Ride to the sound of the guns. Our people are scared. I hate that."

Eddie continued. "Attached is a list of the alternates and key influence points we ran on each using our own circle-of-influence logarithms. As you know, each alternate, like most delegates, is not legally bound to support the vice president and can switch allegiance to any candidate. That includes candidates not in the race."

"So these sumbitches can really vote for whomever the hell they want?" Dick Shenkoph asked. "Even if they were elected as Hilda Smith alternate delegates, they can flip on us and go to that bastard George?"

"Pretty much. But there are technicalities in some state laws that we might be able to contest," Eddie responded.

Every state party had its own rules for electing delegates, approved by the national party. It was a complicated, confusing mess. We had a staff of eight election law specialist lawyers who did nothing but focus on what it took to get Hilda Smith on the ballot—not an easy process—and tracked the frequently changing rules for each state's primary or caucus. It was an absurd way to pick the nominee of the party, but no one seemed to know any way to scrap the system and start over. It was like a rumbling giant airplane that had started out with a World War II frame—say, a B-17—and been constantly altered and modified to an unrecognizable state.

"Oh great," Shenkoph said. "We're going to sue our own delegates to vote for our ass?"

"They have to stick with us unless they want to die a slow and painful death," Kim Grunfeld said.

"We could threaten them with having sex with you," Shenkoph said.

"Cute."

"Half are women," Eddie said.

"All the better," Kim said, without looking up. It was a subject of fascination to Shenkopf whether Kim was gay or straight. No one else seemed to care, but he had brought it up on more than one occasion. She knew it and loved to taunt him with whatever fantasies he might have. She walked over to the long table, which was filled with coffee and awful-looking pastries. She poured herself a cup of coffee and walked back toward her chair. As she passed Shenkoph, she poured most of the hot coffee into his lap.

"Jesus Christ!" Shenkoph jumped to his feet.

"Stephen Stills?" Kim read, ignoring Shenkoph. "Somebody likes Stephen Stills." She looked up at Eddie. "He's still alive?"

In the bathroom, we could hear Shenkoph splashing water on the front of his rumpled suit, cursing in a low, steady stream. I looked at Lisa. We both tried not to laugh.

"Mr. Ted Jawinski is a great fan of Crosby, Stills and Nash. He has been to over a dozen concerts."

"How do you know that?" Lisa asked.

Eddie looked pained, like he had been asked how he knew that gravity really existed. "He writes about it on Facebook all the time. And he buys all their albums on Amazon."

"You have Amazon data?" I asked. This I didn't know. "Is that legal?" Eddie shrugged. I let it drop. At this point, if Eddie had bought sex tapes from ex-boyfriends to use, I was all for it. That's how campaigns work. You start out trying to win in the right way and end up trying to survive in the worst way.

"This is creepy," Kim said, a note of admiration in her voice.

"You ought to see what Eddie has on you, Kim," I cracked, and everyone laughed. Except Kim.

I loved Eddie Basha. He was from the Mississippi Delta, a second-generation American of Lebanese extraction. He had the management skills of a COO of a major corporation and the soul of a very efficient assassin. I'd brought him in at the beginning, starting with that Wednesday in New Hampshire. We had worked together in over a dozen gubernatorial and congressional races and never lost. He was my good luck charm. We had met years ago in a special election to replace a congressman in north Mississippi who had resigned after cops caught him with his old high school girlfriend, both half naked, in a lovers' lane parking spot outside of Pontotoc, Mississippi. Instead of trying to tough it out and beg for forgiveness, the congressman announced that he was resigning, divorcing his wife, and moving in with his old girlfriend. I always sort of admired that honesty. He was forty-two years old, took a look at his life, didn't like it, and changed it. Now he was a high school football coach in North Florida, and I hoped he was happy.

But that had opened up a congressional special election in a district that had been Republican and was likely to stay that way. I did what I did a lot of in those days: I went candidate hunting rather than waiting for somebody to call me. There were a couple of sort of wealthy candidates already in the race who had hired big-name consultants, which I certainly wasn't. There were a couple of state representatives and one small-town mayor. But I had an idea—a sort of crazy idea, but I figured it was worth a shot.

I flew down from D.C. to Memphis, rented a car, and drove to

Oxford, Mississippi. It was summer and even hotter than D.C. but still felt fresher. I drove onto the Ole Miss campus, parked in front of the football stadium, and found my guy running stadiums. I'd read that he did this every day at noon, even in the hottest part of the summer. The stadium was unlocked but empty. Except for my guy, sweating like a bastard and running up and down the steps. He moved with the grace that had made him an All-American at Ole Miss, just over six feet, with huge hands that pistoned by his legs as if they were pulling an invisible rope up the stadium steps. I had watched him play in this stadium many times, heard his name chanted over and over. The night he'd shattered his leg when a three-hundred-pound tackle landed on him just the wrong way, they said you could hear the bone crack into the seats. That had ended his pro career, and brought him into the Marines. Even with a leg that would never be perfect, he flew through basic and was sent to Afghanistan. That was after most of the fighting, but five months in he caught two bullets from an Afghani wearing the right uniform but eager to kill Americans. That was two years ago, and he was back at Ole Miss now, an assistant coach, working on a graduate degree in business.

I waited for him to finish and handed him a bottle I'd iced. He took a sip, frowned. "Not Gatorade?"

"Gatorade is poison. This is far better." Which was true. It was HEED, one of the special endurance drinks I'd learned to love in bike racing.

He looked at me, sweating, enjoying the coolness of the new drink. "You a grad student? Checking the place out?"

I shook my head and smiled. "Eddie, have you thought about running for Congress?"

As it turned out, Eddie Temple had thought about running for Congress but didn't really know how to begin. But to me it looked easy: he had been the first black student body president at Ole Miss, he was a football star and wounded vet, and, most importantly, people liked him. To meet him was to be drawn to him. He had that "thing." Life and politics imitate high school, and Eddie Temple was the guy you wanted to hang out with in high school. When he ran for Ole Miss student body president, a nerdy undergrad named Eddie Basha had run his campaign. It was the "Two-Eddies Campaign," everybody joked. When I asked Eddie Temple if he would run for Congress, he had one condition: Eddie Basha had to be involved. And that's how I met Eddie Basha. We won that race with the first black Republican congressman from Mississippi since Reconstruction, and we'd be dining off that for years. I loved the guy.

"Someday," Kim said flatly, "someone is going to explain to me how a squeaky-clean ex-governor of Vermont and vice president ended up with the good ol' boy southern mafia running her presidential campaign."

Eddie raised his hand and looked at me. "I'll volunteer to answer, chief."

I nodded.

"Because we win."

Dick Shenkoph's applause and hoots of approval didn't drown out Kim's loud "Fuck you."

He was waiting for me when I stepped off the elevator in the lobby of the Windsor Court.

"Brother, dearly beloved, let us gather together!" he shouted.

The lobby was jammed with delegates, alternates, political groupies, reporters, and security. I quickly counted a dozen cops in uniform and what looked like more than twenty additional Secret Service agents.

And in the middle, there was my brother Paul Callahan standing there with his handsome head cocked, that Irish half-mad glint in his eye that made him look so much like our father.

"Hey," he boomed, "nice try with that bomb."

For an instant, I closed my eyes and tried to will him away. It didn't work.

"Kind of a dud, huh? Keep going, you'll get it right next time."

Everybody in the hotel stared at us, and the volume level of conversation plummeted. These were all out-of-town delegates and visitors and none of them recognized my brother, a small grace for which I was thankful. The Secret Service agents looked at me, and I pointed to my hard pin security badge—the little gizmo the Service used to identify those who were pre-cleared for any event or space—and nodded, trying to come up with a smile.

"Jesus Christ." I grabbed my brother's arm and steered him toward an exit.

When we stepped outside on Canal Street, he threw a thick arm around my shoulder. "Come on, show you my office." The mad glint was gone, replaced with a flat seriousness that I couldn't remember seeing before, but it had been just over three years since I had laid eyes on him. The last time had been for our father's funeral, and we had both been glad to flee from that little horror of regret and sadness.

At six four, he was almost half a foot taller than I was, and even though he limped a little now, I had to admit he still had a certain natural grace, like a big cat loping slowly down the street. At LSU they had called him "Two Speed," because he always seemed to be hardly moving or blasting through the line with shocking quickness. He only ran the forty-yard dash in 4.7 seconds, respectable, not spectacular, but he was quick for a big man, very quick. "He got there before you did" had been written about him scores of times by adoring sportswriters.

"You look different," I told him as we were sliding into a booth at McGuire's bar around the corner. "Different but the same." At McGuire's there wasn't a single delegate and there probably wouldn't be for the entire convention. There was no air conditioning, never had been. No bar or restaurant without air conditioning would ever see a single delegate. Instead there were the usual half-dozen regulars spread around the bar looking like they were waiting for Edward Hopper to show up and finish the painting.

"Yeah?" Paul asked. "Different from my campaign posters? We airbrushed 'em," he snorted.

"No, tired," I said. "You look tired and you even have some gray hair." I reached out toward a streak of gray speckles in his dark brown hair.

"Fuckin' A," Paul said, swatting away my hand. "You bet I'm tired. I'm working my goddamn ass off out there." Paul pushed a folded copy of *The Times-Picayune* across the scarred table. "I work my ass off and you still get better ink."

"What the hell?" I muttered. Being with my older brother made me feel like I was sixteen again, and I hated being sixteen.

"Your old girlfriend," Paul said, thumping the page with a big finger.

The newspaper was folded to reveal a column called "Window on the World," by Jessie Fenestra.

"Girlfriend?"

Paul read from the column. "'He was a sophomore when I was a senior, but I remember J. D. Callahan well. He was tall and skinny and interested in two things: guitars and bikes. As in bicycles, not the much cooler motorcycles. My girlfriends all thought he was cute but shy.'"

"I know this woman?" I grabbed the paper from my brother, staring at the small photo next to her column. It was a pleasing face, pretty but not gorgeous, with a lift to one eye that struck me as ironic, somehow bemused. She looked familiar in the vaguest sort of way.

"You remember her from high school," Paul said.

"Ahh." An image from high school floated through my head. "Jessie Fenestra and her girlfriends thought I was cute? Why'd they keep it to themselves?"

I was remembering her now. She was older, a world apart, a hipster. Pretty.

"I think she went for jocks," Paul said with a little edge. "She married a guy I played with. Cajun. Wayne Thibodeaux."

"What happened?"

Paul shrugged. "Life. You know. Same thing that happened to all of us. The cheering stopped." He said it with a mocking, self-aware tone that surprised me. When he saw my questioning look, he said, "I heard that Wayne took to drinking a lot, and then when he quit, he wanted Jessie to quit too. That didn't seem to work out too well." Paul read the column: "'You may have heard of him as the poor schmuck who was dumped by the so-very-glam-and-famous Sandra Juarez. The boy threw a tantrum on *Meet the Press,* which is not the sort of fate this shy, guitar-and bike-loving boy deserved. But life isn't fair. What a shock.'"

I groaned. "Why is she writing this?"

"You're lucky," Paul said. "She's normally the biggest bitch in the city. For some reason she seems to like you."

"You want to tell me what the hell this is about?" I held up the envelope that Ginny had given me and tilted it so that a grainy black-and-white photograph fell out onto the Formica table. It was a photo of our father with a young teenage girl and three boys. It was taken in front of the big Cadillac that he always drove. I felt sick just looking at the photo.

"I thought that'd work," Paul said, and chuckled. "Can't believe this is what it took to get your attention. How long have I been trying to get in touch with you?" he asked, a big crooked grin on his face, the same likable, aw-shucks grin he used to give when reporters asked him if he was the best there ever was at LSU. It said, "Who, me?"

"I'm running a presidential race, for Christ's sake." But I felt a pang of guilt that annoyed me. I had ignored him and he was my brother.

"Heard that. Saw it on the news. Read about it in Jessie's column. How about you, you hear I'm running for public service commissioner?"

"Paul, look—"

"You're a star, little bruth. Everybody writes about you. I got reporters calling me all the time about you. More interested in you lately than me running for public service commissioner. But the thing is, me running for public service commissioner is a big deal. To me."

For the last eight months I'd listened to people who wanted

something from me. Congressmen who wanted Vice President Hilda Smith to raise money for them, governors who wanted Hilda Smith to drop out of the presidential race, big-time party fundraisers who wanted Hilda Smith to run as Armstrong George's running mate—as if that was ever going to happen—endless delegates who needed a picture of Hilda, a cousin on the Battlefield Commission, a job in the campaign. It seemed at one time or another everybody in America wanted something from me, and I had developed a highly accurate sensor as to when the bullshit was ending and the pitch was coming. Now I knew it was time for Paul's pitch. It would be nice to think he really wanted to see me because we were brothers or, yes, nice to think I wanted to see him. But this was transactional. He wanted something. Like they all did.

The waiter brought breakfast. I'd ordered Raisin Bran, Paul a full plate of two eggs over easy, ham, grits, and a side of pancakes. "Jesus Christ," Paul said, "you're eating like a goddamn girl. That like a bike-racing thing?"

" 'That bike-racing' thing almost got me into the Olympics." Which was a gross exaggeration. I was a really good bicycle racer for New Orleans, which meant I was a moderately good racer for the region and a not-so-great one by national standards. But I knew that Paul followed, and cared about, bike racing as much as he was into Indian cricket leagues, and I could get away with a fair amount of BS.

"Yeah, like we almost beat Notre Dame." Paul paused for a moment, toying with a memory, then moved ahead. "The thing is, all these reporters, they seem to have this funny idea about our family."

"Our family *is* a funny idea."

"They got it like some kind of goddamn Disney movie: Pops, the big civil rights journalist; me, the big dumb football player who screwed up but is coming back; you, the hot-shit genius, kind of eccentric. Christ, they even think you're some kind of athlete!"

"What is it about the bikes that really bothers you?"

"Bothers me? It's ridiculous. Bunch of skinny gay guys in tight shorts riding fucking bicycles! Gimme a break."

"Don't forget the jerseys. Wearing jerseys with all these gay colors."

"Rest my damn case! You win in this sport and you get to wear yellow? What the hell kind of sport is that? You get your ass kicked, they make you wear yellow, that's more like it."

"Yeah, yeah, yeah." I looked up at the television over the bar. It was tuned to ESPN. "Hey," I called to the ancient waiter, "you mind changing channels to CNN and turning up the sound?"

"Why?" The voice from the old man was surprisingly deep, an Irish Channel rumble.

"The president may give a speech."

"So?"

Paul laughed. "I think you are confusing him with somebody who gives a damn about your president." Paul chuckled and then said to the waiter, "Hey, Jimmy, he's my kid brother. Humor the boy."

"For you, Paulie," he answered, and shuffled over to the television.

"So I was thinking, you in the spotlight and all, this little family fantasy must be kind of important. I mean, you got your own little comeback working."

"Oh Christ, Paul, what do you want? Just come out with it. I'll try to help any way I can." I thought he'd appreciate my being direct, but there was just a quick flash of anger.

"This is about protecting both of us, goddamn it. I'm a willing and happy extra in this little movie, but you got to remember these journalists are calling me because I am your brother."

"Whether we like it or not."

"And when I was beating the crap out of anybody who fucked with you when you were a skinny shit, and I was the big stud fullback, you mind admitting I was your big brother then?"

He was right. I had wanted to be Paul Callahan for the first eighteen years of my life, now I was hoping we'd just pretend we didn't know each other. Maybe it was politics that had made me a self-centered, shallow shit. Or maybe I was good at politics because I came to it as a shallow, self-centered shit. Maybe there was just too much history between us.

"I gotta win this election, J.D.," he blurted, with a suddenly desperate look.

"Why in God's name do you want to be on the public service commission anyway?" I asked. To my surprise, he had an answer. A good one.

"Because I'm going to be the meanest rate-cutting, rabble-rousing populist bastard you ever saw. And I can pull votes from Metairie and pull 'em from up north where they still remember how I used to make 'em hoot on Saturdays. Then I'm gonna run my ass for governor and I'm gonna win."

"Governor?"

"Don't sound so goddamn skeptical. Look at the assholes we've elected governor. We're grading on the curve here, brother."

"That's a slogan: 'Not the Biggest Asshole We've Ever Elected.' "

"I like it. A little long for a bumper sticker, but we could work with it."

"You don't think people will be bothered by the fact"—for a second I thought about trying to sugarcoat the question but then gave up—"that you're a convicted felon?"

"Pardoned by the governor himself, fuck you very much. That makes me an *ex*-felon, white, forty-one, and free to do whatever the hell I want as long as my knees hold out."

"But—"

"Look me in the eye and tell me this state could give a rat's ass from Sunday if they elect a convicted but pardoned felon governor. For a minor indiscretion like gambling? In Louisiana? Not if they like the son of a bitch."

"Okay," I said, and laughed. "Okay."

"Fuckin' A, okay. And I'm the kind of son of a bitch they like. But first I got to win this public service commissioner's race and I got a problem because this asshole McGreevy I'm running against happens to have picked his parents better than you and me and he's spending a fucking fortune of his daddy's money."

"Ah, yes, but you have the legacy of our father's heroic civil rights stance to propel you to victory."

"Yeah, right. You take a look lately at what kind of vote David Duke used to get in this state? And all these troubles, from the fuckin' A-rabs to the illegals taking all the jobs, they haven't exactly made people feel like they need a dose of peace and love. I don't want to upset your day, little bruth, but Armstrong George would kick Hilda Smith's ass in this state. It's simple. And that stuff about sending all those brown people back over the border, they like that around here."

"You trying to tell me you plan on endorsing Armstrong George?" I cracked, annoyed to be hearing anything from my brother that I knew was true. "I guess I can tell Hilda this thing is over, huh?"

"You still condescend to my ass. Just like always." He shook his head. "No, what I'm trying to tell you is that I need money."

"A candidate who needs money, what a shock. Look, I'll be glad to contribute to the cause."

"I'm touched. But I need a little more help, kiddo, than one person can give me under these new do-good laws. I need some heavy support from the party. And I need some soft money."

"What are the limits you can give?"

"Goddamn thousand dollars per person. These new limits are killin' us."

"How much have you raised?"

"Four hundred and twenty-eight thousand," Paul said.

"Not bad. Cash on hand?"

"Three hundred and ten grand, give or take."

"Give or take what?" I asked. I knew from years of campaigns that no figure was as fungible as cash on hand. Everybody wanted it to be higher than it was. Nothing in a campaign was lied about as much as cash on hand.

"Give or take how much you eat for breakfast, if I'm buying. Look, I'm not a fucking idiot. You think I'm a fucking idiot, but I'm not. Some might say that's one of our fundamental problems. Little Bruth thinks Big Bruth is a moron."

I held up my palms. "I surrender."

It was well over one hundred degrees in McGuire's and my brother started to sweat. Veins in his thick neck surged. "All these fucking years you had me down for a stone-cold dunce, you ever stop to think there might be a little more to it than that?"

"More than you being a stone-cold dunce?"

"Screw you. You think blowing off your family makes you a tough guy?" Paul's voice was loud, carrying across the bar; a few of the regulars at the bar turned around. "Maybe I'm thinking you got me pegged for a dumbski because that way, you don't have to feel bad about never coming home and, when you do, trying to show up your big brother in the brains department. Jesus Christ, you got no other way to compete with me, J.D. You never got out there and knocked heads like the rest of us, but you like to compete. You took up that silly bike because you knew you could never get out there and do what I did, but maybe you could pedal that bike pretty fast. You know what I think? I think the big joke between us is that everybody thinks I'm the guy who would run into a freight train not to lose, big-time stud athlete and all that, but I ain't got nothing on you, little brother. You would do anything to win, anything to protect your precious reputation, which, believe you me, is a compliment in my book under the circumstances. Which is why . . ."

Paul took a deep breath, wiping his dripping forehead with tiny paper napkins. "Which is why you will help me."

"It is?"

"Because helping me is the easiest way to deal with me."

"Paul, look—"

"J.D., you can do this." He reached over and took my arm.

He was still incredibly strong. "I'm asking for your help, J.D." He looked at me with a clear-eyed intensity that I remembered from when I was a kid and watched him play high school football. He'd be on the sidelines with that same look. I nodded.

"What can I do?" I asked.

He relaxed. "I've got me a little independent expenditure group. Okay, it's not my committee, because that would be illegal and I don't do illegal shit since that little gambling fuckup, but let's say that I am aware of a group of concerned citizens who have organized a little independent expenditure committee and that little committee, though full of goodwill and a desire to serve the public good, is a little short of resources. You can get some resources into that committee, and while you are doing it, make sure they don't step on their dicks and waste the goddamn money."

"Who's running this independent expenditure committee?"

"Tobias Green."

I had to moan. "He's still alive?"

"And thriving, more or less. At eighty-five."

"How can you trust that guy?"

"He is a great American who is supporting my campaign because he realizes that the tragedy of high utility rates assails minorities in disproportionate numbers."

"You do have the rap down."

He smiled. "It is an honor to be on the same side as a true civil rights hero who was a comrade-in-arms with our crusading civil rights father."

"You better move a little to the right," I told him.

"What?"

"Because I'm going to throw up any second."

"I knew you would grasp the concept." He looked very pleased with himself. He reached down and picked up the photograph that had spilled out of the envelope that Ginny had brought to me. The small black-and-white Brownie snapshot with the white deckled edges was worn and creased, as if it had been carried in someone's wallet or purse. It showed a strikingly handsome couple, a big man in his mid-fifties in an elegant suit and rakish hat, his arm around a much younger woman, large-breasted, with long brunette hair hanging over her shoulders like a shawl. And with them were three children. One of them was me, nine years old, peering out at the world with a confused, hesitant look. Next to me was Paul, at thirteen already big for his age, bursting out of his white T-shirt, and, next to Paul, a toddler in a torn Mardi Gras bib.

"This is the only picture of all three of us together," I said. "The only one I've ever seen."

"Just one big happy family, huh?" Paul chuckled. "Well, except Mom didn't make the photo . . ."

Our mother had separated from our father when I was about six. Moved back in with her parents and died when their fancy sailboat went under out in the gulf. Paul remembered her, I figured, but he rarely talked about her. Me, I didn't really remember. Not much anyway.

He got up, leaving me with the photo, then came back to toss a business card on the table. It was a glossy card with images of large-breasted women touting a strip club called "The Body Shop."

"That's Tyler's place," Paul said.

Sitting in that ridiculously hot bar, I tried to conjure up my favorite image of our father: a large man sitting at his typewriter wearing his Marine aviator's flight helmet, typing like mad to finish his column. There would always be a bottle of George Dickel nearby, and he would dictate the column to an imaginary flight control officer on deck in the imaginary carrier below. *The trouble with this state isn't that we live in the past, it's that our past wasn't worth living in in the first place.* Great rants, Dickel rants, rants that were funny sometimes, sad others, but rants that always managed to piss off somebody. It was every Tuesday night, when the column was due for the Thursday papers. One thing Paul would tell me about our mother is how she always said she was raising children in a world that ended every Tuesday night.

"Hello, J.D." The voice was deep and startling and one I remembered very well.

I looked up and saw a tall, painfully thin black man who looked ancient. He was smiling.

"Do I look that bad?" the man said in a wonderfully resonant voice. It was a voice from my childhood.

"I guess I look that bad," he said, and his smile broadened. He put his hand out and covered mine. This was something I remembered as well: a gentle touch, though his hands were rough and large.

"I'm old and sick as a dog," Tobias Green said. "But they ain't buried me yet. Come on, I got something to show you."

It was a storefront just off Canal, not far from the abandoned casino. A large banner read CITIZENS FOR JUSTICE, and the space was filled with cheap furniture and kids in their twenties. It was like a campaign, but the kind of campaign I hadn't done in years: a grassroots, bootstrap operation where the yard sign budget would be greater than the media budget, and there probably wouldn't be any television, just digital, and then only if they were lucky. I liked this kind of place; it was where I had started. When I defied my father by working for a Republican running for the New Orleans city council, back when I was twenty or so and still at the University of New Orleans, we had worked in an office just like this. We got killed in that race, and it pleased my father immensely. He hated Republicans—which, if I was honest, was part of the reason I'd ended up working that side of the fence.

"We called the air conditioner repairman the first week," Tobias Green told me. The space was stifling hot with a battery of old fans stirring the dead air. "He left laughing after a few minutes. Told us we didn't have no air conditioner to repair. Still charged us forty-two dollars fifty for the call." Tobias Green chuckled, a raspy sound that turned into a deep cough. Several of the workers looked up, concerned. He pulled out a wrinkled handkerchief and coughed into it, wiping the corner of his mouth assiduously. He was still a proud man.

"Tobias," I asked, "just what in the hell do the Citizens for Justice actually do?"

"I am shocked that the son of the great Powell Callahan even has to ask that question." He was smiling.

Tobias took my arm and led me into the small, glass-enclosed space that was his office. There were pictures on the wall of Tobias Green with every Republican president since John F. Kennedy. And a large one of Tobias and my father taken at the

Republican convention of '68 in Chicago. They were wearing what looked like identical snap-brim hats and seersucker suits. It was as remote and strange as a Victorian lithograph.

"He was a great one," Tobias said.

"He was an alcoholic who couldn't keep his hands off any woman in a six-mile radius."

Tobias laughed. "We've all had our problems with women."

"Are you talking about me?" I asked. "I got dumped. I never screwed the babysitter."

Tobias held a finger in front of his lips. "Sssshhhh," he whispered. "We must give great men their respect."

"Hey," I said, "you don't have to worry about me. I'm holding the party line. Straight down the middle. I'd talk to Paulie, if I were you. He's the one who seems to want to start talking about family secrets."

"Soon to be Commissioner Callahan, then governor," Tobias said. "A great one in the making." He paused for a second. "You asked about Citizens for Justice. We're a grassroots activist organization working for the oppressed in our community."

"What does that really mean, Tobias? Who's paying you?"

"We were involved with the gaming industry for a while."

I laughed.

"The gaming industry is a great employer of minorities and supports the minority community."

"You mean they paid you a ton of money."

"They were appreciative of our commitment."

"Tobias, I love you. You delivered votes when there was a pro-casino initiative on the ballot."

"Exactly."

"And now?"

"We're expanding into utility rates."

Ahh, what a scam. This was too good. "Utility rates?"

"High rates oppress the poor, Brother Callahan. That I assure you. We are very desirous to support your brother's campaign for public service commissioner. We are confident he will represent the little people when he's on the commission."

"Right," I said. "Of course. But you are running a little short of funds."

"J.D." He sighed. "I can make you only one promise."

"What?"

"If you help your brother, you will feel better about your life."

I started to object, but he held up his hand.

"You should go see Tyler," he said.

"How bad is he?" I asked.

"Bad? How do you mean bad?"

"Nuts, for instance. Crazy racist skinhead nuts. How's that for starters?"

Tobias sighed. I was shocked that he actually looked pained. "I have always believed that Tyler had a good heart."

"So that jackboot-wearing, skinhead, neo-Nazi shit was just his way of getting attention? Is that it?"

He shrugged. "He has love in his heart."

"Yeah? You think so?"

"I will always stand up for your family." He said it with solemnity, like he really meant it. But that was the thing about a guy like Tobias Green. He had been acting for so long it was hard to tell where the real person began and the act ended.

"Yeah? Well, maybe you'll get your chance," I grumbled.

Tobias reached out and grabbed my arm. He looked hard right in my eyes. "Your brother needs help, J.D. He's had a rough time. If he can win this race, it will get him back on track."

"Rough time? Like I've been on a cruise or something?"

"You were always the chosen one, J.D."

"Me? That was Paul, for Christ's sake. He was the big football star, oldest son. He owned the world until he went and screwed it all up. Me, I was a geek."

"Paul and your father were very much alike, J.D. Both were warriors on a great battlefield, and once the battles ended, they were lost."

"Oh, for Christ's sake, Tobias. A lot of people did the right thing in the civil rights days and then went on and didn't fall apart and put their families through hell like Powell Callahan." Tobias sighed and didn't seem to be listening. It was always that way with Tobias. He was so accustomed to just talking that he had forgotten how to listen. I leaned in close to him. "After all the women, all the times ignoring it, that's what broke my mother. You know that. He screwed the babysitter, Tobias. She was fourteen. Tyler's mother was fourteen. The great civil rights hero, my father, wasn't just a cheater, he was a child molester. And I've got a nutjob half brother. He's out there, and he never really had much of a chance."

Now Tobias had heard me, and he looked so sad I thought he might start crying. "It's a terrible thing not to have any battles left to fight." He looked around at the dingy office and the scurrying kids. Then he straightened himself up and tried to smile. "But the Lord works in mysterious ways. We soldier on."

He hugged me. I could feel his skin moving over his bones.

"I'm praying for him, you tell Tyler that," Tobias Green told me as I was leaving. "If you see him, you tell him I'm praying for him."

"Right."

"We are all sinners, J.D. We should never forget that."

"But don't you think some of us are more sinners than others?" I asked. "Don't they have a scale for measuring just how sinful a sin is?"

"You three brothers be good to each other, you hear? You all you got in the world."

"That's a depressing thought."

I left him shaking his head and eyeing, with more than casual interest, one of the attractive young women working for the Citizens for Justice.

Chapter
*
Four

ON THE WAY TO THE STRIP CLUB, I called Eddie and told him I'd be gone for an hour or so.

"What the hell, J.D., we've got a delegate-counting meeting in ten minutes and then a final walk-through at the Dome. The bastards are adding security."

"I know," I said. "I went there after I saw the veep last night. It's a shit show. Look, I just have to do something. It's stupid family stuff." I could have come up with some elaborate lie for Eddie, but we had been through too much. And he probably wouldn't believe me anyway.

There was a long pause, and I could see Eddie holding his phone, pacing. He always paced when he was on the phone.

"Just tell me one thing," he said. "Does this have to do with Sandra?"

"Jesus, no. Why the hell would you think that?"

"Why? Because you still have a thing for her and she saw you last night after the bombing and for Christ's sake, J.D. You don't think I know you better than yourself? Are you giving her some kind of scoopy scoops thinking it'll impress her?"

"Christ." I sighed. "I would do something like that, wouldn't I?"

"For Sandra, hell-goddamn-hell yes."

I laughed. "You do know me."

"Better than you do," Eddie said.

"That's not what I was going to do. But now that you brought it up, I think I will," I said. I hung up while he was starting to shout into the phone. "J.D.!"

Sandra answered on the first ring. "Bitch? That Ginny girl called *me* a bitch?" Then she laughed. "I can't believe you are calling me. I'd like to think it means you are done hating on me, but I'm a big girl, so I know you're really calling because you want me to do something for you. So what is it?"

I almost hung up. But goddamn, she was so dead-on. "Off the record?" I asked. It was so weird to be asking a woman I'd lived with if we were off the record, but there were rules between reporters and campaign operatives, and sex and love past, present, or future didn't change the rules. It was what you learned in politics, particularly with reporters.

"Oh, good," she said, with that excited tone she got whenever she thought there might be a story, "you do have something. Yes, of course, OTR."

"In about an hour, the vice president of the United States is going to be making an unannounced drop-by at the Ochsner Hospital to see the bomb victim."

"Does anybody else know this?" she asked immediately. I knew she would. Every reporter did. If you told a reporter like Sandra that it would cost her one of her kids for an exclusive, her reaction would be, "Can I pick the kid?" But of course Sandra didn't have kids, which I admired about her. "Who the fuck would want me as a mother," she'd said the one time I asked her about it. I was so relieved by her answer that I never brought it up again.

"No, just you."

"Thanks. Keep it that way." She hung up.

"Bitch!" I yelled, banging the steering wheel. Why did I do this?

I found the club on the road to the airport in a stretch that I'd always found as depressing as any in America, a messy collection of dingy convenience stores, off-brand gas stations, tattoo parlors, and massage parlors. The Body Shop stood out like a UFO that had landed by mistake on Airline Highway: it was huge and brightly painted, with a flashing neon sign that towered over the strip.

I drove by three times before stopping, trying to make sure a reporter wasn't following me. It was doubtful, given the general laziness and pack mentality that pervaded the press covering an event like the convention. But there was always the remote chance that some hotshot had read *All the President's Men* one too many times and actually taken the initiative to shadow Hilda Smith's campaign manager for the entire convention. It was also possible that dear brother Paul had already put a word in some reporter's ear.

I parked in the rear, out of sight of the road. The asphalt of the parking lot felt sticky, as if on the verge of melting and swallowing me whole.

Inside it was twenty degrees cooler, a dark world of time suspended. Music blared, a medley of nineties hits. A large white man in a black turtleneck and blazer guarded the door.

"Where's Tyler?" I asked.

The big guy, who was perhaps thirty but looked older, with the overdeveloped muscles and thinning hair of a heavy steroid user, looked down at me with heavy eyes, a look that made it clear he was not interested in just another guy who wanted to see Tyler. Everybody wanted to see Tyler.

"Name?" he asked, in a thick country accent. This was not a New Orleans boy, probably from north Louisiana or maybe Mississippi.

I paused, thought about lying, and then just said, "Tell him his brother is here to see him."

"That the truth?" he grunted, and looked almost awake for the first time.

"You get a lot of people here claiming to be Tyler's brother?"

He stared at me for a long time, then grunted again. "Ha. Ha." He turned away to watch a pair of dancers walk by. One, a tall Asian woman, winked at him. She was easily one of the most beautiful women I had ever seen.

"I thought the women at these clubs were supposed to be skanky," I said to my new friend.

He turned and did his long-stare thing. This was something he was quite good at, actually.

"Man, you can't be Tyler's brother if you that ignorant."

"I'm the slow one of the family, that's all. Look, I really am his brother and really do need to see him." This time I put twenty dollars in his shirt pocket.

He took the money out, looked at it. "Wow," he said flatly.

"Oh, Jesus Christ," I mumbled, handing him two more twenty-dollar bills. We were in the midst of the biggest economic crisis since the Great Depression in a town that had unemployment through the roof, and I couldn't get some good-ol'-boy thug to let me talk to my own brother for twenty dollars. What the hell was happening to this country, anyway?

The large man nodded his head toward a door across the floor of the club, where several women were doing their best to coax tips from the desultory crowd. I'd always avoided places like this, finding them sad and depressing, like a permanent bachelor party refusing to end for fear of the wedding. But I had to admit, these women were impressive. It wasn't the ones with the large, fake breasts that I liked. It was the taut, athletic women who looked like more sexual versions of pro volleyball players or gymnasts. Like the two dancing together in front of a pair of Asian businessmen in their fifties. It was an aerobics show with sex. This I liked. If only it weren't out here on Airline Highway in this dark cavern with lonely Japanese businessmen. What in the world were Japanese businessmen doing in New Orleans, anyway?

The door led to a drab hallway lit with bright fluorescents, the sort of hallway you'd see in any cheap New Orleans office building: brown carpet, Mardi Gras posters hanging on the wall, a row of plain doors. Somewhere very loud, grating music was blasting. Out of one of these doors stepped two women dressed in shorts. One wore a Loyola T-shirt, the other a New Orleans Saints jersey with cutoff sleeves tied at the waist. They looked like two young women headed for the Galleria Mall, which had been not too far away before it closed after the Crash. I realized that I had been watching them pantomime sex together a few minutes earlier.

"Do you know where Tyler's office is?" I asked.

"You hear that shit music?" the blonde in the Loyola T-shirt asked. "That's Tyler's shit."

"He always had the worst taste," I said, hoping they'd stop and talk. It suddenly occurred to me that I couldn't remember the last time I'd had a conversation with an attractive woman who wasn't involved in politics in some way. A stripper seemed like as good a way as any to break a bad habit. And they were both very attractive.

"Yeah?" She smiled, her mouth lifting up to one side, sort of an ironic smile. An ironic stripper. This was getting better. "You been knowing Tyler long?"

"All his life," I said.

"No shit? You don't look like one of his friends. You got some tattoos under that suit? Some kind of ring-a-ding metal hanging? Huh?"

I blushed. So help me, I did. The women I talked to in politics, they didn't talk like this, at least not in the first two minutes of conversation. Not even Ginny. Or Sandra. And they were two tough women.

"He's shy," the other said. She had red hair and the developed arms of a gym buff. "Cute." She reached out and touched my cheek. "Blush, blush," she said, peering at me with striking green eyes.

"He's here?" I asked, pointing toward the door, which seemed to vibrate with some of the worst music I'd ever heard.

"You're not a cop, are you?" the redhead with the strong arms asked me.

"Do you like cops?" I asked. "If you want me to be a cop,

I'd be happy to be a cop. You want me to be a fireman, I'll be a fireman."

"He likes you," the other woman said.

"Sure he does. This one likes girls, you bet."

I shrugged. In my pocket I could feel my iPhone vibrating madly. God knows what was happening while I was in here. Delegates could be changing sides right and left, more bombs going off, Armstrong George announcing he liked to wear a dress around the house to relax. But at the moment I didn't really care.

"FBI," the red-haired woman said. "You could be FBI."

The other girl pulled at her T-shirt. "Let's go."

"Why FBI?" I asked. The way she said it and the reaction from the other girl struck me as curiously genuine. She didn't seem to be kidding.

The redhead raised her eyebrows. They were carefully groomed. "You never know," she said.

"Does the FBI hang out with Tyler?" I joked, but they knew I wasn't joking and they had turned away, heading down the hall. The redhead waved behind her back without turning around. I waited until they were gone and then opened the door to Tyler's office.

It was a large, bland office, with only two notable features: a metal gun case the size of a large refrigerator and a tattered Confederate flag hanging behind the metal desk. The one photo was a framed picture of Tyler with army buddies. They were all wearing camo pants and sweaty T-shirts. This was before Tyler had been "blown to hell," as he put it, in a training accident, and he looked impossibly young and, well, perfect. He waved when I came in but kept yelling into the telephone.

I'd seen him maybe three times since what he called his "accident." He claimed it didn't really bother him, that it gave him "character." But it still made me ache to see him. He was tall and thin and didn't look like a kid anymore. He'd always had an impossibly pretty, boyish face with an elfish sort of glint in his eyes. Now it was hard to look at him, at least if you had known him the way he had been before. The right side of his face was scarred a bright red that twisted his mouth into a permanent half smile. His right arm hung limply down from his shoulder. I knew when he stood up he would cant to the right, the muscles in his right leg not strong enough to support him equally with his left.

He hung up the phone and sat back, looking at me. Yes, you could still see a little of that sparkle in his eye. He wore a tight, sleeveless white T-shirt and black suspenders, just like the last three or four times I'd seen him. I knew that under the desk there'd be the same heavy black boots with the stacked wooden heels he'd worn since he was sixteen or so. He looked at me for a second, head cocked to the side so that more of his unscarred side showed—I wondered if he realized he did this—and then said to me, yelled at me, really, since the music was so loud, "You know the hottest businesses in this town? Security guards and dancers. You can't lose money in either no matter how stupid you are. And believe me, some stupid people have tried. Economy's gone to shit, got unemployment like forty percent, don't believe those happy-talk numbers, total bullshit, and people can't hire enough guards or girls."

I reached over to turn off the CD player. The sudden silence was extraordinary. My ears were ringing. "That's the worst music I've ever heard."

"You used to like my stuff," he said, smiling a little more. "That's my old group, you know."

"Trust me, I know. And that's a lie. I always hated it. Maybe I pretended to like it to be nice, but I always hated it. And, hey, it's great to see you, too."

The tall, scarred man who was my half brother stood up from behind the desk, holding out his hand. When he had mine in his grip, he pulled me toward him and pounded me on the back. He was very strong.

"We're Irish, not Italian, what's with this Godfather crap?" I teased him, pulling back to look at him. I always tried to make myself look directly at him so I wouldn't be one of those people he had talked about once, the ones who look the other way. He had laughed about that, of course, about how all his life he had been trying to shock people, and now it looked like he might be succeeding.

"What about a stripper who's also a security guard?" I asked him.

"What the hell are you talking about?"

"A stripper who doubles as a security guard, wouldn't that be a good business?"

"Dancer. Dancer, dancer. Got to get with the lingo. It's a world of professionals, J.D. You know there is a goddamn dancers' union? Like the Teamsters or something." He shook his head. "Unbelievable. So I haven't seen you in how long? I don't know. You've been in town for days, you don't get in touch, and then you turn up here in the middle of the goddamn afternoon when you're supposed to be electing that silly woman president. So you want something. Right? Don't lie to me, J.D."

"Tyler." I laughed. "It is good to see you."

"You sound surprised. Why shouldn't it be good to see me? I'm a wonderful, caring, loving individual who values friendship and the love of my brothers above all else!" He held me out at arm's length. "So tell me what you want. Enough kissy face."

"Yeah, I want something," I admitted. "I'm just not sure what."

He collapsed on a sagging couch in the corner. "That's very goddamn helpful. You know what I like about being in the security and girl business? Everybody knows what they want. It's real clear. I want to make sure some out-of-work asshole doesn't break into my business, so I need some security. I'm having a party and don't want some maniacs crashing it just because I got a band they like playing. That's easy. That I can do. Or I need some dancers who know how to do what they do, that I can handle. But this existential shit, you want me to tell you what you want, that I don't do."

"You're a good talker," I told him, and I meant it. "I forgot what a good talker you are."

"Yeah? Like maybe I got it from our father, huh?" We laughed again, but there was a little edge to it, a little ouch for both of us. "You having any fun?" Tyler suddenly asked me. "This is your big wet dream, right? Elect yourself a president, even if it is some weak sister socialist like Hilda Smith. Christ, J.D., what are you doing? I got strippers who I'd vote for before that woman."

"Dancers."

"Damn straight. 'I think Armstrong George represents the

dark side of America,' " he mimicked in Smith's voice. "Give me a break. My girls are armed to the teeth and damn proud of it. Not a one of 'em doesn't have a gun and would just as soon blow your ass off as not, you mess with 'em."

"I'll try to remember that. And you can rest assured that Hilda Smith is a firm believer in Second Amendment rights."

" 'Rest assured.' " He mimicked me now. He was good at voices, always was. "Don't give me that crap! She wants to give a goddamn IQ test before you can buy a gun. Get a note from your mother. And your priest. Christ, a goddamn communist."

"There aren't any more communists. And they love guns in Russia, everybody has one."

"See! She's worse than the Russians! Christ!" We chuckled. "You're a famous son of a bitch," Tyler said. "See you on television all the time." He paused, then started laughing. "Why in God's name did you make such a fool of yourself over that television woman? Sandra? She looks meaner than a snake and is old enough to be your mother."

"Maybe it's in my genes."

"That Callahan screw-up-with-women gene thing going, huh?"

I didn't answer, didn't want to think about it, really. "What about you? You married or anything?"

He shook his head. "We going to stand around here all day or are you finally going to tell me what brought you out here in the middle of the day? I know. You want me to make a speech at the convention, right?"

I must have flinched for an instant, even though I didn't realize it. But Tyler was smart and he knew me. Had known me, like I told the dancer outside his office, all his life.

"I get it," he said. "Jesus, of course. You're worried that some-body might find out I'm your brother—half brother, okay—and make some stink about it, right? Embarrass you, right?"

"It's not about embarrassment," I blurted, but I knew he knew I was lying, at least partially. "This thing is just a death struggle. People are going crazy."

"Don't give me that crap," he sneered. "You guys in politics, you always try to make everything you do so goddamn dramatic. Death struggle, my ass. It's an election, that's all. Nobody's going to die. Oh, Jesus, what a look."

"You don't really want that fascist thug Armstrong George to win. I know you don't."

"The hell I don't." He started to laugh. He had a quick, manic laugh. "I hope Armstrong George does win this thing, I really do."

"You don't mean that."

He barked out a laugh. "Hell I don't. I can't stand that woman you work for and that Democrat is such a phony he makes me want to puke. The only reason I would even entertain the idea that maybe it wouldn't be so bad if Hilda won"—he played with the name, raising his voice in a mocking soprano—"is that you work for her and I suppose if she wins you would be a big god-damn deal in the White House, and you could help me get good concert tickets and shit. That's it."

"I could do that." I sat down in the metal chair in front of him.

"Be careful," he said, nodding at the chair, "I just had sex with one of the girls in that chair and it might be kind of a mess."

He cracked up when I shot up out of the chair.

"Forget about it. I wish. Worst thing you can do in this busi-

ness. Screw the help. Not that I care about business that much."
He chuckled.

"You in trouble with the FBI?" I asked.

"Well, that came out of nowhere. Why you asking that?"

I didn't say anything and then he smiled. "I know. One of the
girls said something, right?" He held up his hand. "You don't
have to answer. But yeah, they did come out to talk to me."

I kept waiting for him to laugh and say he was joking. But he
didn't. He looked at me, enjoying the moment. Finally I had to
ask. "Why?"

"Because I'm on some list they keep of Bad Boys and they
wanted to make sure I knew they knew."

"What list?"

"Hell if I know. But it probably comes with my 'known asso-
ciation with undesirables.' "

"Like?"

"Come on, J.D. All the whack-job skinhead white power crazies I've hung out with over the years." He smiled proudly. "Us
gun-loving nuts. You know. The kind that Hilda Smith thinks
are . . . *radical extremist.*"

I didn't know what to say. But I knew he was right. It made
perfect sense that a guy like Tyler would have lit up some warning lights in his day.

"I know what you're wondering. Did they know I was your
brother. Half brother. Isn't that what you were wondering?"

"Oh, Christ, Tyler." I hated that I was so obvious.

"The answer is that if they did, they didn't mention it. Look,
J.D., as far as I'm concerned you're the son of the famous Powell
Callahan, who was a crusading goddamn civil rights journalist,

devoted family man, a giant among men. You had a good Christian mama, God rest her soul, envy of all the Garden Club. You got a football-hero brother who had a little problem but is coming back. Great goddamn American story."

"Yeah," I said. "Great American story."

"But let me tell you something, brother dear. You got it all wrong. You think I'm the embarrassment. You ever think it might be the other way around? You know what kind of crap I'd get if my pals thought I was related to the guy who was trying to help elect *Hilda Smith*?" He laughed.

"So I guess we're good."

Tyler shrugged. "Your father"—he paused, smiling, seeming to enjoy it, and I wondered if he did—"my father was the perfect idea of a liberal savior. Don't try and tell me that's not one of the reasons you became a Republican. You wanted to show the Old Man. And me, I did my own thing too. So really we aren't that different, J.D." He smiled again. "I just get laid more and have a lot more fun."

"Tyler," I said, "I am absolutely sure that's true."

He looked at me like he was going to say something else, then stopped. "You got to get back, I know. You got that 'I've got to get back and do important work' look. Happens all the time in here. Mostly after some guy sneaks away from the office and has himself a little lap dance and then starts thinking, Shit, what the hell am I doing out here on Airline Highway in the middle of the damn day? They get that same look you got right now."

"Tyler, look . . ." I felt like I should apologize.

"Hey," he grinned, "there's your girl." He pointed behind me to a silent television sitting on a Dixie Beer box.

"Jesus," I mumbled, reaching for the sound. Right away I could tell nothing good was happening. It was at the hospital. Hilda was stepping from a town car in front of a seething scrum of reporters and television cameras. Sandra was there, but how did all these other reporters know? Worse, off to the side with a bemused look on his face was Armstrong George, who was just wrapping up a press conference. Right behind him was his son Somerfield, looking impossibly smug.

"I am here to see a friend and supporter who has had a very traumatic experience," Hilda said, looking startled. She hadn't been expecting this, that was clear. She was looking around, blinking in the sun, trying to take it in. Her eye landed on Armstrong George, and you could see her mouth tighten, her eyes narrow. This was an ambush. *She could blow up,* I thought. *Oh God, this could be it.* I instinctively reached for my iPhone and started dialing Lisa.

"This is not a political visit," Hilda Smith said carefully. Behind her, Secret Service agents looked miserable. Quentin Smith stood to the side with Lisa Henderson. The press herd, realizing that they had stumbled upon that rarest of events, an unscheduled appearance by a serious presidential candidate, attacked in full fury.

"But Ms. Vice President, you are running for president. Governor George just told the press that this bombing is further proof for the need for his New Bill of Rights and the measures of the Protect the Homeland bill."

"I am not here to make a political point. Or hold a press conference."

From behind his desk, Tyler cackled. " 'I am not here to make a political point,' " he mimicked. "Christ, J.D., how do you work for this woman?"

The camera panned over Armstrong George, who was still looking calm and superior. "Because of that asshole," I said. "I hate that asshole."

"Bullshit," Tyler barked.

"What?" I whirled around.

Tyler was grinning. "You'd work for Armstrong George in a heartbeat if you thought he could win and he asked you to. And if he paid you a bundle."

"You are so full of shit," I answered, and turned back to the TV. But I wondered if he was right. But so what? Lawyers work for anybody and manage to turn it into some kind of admirable duty. Why couldn't I do the same?

"So is it fair to say that this latest incident has not changed your view on the need for new laws to protect Americans?" Paul Hendricks had that Boston above-it-all tone in his voice. I could have strangled him. This was a disaster. Why didn't Lisa stop it? Jesus God, she was standing right there. Pull the plug, get out, and get her inside the hospital, away from the pack. I'd tipped Sandra so she could get a nice exclusive, put it out there that the VP had gone by the hospital. Now this? What had she done?

"My position is clear. We cannot sacrifice American values to protect American values. We must defend both."

Sandra Juarez jumped in with a follow-up. "Yes, but polls show overwhelming support for the steps Governor George is calling for."

"I know the governor's position," Hilda Smith interrupted, and her eyes narrowed slightly, her face visibly tightening. "And he is entitled to it. His freedom of speech is protected by the real Bill of Rights, the same Bill of Rights that he seems determined to undermine—"

"That Sandra bitch doesn't look so bad," Tyler said. "I mean, for an old woman."

Lisa Henderson stepped forward and took Hilda Smith by the arm. "The vice president is here on personal business. This is not a press conference. Thank you." She pulled gently on Hilda's elbow.

"Why are you refusing to answer the question?" Sandra Juarez demanded.

The vice president started to turn and follow Lisa, ignoring the shouted questions. But then she stopped, face flushed, eyes flashing.

"I came here to visit a friend who was wounded in this futile attempt to disrupt our democratic process. The very notion that anyone could even consider holding a press conference in front of a hospital to score political points is barbaric." She pointed a finger at Armstrong George, who had placidly watched it all unfold. "Ask that man how he could do such a thing."

She turned, shaking off Lisa's hand on her elbow, and disappeared angrily in a scrum of Secret Service agents into the hospital. Her husband followed.

"God." I sighed. "That was horrible. 'Futile attempt to disrupt our democratic process'? This is a convention, not democracy." I turned around to look at Tyler. "Don't you think that was horrible?"

"Depends," Tyler grunted.

"Yeah?" I was suddenly hopeful. Maybe I was being too critical. Maybe it wasn't that bad.

"If you were for Armstrong George, it was a hell of a thing."

"Fuck you."

Tyler shrugged. He got up and teetered for a moment on his bad leg. "You ever get to know that son of his?" Tyler asked me.

I couldn't get the image of Hilda's startled look out of my head. "Somerfield? No, not really. Why?" Tyler followed me out of his office and back into the club.

"He seems to love to get in all the shots." Tyler slapped me on the back as we moved through the dance floor. "Buck up, Buckaroo." There seemed to be beautiful women everywhere. How did Tyler get used to this? "She's weak, admit it. Not just a woman but a weak woman."

"Thanks for reminding me. Great."

Tyler shrugged. "I'm just a dumb ex-skinhead who manages a tittie bar out here on Airline Highway and has a little muscle-for-hire business on the side. You can't expect me to understand anything very deep. But you always did think you were smarter than any of us."

"Paul told me the same thing," I admitted. Tyler was smiling. I couldn't tell if he was smiling at me or at the dancers who swarmed around us, teasing like younger sisters.

"Look out, girls, here we come. Hey," Tyler said to one stunning brunette who towered over him, "have a drink. Have a couple of drinks, I get better looking."

"Oh, I love you, Tyler, just like you are," she said, reaching out to brush her hand over his scarred face. For a moment they made a striking tableau, the showgirl beauty and the guy who looked like he'd been dragged behind a car through flames.

"It's not such a bad job," Tyler said to me at the door. "I get by."

"You want to come down to the convention, let me know, I'll get you a floor pass."

We looked at each other for a moment, then both laughed.

"Yeah, right." Tyler laughed. "Great fucking idea. Maybe I'll give the keynote or something. 'My Life as a Misunderstood, Half-Fried Skinhead.' It'll bring down the house. I have a dream," he suddenly shouted. "A dream of quality strippers for all mankind."

On the way back to the Windsor Court, just as I turned on Camp, past the waiting homeless sprawled on the sidewalk in front of the Presbyterian Mission, I spotted Tobias Green walking toward his storefront office. I tried to duck, but that's hard when driving, and Tobias spotted me, and motioned frantically for me to stop. He was so thin and frail he looked like a black scarecrow flapping in the breeze. Except this was August in New Orleans in the hottest summer in a hundred years and there was no wind. I kept driving.

I got back to the Windsor Court a little after noon. They were waiting for me in Hilda's suite, Lisa Henderson not even trying to hide that she was furious and Quentin looking remote and calm, like he always did. They had been texting and calling me for the last hour and a half. Lisa made that point as soon as I walked into the room. Hilda was meeting with delegates and wasn't there, which was a mild blessing.

"Where have you been?" Lisa demanded.

"At a strip club, actually. How was the hospital?"

"You don't know?" she said, eyes widening, then saw my

look. "Of course you know. Funny," she snapped. "Very funny. That man Armstrong George should be shot."

It made sense that Lisa would blame that little horror show on Armstrong George and not Hilda. That was her greatest weakness as a handler. She was too close to Hilda. She'd made the fatal mistake of falling in love with the meat.

"So you've seen it?" Quentin Smith asked. He pointed to the television, where Hilda's disastrous hospital appearance was playing silently. He was calm, but then he always was, a low southern voice, steady, not particularly friendly or inviting but not openly hostile, either. A voice in control.

There was Hilda Smith stepping out of her town car and the rush of the reporters. She looked terrible, first startled, then angry. We watched in silence. It was almost pornographic, a political snuff film, horrifying, riveting.

"Any idea how Armstrong George knew to be at the hospital?" I asked. But I had the awful feeling I knew: Sandra Juarez would have tipped him off so she could have a more dramatic moment. She had probably told them not to tell any other reporters, but they had turned around and screwed her just like she had screwed me. It was all so perfect and predictable. And it was all my damn fault.

"George was holding a press conference in front of the hospital, attacking Hilda for opposing the national death penalty in his New Bill of Rights, when Hilda showed up," Lisa said. "He even brought that little shit of a son with him. I hate that twerp."

"Why didn't our advance warn us that George was there?" I asked, more to myself than them.

"So this is my fucking fault!" Lisa erupted.

"No," I said, and the sincerity of my reply seemed to surprise her. She stopped.

"We didn't send advance. Hilda wanted it to be personal." Had Eddie Basha known about the visit, he would have sent advance anyway. But I didn't tell Eddie and no one else did either. My little game playing had come close to blowing the campaign. Quentin Smith looked at me as if expecting an answer or explanation. His face was worn with long days outside in the winter. He had blond hair, going gray at the temples, and dark eyes. He was a handsome man.

"We got ambushed," I said, shrugging.

"Ambushed or set up?" Lisa Henderson spat out. "Armstrong George had to know we were planning to go by the hospital. Had to."

She was right, of course. But there was no way I could come clean. "Why?" I asked.

Lisa sputtered. "Why? Why? He was waiting for us, that's why."

"He was there," I said, "yes. But that doesn't mean anything. He didn't have to know Hilda was going to the hospital. It's not such an odd thing for him, holding a press conference at the hospital. This bombing was what he needed. It's a natural for him." It sounded good enough that for a moment I wondered if maybe that was actually what had happened. Maybe Sandra hadn't tipped him off. But I knew. She had to have.

"It does seem . . . odd," Quentin Smith spoke up. "To be there at the right time, at the right entrance." He shrugged.

"The front door?" I responded sharply, then regretted it. I was crazy to spar with Hilda Smith's husband. It was the first rule of consulting: never, ever cross the candidate's spouse. It was always a loser. And though Quentin Smith hung in the background and was rarely seen in public with his wife, he was still a powerful force, a guy who was used to getting his way. It was his money that had guaranteed Hilda Smith's election as governor, as much as Lisa Henderson and all the Hilda Smith acolytes liked to think otherwise.

"Sandra Juarez was the worst," Lisa blurted, then looked at me accusingly.

Quentin Smith raised an eyebrow.

I started to say something, then stopped. I wasn't going to give her that satisfaction.

"There's one other thing," Quentin Smith said finally, after exchanging a look with Lisa.

"Yes?"

"The FBI wants to talk to you," Quentin Smith said.

They were waiting on the ground floor of the Windsor Court. It was a windowless room that had been taken over by the Secret Service as their command post three weeks before the convention began.

Ernie Hawkins was hovering outside the presidential suite to lead me to where the FBI was waiting. There was something reassuring about seeing Ernie, but he only grunted in response when I asked him what the hell was going on. Then a gaggle of delegates and a couple of reporters packed into the elevator and immediately pounced with the usual mixture of advice, criticism, and requests for floor passes. Jammed up near the ceiling of the elevator, the six-five Hawkins watched it with a fixed expression that seemed halfway between disgust and amusement.

"Listen up, J.D."—a delegate stuck his flushed face inches from mine—"when you needed us we were there, and goddamn it, we need you now. My daughter has been working her ass off for Hilda and that prick Basha won't even give her a floor pass for one damn evening! For this I raised your ass over fifty thousand? You and I go way back, J.D., and let me tell you, on a strictly personal level, this bothers me no small amount."

I couldn't remember ever seeing the man before in my life.

"Your daughter is . . . ?"

"Ricki Simmons. Junior at Stanford."

"Right," I nodded, and found myself wondering if she was good-looking. I'd have to ask Ginny. She might know her. I took a card out of the pocket of my tired sport coat and jotted down her name. "Where's she staying?"

Ernie Hawkins looked down at me and winked. He got the joke. The elevator stopped on the lobby floor and everybody got out. Ernie put a key into the control panel and took the elevator down a floor to the basement. This was where the Secret Service had set up one of their command centers. I'd been down here once before, when Ernie and our advance staffer who worked most closely with the Service gave us a walk-through of the hotel set-up. At the end of the long, dim corridor was a secure room they had set up as the emergency fallback in case there was some kind of threat and they were unable to get the VP out. The Secret Service's first response was always to get the "protectee" out of the area as fast as possible. In any motorcade of black SUVs, a couple of them were filled with a tactical response team, a Service unit that had the job of fighting off any threat and staying behind while the lead agents extricated whomever they were guarding.

But there was always a fallback plan in case they couldn't get out. At every stop of anyone high up on the food chain of protection—and a VP was almost as high as it got—a location was picked to use and defend until it was possible to leave. Everybody called it "the Alamo," as in, "Where's the Alamo going to be?" The Alamo at the Windsor Court was down the hall, where an agent with an automatic weapon stood almost casually by the door. I nodded, and he waved back.

Ernie led me inside to one of the command rooms. There was the usual line of radios charging and locked gun racks with automatic weapons and maps of New Orleans on the walls. It smelled like bad coffee and Chinese food. A short man built like a fireplug stepped forward. I'd never seen him before. His black hair was longish in the back, his face framed by sideburns that swept past his ears, pointing to his small mouth. "Joey Francis," he introduced himself. "I'm the bomb guy."

I nodded. There were a couple of other men in the room, one black, one white, both muscular and staring down at their phones. They were doing what you do when you want to listen but don't want to look like you want to listen. There were metal chairs and desks in the room, and Ernie sat down on the edge of a long table.

"I was one of these kids, always knew where the best illegal fireworks stands were." The guy with the Elvis sideburns was talking to me. He had a funny half smile, like he knew some secret that amused him no end. "Loved that shit. M-80s. Cherry bombs. Made my first pipe bomb when I was nine. A piece of lead pipe stuffed with Red Dot shotgun powder, candlewick for a fuse. Tossed it into a gutter on our street, and when it blew it caught the methane gas and every manhole cover up and down the block blew up in the air like big dimes being flipped. That was it. I was hooked."

"Quentin"—I stopped, correcting myself—"Mr. Smith said the FBI wanted to talk to me. But you're with the Service?"

I saw the black man in the back shake his head slightly, as if this amused him.

"Nope," Joey Francis said, putting out his hand. "I work for a living, so that means I'm with the FBI."

"Funny," the white man in the back said, "very funny." He looked up at me from his phone and shook his head. This didn't seem to bother Joey Francis.

"I wanted to ask you, J.D., you have any idea who might have wanted to kill the vice president's delegates?"

The question didn't make sense to me. "Don't you think if whoever did this was trying to kill a bunch of delegates, they'd be dead? This was psychological warfare, right? Scare people. Freak 'em out."

He shook his head as if humoring me. "Fine. I'll rephrase. Do you know anyone who would want to frighten the vice president's delegates?"

"We do that all the time to keep them in line. I have a whole staff dedicated to scaring delegates."

He stared at me.

"You're wondering how I got this job?" I said. "Either that or why I'm being an asshole."

"Both."

"I win elections. Beyond that, I have no socially redeeming purpose."

"Which means that if you lose—"

"I'm a loser, yep."

"Good to know. Is there some kind of master list of delegates and who they are supporting? Can anybody get that?"

"No offense, but doesn't the FBI know these things?" My phone was vibrating constantly. I had already wasted half the day with my brothers, and being in this dark basement talking to a bureaucrat was suddenly seeming like an immense waste of time. I thought I heard one of the two guys in the back chuckle.

"If you could get us a list, I'd like to match it against the one we have. And a list of where they are staying."

"Sure. We have everything from their cell phones and email to underwear sizes. No problem."

Joey Francis nodded and looked a little surprised that I was agreeing so easily. But what did I care?

"Another question," he said. It drove me crazy when people announced that they were about to say something instead of just saying it. It was a favorite rhetorical device of bureaucrats, as if they were afraid they wouldn't be understood without a pre-amble. "Do you think your brother is dangerous?"

I stared at him. A little river of sweat was starting to run down my back. It was hot down here. The builders had not wasted money on air conditioning for the basement. "Paul?" I asked.

I could feel my phone vibrating. Why couldn't people just leave me alone for five minutes? Then I wondered if the president had finally gone ahead with his delayed address and I wanted to get out of this room in a hurry.

Joey Francis was just smiling at me. I hated how this made me feel, defensive and off-balance. I wasn't used to this. I was the guy who prided myself on making others feel defensive. I had made a lot of money advising clients how never to be on the defensive. I stepped in closer to Francis.

"What are you trying to say, Mr. Francis?"

"You have a reputation of a guy who will do anything to win. You have a brother—half brother—who is—"

"Crazy," I said.

He shrugged. "Extreme. It was suggested that we talk to you about him."

"Suggested? By whom?" He just stared at me. "Look, let me explain something about politics. What happened last night was a goddamn disaster for my campaign. Yes, I'm a guy who *will* do anything to win. I'm that obsessive guy who cares about nothing in the world but my campaign. Would I blow up the other guy's delegates if I could get away with it? Hell, I'd burn their houses down, kill their spawn, and sow their fields with salt. I'd drop uranium isotopes in their drinking water. I'd do anything possible to help my candidate win. But this bombing was terrible for us."

He let me finish, not changing his expression. "Sounds good," he said, then held out his hand. "Thanks for coming by."

"That's it?"

"That's it."

I left, with a quick nod to Ernie Hawkins.

———

In the hallway, I realized my heart was pounding and I'd broken out in flop sweat. I was getting into a service elevator near the kitchen, my standard way of avoiding the crowd in the Windsor Court lobby, when the black agent who had been in the command center stepped into the elevator.

"You don't remember me, do you?" he said.

"You were the guy in the room who pretended not to be listening to that Joey guy give me a hard time. So, yeah, I remember you."

"Your brother's right, you know."

Boom. There it was again. *My brother?*

"He says you're one smart smartass. But come on, you don't remember me at all?" He took a key out of his pocket and locked the elevator to keep it from moving. "Old Indian trick," he said.

I stared at him. I'd slept less than two hours the night before, not more than four or five hours every night for the past month. All the faces of all the people I'd met during the campaign swirled before me. I tried to focus. There was something familiar about the guy.

"You see," the black man said with a smile, "it's what I always told your brother. The big slow white boys are heroes for life and us fast nee-gros are invisible. He's lumbering up and down the field like a truck and I'm a ninja night warrior. Invisible. Deadly."

It was quite a little speech. I stared, feeling the grip on my arm relax. Then the man broke into a deep, loud laugh. "Ninja," he said, chuckling at his own language. "I like that."

Suddenly a face and name swam out of my subconscious. "Robinson," I said. "Walter Robinson."

"Hallelujah," the man said. "Praise the Lord. His children have wandered in the wilderness long enough."

"You were great," I said, actually excited now. "The fastest guy I ever saw." Walter Robinson had played with my brother at LSU. He had been a tremendous defensive back until something had happened. "You got hurt, right? Your knee?"

He nodded. "Bad ACL, bad doctor. Bad redo. Zip, it's over."

"Man, you were fantastic."

"Your brother wasn't bad. But you know why he got all the glory?"

"Did it have something to do with winning the Heisman?"

He shook his head. "You are confusing the effect with the cause. It was Title Seven in reverse."

"Title Seven?"

"Quotas. Reverse discrimination. Call it what you will. Your brother was a freak—"

"Still is," I agreed.

"He was a freak because he was WHITE! And a RUNNING BACK! Nobody could believe it. And a decent running back, at that."

"Walter," I asked with a sigh, "why are we having this conversation? You followed me in here for a reason." I held up my phone. I couldn't count the number of text messages and emails that had come in during the last forty-five minutes. "Are you with the Secret Service now?"

"A cop. And because I am such a charming son of a bitch and because I am a former football great—your momentary lapse of recall being the exception—and because I am a black man in a city that likes to call itself black and because the big boys in the department do not believe I am dealing drugs or killing people on the side for extra cash, they have made me the NOPD designated liaison with the Secret Service–FBI total federal goat rope during this little celebration of democracy."

"So can you tell me what was going on with that guy? Why did he really want to see me?"

Walter Robinson grinned. "It was all about Joey Francis proving that he wasn't going to be intimidated by anybody, even the vice president's own campaign manager. This is his town, not some Washington big shot's."

"That's crazy."

Walter Robinson leaned in intently. For a terrible moment, I thought he was going to kiss me. Instinctively, I pulled back.

"Can I trust you?" he finally asked.

"Trust?" I asked. "Trust?"

Walter Robinson nodded. "You and me."

"God, no," I shot back instantly. "Of course not."

Walter Robinson kept staring.

"Trust?" I repeated. "Like you were going to share something with me and I was supposed to value this something and then somehow take that something into consideration?" Walter Robinson shrugged. "No way. Not going to happen. All I care about is one simple thing: in seventy-two hours Hilda Smith is going to have more delegates voting for her than that psychotic asshole Armstrong George. That's it. Period. That's my sad little mission. And I am taking on no passengers or excess baggage. So anyone would have to be out of their mind to trust me unless that trust helped me get what I need to get done."

"I think I'm not hearing the truth," Walter Robinson said. "I think there's one thing you care more about than Hilda Smith getting those delegates to vote for her."

"Yeah?" Suddenly I wanted out of the suffocating elevator in the worst way. I was sick to death of this man leaning into my face. "Well, let me tell you something: if somebody told me that I had a choice between a cure for cancer and electing Hilda Smith, I'd laugh out loud, the choice would be so easy. And that's the God's honest truth," and while I said it, I knew that it was the truth. There was a time when such a realization might have troubled me in some deep way, but I'd reached a point in the campaign—and my life—when I just didn't care.

"I still think there is one thing you care about more than this election," Walter Robinson repeated.

"Am I being kidnapped?" I asked, and reached for the control panel. His hand shot out and stopped me.

"You care about you," Walter Robinson said in a quiet but menacing voice.

I paused for a moment, then burst out laughing.

"Well, earth to Walter, come in. Of course I care more about myself. I'm a political consultant, for crying out loud, not a missionary. I'd get run out of the damn consultants' union if it didn't put me numero uno. So what?"

"So, can I trust you if it's in your best interest?"

I put a hand on Walter Robinson's shoulder. It felt like a warm piece of iron. Paul might be melting a little around the edges since his playing days, but Walter was still doing something right. "Walter, you can always trust me to put my interests first. Of that you can be sure. Now can I please get the fuck out of this elevator before I lose my goddamn mind?"

"I've got a letter from the bomber," Walter Robinson finally said. "It talks about your girl."

"My girl?" My heart started to race. "Sandra? The bomber talks about Sandra?"

He frowned. "Who the fuck is Sandra? Your girl. Hilda, the vice president." Walter smiled a little. "It seems our boy don't like your girl too much."

Chapter

★

Five

EDDIE BASHA GRABBED ME as soon as I stepped out of the service elevator.

Walter Robinson smiled at Eddie and waved, just before the elevator doors closed. "Who the hell is that?" Eddie demanded. "Is he with the FBI? And what's this shit about you getting interviewed by the FBI, anyway?" Eddie insisted, not waiting for my answer.

"How the hell do you know about that?"

He looked at me with a smirk. I didn't like this look. It made me feel like he knew something I didn't know, and I was supposed to know everything. That was my job.

We were standing in the hall of the Windsor Court, on the floor completely taken over by Hilda Smith staffers. We had compressed an entire campaign into this floor and the trailers over at the Superdome. One room was devoted to nothing but the tracking, care, and feeding of delegates. Another room was filled with the finance staff, who were consumed with making sure the heavy-hitter donors felt special while also setting up fundraisers for the general election. I loved that group. They were a combination of boiler-room hustlers and special forces, incredibly driven and focused. Most of them were in their twenties, and there wasn't one of them who, if not already rich, wasn't sure to be absurdly so. Next to them was speechwriting. The two groups eyed each other with bemused suspicion. While the finance staff was banging the phones and making side bets on how much they could raise, the speechwriters would wander the halls in a daze, chewing on pencils and looking like every lost grad student who hadn't slept in months. The advance staff was next to the speechwriters. They were the guys and girls who prided themselves on always making events look good. They were famously arrogant and known for partying hard after an event they had spent days putting together. I'd bailed out more than one from jail. Then there was the legal department, a small law firm that handled everything the campaign touched. It was a strange, highly functional family that was brought together not by idealism or ideology so much as a burning desire to win. And now we were close. Very, very close.

Eddie steered me away from a passing intern. She was pretty. As political director, Eddie Basha had made sure that every female intern was a looker. This did not go unnoticed or unappreciated by women like Kim Grunfeld and Lisa Henderson. They went out of their way to make life miserable for the young women.

"Come on, Tommy Singh has got numbers for us."

Eddie pulled me into his room, just down the hall from the war room. Tommy Singh was sitting on the bed studying numbers on his phone. He was always studying numbers on his phone. If he died tomorrow, they would erect a statue of him peering at numbers on his phone.

"This bombing is bad for us. Very bad," Singh pronounced.

"This is news?" I asked.

Eddie spoke up. "Don't try to be sincere. Listen up, Tommy did a poll on the bombing."

"This is the poll we agreed you were not going to do, right, Singh?"

"That would be correct, yes."

"Jesus Christ," I erupted. "Have you lost your goddamn mind?"

"I will not charge the campaign," Tommy Singh insisted. "I would never do that, J.D."

"That's not the point. If it gets out that we are polling—"

"But you aren't. I am," Singh insisted.

"Oh, that will help. Everybody will buy that. The campaign didn't poll, just the pollster. Oh, that's just great. And by the way, if you paid for the poll, then we're violating federal election law and we're all going to jail."

"Armstrong George wants to abolish the FEC," Singh said.

"He also supports torture, so he's probably cool if I waterboard you."

This seemed to confuse him. He shrugged and started to read from his poll. "'Does the recent bombing at the Republican National Convention make you more or less likely to support stronger measures to protect against crime and terrorism, including wiretaps, detention without bail, etc.?'" Singh looked up. "More likely: seventy-eight percent."

"So?" I asked. "Did you poll whether or not blowing up Armstrong George made you more likely or less likely—"

"I'm thinking you shouldn't keep joking about that stuff," Eddie sighed.

"I can continue," Singh insisted hopefully. He was like every pollster. Nobody ever paid any attention to him except when he was reading numbers. So he liked to read numbers. A lot. Slowly.

"But the bottom line," Eddie said, "is that Tommy's numbers make it clear that as long as everybody is focused on the bombing, we are screwed. Now, here's my latest state-by-state breakdown of delegates."

Eddie laid a printed chart on the bed. It was a list of every delegate and their likely voting status. For the next hour, we debated each delegate, all 2,242 of them and another 2,180 alternates. What would it take to crack each Armstrong George delegate? Was it hopeless, possible, likely? For each Hilda Smith delegate, we tried to imagine if we were working for Armstrong George, what we would do to get one of the Smith delegates to flip. As VP, Hilda Smith had certain toys we'd already used to scarf a few of George's delegates. We invited a half-dozen from California to ride with her on Air Force Two from LA to San Francisco in May, and four of the six had flipped. Nobody seemed to care about visiting the vice president's residence on Wisconsin, but we'd been able to give a handful of delegates special tours of the White House when the president was at Camp David, followed up with a lunch in the White House Mess. The White House Mess seemed to always really get them, despite the mediocre food. Then some of George's big donors who were also heavy hitters for the president had heard about it and leaned on the president to cut us off.

We went through the database on each delegate. Some stuff was routine: lawyer, involved in environmental causes, married, lost lots of money in the big crash. Lots of it. Some was dark, closet stuff and it was creepy that we even knew about it: what websites a delegate liked to frequent late at night, what sexual harassment lawsuits had been settled out of court, who spent too much time and money in Vegas. But tantalizing as the personal stuff was, it was always hard to find a way to use it. Like a nuke: great to have, hard to use without blowing yourself up.

After an hour, we had evaluated every delegate and narrowed the universe to just thirty-seven delegates we thought might be likely to switch. But of those thirty-seven, only eleven were Armstrong George delegates that might possibly switch to Hilda Smith. That left twenty-six delegates who were technically committed to Smith but were likely to switch to Armstrong George if it looked like he was going to win.

"This is not good," Tommy Singh observed in his annoying, neutral tone.

"Thanks, Tommy," I grumbled. I was still pissed at him for going ahead with the survey.

"We will lose unless something changes," Singh continued, undeterred. "That is clear."

A long silence ensued.

"We can shake it up," I said. I wasn't sure if I believed it at all, but I needed to be cheered up, and if nobody else was going to do it, I would have to try it myself.

"How?" Eddie asked.

"I've got some ideas," I insisted. It annoyed me how skeptical they looked. "What ever happened to believing in your campaign manager to work miracles?" I chided them.

"I believe in delegate counts," Tommy Singh said dryly. But he said everything dryly.

They waited for me to continue. When I didn't, Eddie just said, "Well, good. Because otherwise, I think we are fucked pretty."

"We keep these numbers to ourselves, right?" I looked at each of them hard. "The world thinks this is a three- or four-vote deal. If it gets out how soft our numbers really are, this whole thing could collapse on us."

"J.D.," Tommy Singh said in his flat, unemotional voice, "it is time for rabbits out of hats. These numbers are not encouraging."

"Thanks, Tommy, I'll try to get serious about this now. I promise."

I turned and left.

I met them at a coffee shop on St. Charles just up from Lee Circle. Big brother Paul and Walter Robinson were sitting in the middle of the empty shop when I walked in.

Walter tapped his watch. "You're late."

"You guys," I grumbled, "don't have much to do. I do."

"Ungrateful, I'd call him," Paul said. "Downright ungrateful."

The coffee shop was bland and hip, with prices that were high for New Orleans. "Nobody ever comes here," Walter explained. "It's owned by a guy who has some clubs in the Quarter and he uses it to wash money he takes under the table at the clubs."

"Glad you're right on top of it," I said.

Walter shrugged. "He's useful. A lot of people come in those clubs and he helps us out."

Sitting at the table with the two large men, I felt like I was back at the kitchen table when I was a teenager, Paul and his oversized football buddies dominating everything. All that was missing was my loony dad pouring bourbon for everyone, probably wearing his naval flight helmet.

"Can we talk about this letter?" I couldn't stop thinking about that delegate count. We were losing, that was clear. The only good thing was that nobody had realized it yet. But they would. I had to change the dynamic while it was still possible. "It came to me. The guy must have seen my name in the paper or me on television or something. Maybe he knows me. Hell if I know. Can I see it?"

Walter stared hard at me with an impressive ferocity. It was his best game face from the Tiger Stadium days and I had to admit it was an intimidating sight. "So here's the deal," he said. "I've kept the letter tight."

"Tight?" I asked.

"Just me and a couple of my guys. I haven't given it to Joey Francis."

"You're kidding me? You and a couple of NOPD blues are sitting on a letter from a guy who is scaring the crap out of the convention? And, more importantly, is hurting my chances to elect my candidate?"

Paul smiled. "Glad you got your priorities straight." He held up a coffee cup in salute. "Walter doesn't trust the FBI, and Walter, well"—he hesitated and looked over at Walter, who nodded—"Walter is like us. He has some dreams."

"Dreams?" I said.

"Needs," Walter said.

The two of them were looking at each other and smiling. "Oh my God, you want to be the hero and bust this thing, right? That's why you haven't turned over the letter. You want this to be the Walter Robinson show?"

"Well, I—" Walter said.

"Exactly," Paul said.

"Good God. Isn't that illegal?" I asked.

"You remember that black stripper who got sliced and diced and used as crab bait?" Walter asked, leaning toward me.

"That was a movie, right?"

"Exactly!" Walter shouted. "That was my case. But the FBI took it over as a federal investigation. Hate crime, like that made a difference. They got all the glory. I'm not letting that happen again."

"What do you want?"

"I'll tell you what I want. I want to be on ESPN."

"ESPN?"

"You know how they always have guys who were the shit in college in the booth to talk trash about the game? I want to be one of those guys."

"You don't want to be on CNN or NBC? You're a serious guy now, Walter. This thing breaks, you got some big-time respect coming."

"CN fucking N? NBC? Are you out of your mind? Nobody in my world watches the news. We watch sports, man! What kind of people do you think we are? If I can break this thing, get some attention, I figure I can parlay this on ESPN. But I want you to help." He leaned in close again. He liked to do that. "Can you promise me you'll help?"

"Sorry, sorry. Got it. Sure. I'll do everything I can to get you on ESPN." He stared at me like he was deciding exactly where to put the bullet. "I'll get the vice president to make some calls. We'll be all over this."

"The vice president?" he asked. "Really?"

"Promise."

"And she has got some suck?"

"She's the second most powerful person in the goddamn country. What the hell do you think?"

My brother spoke up. I'd almost forgotten he was there. "J.D." He sighed. "Walter is trying to help. He gets paid to deal with little shits every day in his job. Don't be one."

God, it was the same voice I'd grown up with. It was strangely reassuring, to be back in a world in which my older brother was giving me a hard time for mouthing off to one of his friends.

"I don't want to tell him anything else," Walter said. I think he may actually have been pouting.

"Oh, Christ," Paul groaned. "This is ridiculous." He got up.

"The letter beat the crap out of chinks and spics and sand niggers," Walter blurted.

"Yes?" Oh, Jesus, this could be good. Maybe the gods had decided I deserved a gift.

Paul sat back down. "I'll translate. It was an anti-immigration, full-bore hate piece. Lock up the borders. Throw away the key."

"It said that?"

"Calm down, boy," Walter said, grinning. "You biting on that bone?"

"America has to be saved for Americans, you know," Paul added.

The pretty hipster with bright purple hair brought us over fresh coffee and gave Walter a certain look. She was definitely sleeping with him.

"Did your bomber pal mention Armstrong George in the letter?" I asked.

"Might as well have," Walter said. He hesitated. "Other things."

"Like what?"

"All this crap about sovereign nations and purity and honor and crap like that. Signed it 'C.N.'"

"C.N.? What's that mean?"

Walter shrugged. "His initials, I guess. What do you think?"

"Go ahead," Paul told Walter.

"What?" I asked. "Go ahead what?"

Walter paused and sighed. "He enclosed a copy of the man's greatest hits."

"What are you talking about?" I was getting tired of this. It was like they were determined to take up as much of my time as possible by laying it out to me bit by bit.

"The New Bill of Rights. He sent a copy along. Drew a little Confederate flag at the bottom."

"We've got to leak this," I said right away. "Now." Jesus, I mean, an Armstrong George supporter behind this bombing? It was perfect. Hilda could take the high road, make Armstrong George take the heat. Beautiful.

"What about my deal?" Walter demanded. "I got to get some guarantees here."

"Whatever the hell you want, big guy. And I mean it. She wins, you write your ticket."

"And if she doesn't?"

"Christ, Walter. We'll get you famous, don't sweat it. I just have to figure it out. We need to leak it. That's what we need."

"You know how to do that?"

"God, yes." I laughed. "That I know how to do."

"How? When?"

"Let me think about it. Just keep the letter in a safe place."

"Don't you worry, sugar pie. We're covered."

The Secret Service ushered the three delegates into Hilda Smith's suite. Eddie had confirmed that so far only three had left town, so we needed three replacements. Meeting at the VP's suite was part of the strategy, of course, to wow the alternates with the office itself—we didn't want them being reminded that they were about to spend time with the second most important person on earth. She was waiting with a smile and a can of Diet Coke in her hand. That was planned as well, like the personal photos of Hilda and her husband and twin sons that were placed around the room. You wanted them to think they were seeing the personal side of this powerful person, not just getting the standard tourist tour—keep behind the rope, please—but having a chance to walk right into the living room and have a can of Diet Coke with the vice president. She had a glass, but she drank straight from the can, opened it herself, and when they brought around some cookies, she grabbed a handful of the chocolate chips like they were the last food on earth. I had to bite my tongue to not laugh, but it was smart as hell.

The secretary of agriculture was there too, and the secretaries of defense and transportation as well. Agriculture was there because the three delegates were from South Dakota. Agriculture still counted big in that state, and two of the three delegates were from farm backgrounds themselves. Defense was there because he was an Iraq War hero and a regular on the talk shows, so everybody knew him. He helped protect Hilda Smith's right flank, too, being ex–Special Forces and all that; it made her seem less squishy just to have him there looking like a soldier. And though it wasn't like anyone particularly cared about the transportation secretary one way or the other, she was there because it was always good to have one more person around and she had been available. And, besides, she was the former mayor of Orlando and an old college friend of Hilda Smith's, which meant that she understood a little bit about politics and would be loyal, two rare traits for any cabinet member.

The vice president was positioned in an overstuffed chair at the center of a half circle, framed by the cabinet secretaries. Lisa and I hung out on the side, half leaning, half sitting on a bookcase against the wall.

Under my arm, I had Eddie Basha's dossier on the three people who had suddenly moved up from alternate delegates to the real thing. Lisa promised me that Hilda Smith had studied the stuff, but who knew? She didn't like this kind of politics, the sucking up, the stroking, the implied threat. She was no Lyndon Johnson or Bill Clinton, or even George W. Bush.

"I visited Terri Clark this morning at the hospital," she began, after greeting each and making sure they were introduced to the cabinet members in the room.

"I hear she's one tough cookie," Ted Jawinski said. "Hard to scare her." He was not young, somewhere over sixty-five.

"She's a brave woman," the vice president said gently. "She's made us all proud."

"Killin's too good for that son of a bitch who set this thing off, scaring the bejesus out of everyone. You know what I think, Mrs. President? I think we ought to have public executions. Ought to have to do firing squad duty just like jury duty. Civil obligation."

Lisa turned toward me, a sick look crowding her eyes. I wanted to laugh. One of the problems with Hilda and Lisa and their little inner circle from Vermont was how easily they were shocked. They'd never learned to embrace the whole sick joy of the total American strangeness in politics. You needed to love the weird, the deformed, the deranged.

Hilda Smith smiled. "It would be Mrs. *Vice* President, but you can call me Hilda," she said, still in the same soft voice. "I want to be president and I need your help. I need each of you to help."

Perfect, I thought, relaxing a bit. *She can do this.*

"We're formally uncommitted, of course," spoke up Bruce Dent. "Those are the rules."

"I believe," the secretary of defense said, friendly but with an edge, no doubt about it, "that the vice president is well aware of the party rules."

I knew all about this kid Bruce Dent; his "shit sheet," as we called it, was tucked under my arm. I had never met him before but didn't like him. He was twenty-one years old and had been named a Marshall Scholar a few months earlier, not an everyday occurrence at the University of South Dakota. Now he was sitting in a hotel suite with the vice president and cabinet members. He had scored a perfect 2400 on his SATs. The kid was so full of himself it was going to take more than a mild brush-off, even coming from the secretary of defense, to make him cower.

"You know, sir," he addressed the defense secretary directly, in a firm, calm voice, as if he did this every day, "my father served with you in Iraq. Eighty-second Airborne."

Goddamn it, why the hell didn't we know that? I started looking through my folder on Dent frantically. I hated being surprised.

The defense secretary smiled. "Glad to hear it, son."

"He was killed in the first week of the war."

So what, you little prick? I wanted to shout. *You think that gets you off the hook?*

The defense secretary nodded solemnly. "He was . . ."

"Richard Dent, sir. Did you know him?"

I felt like my head was exploding. What in God's name was happening? I tried to get Hilda's attention, motioning her to move on, get going. But she was just staring at this little prick with his plain, almost baby face, dressed in a black suit and thin tie. He looked like he ought to be pushing *Watchtower*s door to door.

"You must be very proud of him," the defense secretary said after a long pause. "And I know you must miss him greatly."

"He always put his country first," Dent said, "and taught me to do the same. That's why this isn't an easy decision for me, who to support for president. I know I was elected as an alternate delegate for the vice president, but given recent events, I find myself rethinking."

No one said anything for what seemed like an eternity. I wanted to throttle the self-important little shit. "Jesus Christ," I mumbled, and got an elbow from Lisa.

"I believe, Bruce," the vice president finally spoke up, "that I very much have the best intentions of this country at heart. I'm a first-generation American. A deep patriot. I love this country with all my heart and soul, and that's why I want to be president."

Bruce Dent nodded politely. "Mrs. Vice President, the country is coming apart. It's just getting worse, even since I ran as a delegate. Now this bombing. You said you didn't want to be president. Are you really ready to lead?"

This kid should die immediately.

Hilda laughed. "Well, Bruce, you were a Boys State president yourself, president of the student body at South Dakota, I'm sure you understand that sometimes in politics you say what you think is politic." She smiled, but the softness was gone from her voice.

Well, at least she has read the briefing files, I thought. That was something.

The "I don't care to be president" quote came when she had suddenly emerged as a vice presidential possibility and was asked about her ambitions. She had said, without thinking about it for more than a moment, that she had no desire or interest in becoming president.

She turned and faced Sue Johnson, who had yet to say a word. She taught ninth-grade American history. "Sue," Hilda Smith asked, "is there anything in particular you'd like to ask me?" She smiled at the schoolteacher. I had to give her one thing, she did have a great smile.

"Well, Mrs. Vice President, there is one issue that we have been working on for quite some time."

Lisa and I fumbled through Sue Johnson's file as if it held the secrets to eternal life. Issue? She had written letters to the editor against school vouchers and had once run for the state legislature opposed to homeschooling. That was all safe enough. Hilda could fudge the school voucher stuff, she'd done that already a million times in front of a thousand different teacher groups, and homeschooling, who cared?

"Yes, Sue?"

"There's a railway crossing three blocks from our school, and we have been trying and trying to get one of those mechanical arms that come down when there are trains, but for some reason, it just hasn't happened. The governor got so mad about it, he's been keeping a highway patrol car there to warn people, but they can't do that forever and that's not right and—"

"I'll look into it personally," the secretary of transportation said.

"It's near the school, is it, Sue?" Hilda asked sympathetically. "I remember when two kids were hit in Burlington by a train. It was terrible."

Sue Johnson was nodding frantically. "Terrible. That's what happened to us. We lost a senior girl that way." Her eyes reddened.

"I know that crossing," Ted Jawinski said. "Hell of a thing, Mrs. President."

It seemed that Ted was determined to be in the presence of the president.

"Do you know about Crazy Horse?" Ted Jawinski suddenly demanded.

"The Indian leader?" Hilda asked, then corrected herself. "Native American leader."

"The statue," Jawinski corrected. "The carving."

There was a pause. "Crazy Horse the statue?" she finally asked. The other cabinet members looked at each other. No one knew what the hell this guy was talking about.

"Crazy Horse was a great warrior." The secretary of defense finally spoke up to cover the silence.

"Hell yeah," Jawinski exploded. "Out near Rapid City. South of Rapid, really. Damnedest thing you ever saw. Like Rushmore, only this Indian up there on a horse with his lance. Hell of a thing. Ought to be a national monument. No doubt about it."

"I see," the vice president said. "It sounds . . . impressive."

"I'm part Sioux, you know," Jawinski announced.

Everyone in the room stared at the man.

"Really, Mr. Jawinski?" the vice president finally asked.

"That's what they tell me. My great-great-great-aunt or something. Just didn't tell me which part!" He laughed heartily. "All kinds of crazy stuff happening out there then, you know? Anyway, this Crazy Horse is really something. We gave some money for it in the Lions Club. No federal money, though, not a cent. Ought to be a national monument for sure. It'll knock your eyes out."

"We'll certainly take a close look at it, Mr. Jawinski. It'll get our attention right away."

He nodded.

Now! I begged silently. *Close the sale now! Ask for the damn order!*

"What I'd like to do," the vice president said, "is walk out of here today and be able to announce that I can count on each of you for your support. It would mean a great deal to me and, I believe, to the country."

There was a long pause. Ted Jawinski looked down at his cowboy boots. Sue Johnson clutched her hands tightly together in her lap. Bruce Dent looked the vice president right in the eye.

"Bruce?" she asked with that great smile.

"Well, Mrs. Vice President, as I think you can understand, I do need to talk with Armstrong George first."

The cabinet secretaries stiffened.

"I would think you know where he stands on the major issues. Tell me, Bruce, do you support closing our borders to all non-Europeans? Do you support English not only first, but English only in all our schools? Do you support withdrawing from the UN? Do you support ending NATO?"

It was a sudden, angry burst. The secretary of defense was so shocked his mouth was hanging open. I liked it. If she showed this side more often, we'd be a hell of a lot better off.

The young man reddened. "I just think it would be best if I spoke with him, Mrs. Vice President."

"Of course, Bruce." She smiled. "Even Armstrong George hasn't done away with the First Amendment. At least not yet."

Yes! Ram it right up the little twerp's ass!

A long silence hung in the room. It was not pleasant. Finally, Ted Jawinski spoke. "Could I kind of get back to you on this thing?" he asked.

"Of course. But let me remind you that the next twenty-four hours could determine the future direction of our country, and you can play a critical, positive role. This is no time to play politics with our national interests."

They all looked down. Playing the shame card at the end was a good move. Maybe I was wrong. Maybe she was better at this than I thought. It was funny how people changed when they had to. I can't tell you how many candidates I've had who started out promising to stay positive, no attacks, but by the end were begging you to just nuke the other bastard and get it over with. Nuke him, nuke his wife, nuke his damn kids if that's what it takes. Just don't let me lose.

As soon as the three delegates left the room, Lisa Henderson started applauding. Everyone joined in.

"If I may say so," the secretary of defense said, "I only wish every delegate at this convention could have been in this room."

"Well, no one committed." Hilda Smith sighed, but it was clear she was pleased. "J.D. has been telling me we have to up the stakes for this nomination, and I think it's time I took his advice."

"I thought I suggested kicking them all in the ass," I said. "I'll be back in a second," I added, and slipped out the suite door while everyone was laughing. It was a dark laugh, nervous and edgy.

I caught up with Bruce Dent at the elevator. "Bruce," I said, waving him over. The young man still looked flushed from his encounter with the vice president. I put my arm around his shoulder and walked him down the hall.

"Listen," I told him in a warm, friendly voice, "you're a Marshall Scholar, right? Smart as hell."

The intense young man did not attempt to dissuade me from this opinion.

"A quick study," I continued. "So here's a little lesson in Crime and Punishment." I smiled and Bruce Dent nodded, focusing on me with his myopic eyes. I felt like grabbing his ears and ripping them off.

"It's really quite simple, you arrogant little shit," I said in the same warm voice. "Come out for us in the next hour and I make you assistant deputy campaign manager, and when we win, you get a nice, juicy position in the White House." I smiled.

Bruce Dent turned red and then swallowed, a process that looked painful. "You're offering me a job for my vote. That's illegal."

I punched him playfully in the shoulder. "That's why we call it Crime. Now here's the Punishment part. If you don't, or if you jerk us around, then I and my entire opposition research

operation will spend the rest of our lives digging up the nasti-
est shit we can find on you and making sure it gets in the right
places."

Bruce Dent's face reddened even more. "That's outrageous."

"Of course it is. So is the fact that sometimes we just make up
this shit and leave it to some poor fuck like you to deny it. Got
a little secret or two there, pal? Maybe smoked a little dope over
there in England? But hey, the choice is yours."

I beamed as if I had just offered my favorite nephew a choice
job. I took my arm off Dent's shoulder and moved in front of
him, gesturing with both hands. "I want to hear a little commu-
nication here, Bruce. The problem with the world today, nobody
communicates enough. I want to include it in my own personal
New Bill of Rights. Humans must communicate more."

Bruce Dent stared at me. "How much does a deputy campaign
manager make?"

"Assistant deputy campaign manager, Bruce. Now we're
talking."

I met Sandy Morrison late in the afternoon at her suite at the
Royal Orleans on Bourbon Street. It was a sprawling space, with
louvered windows and French doors leading out to a balcony
overlooking a courtyard. The curtains were drawn and the air
conditioning was on so high that I shivered as I stepped inside
the room, sweat forming in the small of my back. Somewhere
Brazilian jazz was playing. It felt like a nightclub.

Sandy was wearing a tailored red suit that seemed to match
her fingernails perfectly. It didn't look accidental. In a high wing-
back chair, she crossed her legs and steepled her hands.

"Of course I can do it," she said.

"But will we get caught?" I knew the answer, but I just wanted to hear some reassurance.

Sandy shrugged. "If we use my people, my regular phone banks, maybe. You never know who might talk. Christ, J.D., I have twenty-two hundred people who make phone calls for me in a dozen cities. You think I can nursemaid every one of them? All I can do is strangle them when they fuck up."

She smiled. It seemed to be a notion that had particular appeal to her.

She stood and walked over to the curtains in front of the French doors leading onto the balcony. Pulling them back, she revealed a stunning Asian woman in a string bikini lying on a chaise longue. She looked to have been doused in oil.

Sandy let the curtain drop. "Nineteen," she mouthed, almost shivering in delight. She crossed over and picked up a pack of menthol cigarettes off the wet bar and lit one with a gold cigarette lighter. She snapped it closed with a hard click, inhaling half the cigarette in one long gulp.

I'd used Sandy Morrison phone banks for years before we finally met, when I was running a Texas governor's race and found myself in her home base of Dallas. To my astonishment, she insisted on picking me up in a limo and took me on an all-night tour of Dallas's strip clubs, the "best tittie bar circuit in the world," she'd proudly announced. All the doormen had known her and many of the dancers. I'd never seen anybody have as much fun.

At the final club of the evening, a massive place known as VIP, with what seemed like hundreds of dancers, Sandy had summoned a dozen of the most attractive to a private room known as the Champagne Club and, with obvious delight, told me to take my pick, any or all would be happy to accompany me back to the Mansion on Turtle Creek hotel, where I was staying. More overwhelmed than aroused, I passed.

"You sure, honey?" she'd asked, gently waving a handful of hundred-dollar bills toward the women. Sandy fanned the bills between her fingers, like a Vegas dealer. I wondered where she had learned the trick. "You take that car back, sweetie, 'cause little Sandy is going to have herself some fun. God, I do love being rich."

When I left, she was surrounded by the dancers, handing out hundred-dollar bills like candy to children. She was smiling and looked supremely pleased to be alive.

"We elect your Hilda, she going to take away my cigarettes?" That was one of the accusations Armstrong George had made, that a President Hilda Smith would push to make tobacco illegal.

"God, I hope so," I said.

"Fuck you," Sandy said, lighting up another. She held the smoke for a moment, then blew it in my direction.

"Fuck you, too." I smiled at her.

"Here's how it ought to work," she announced. "What we do is get somebody else to make the calls. I hire another outfit, a small firm, and tell them that I was approached by Armstrong George's campaign to make the calls but couldn't do it because I was already working for Hilda Smith. But I thought she was going to lose and wanted to help Armstrong George, so I was setting it up."

I thought about it for a minute. It was a typically devious and effective Sandy plan. "I like it," I said.

"Okay. Great. How are you going to pay for it?"

"Let's talk about that," I said.

"Okay," Sandy agreed, sitting back down. She always liked to talk about money.

"I can come up with the money from Host Committee funds. It's such a mess, nobody will notice."

The balcony doors opened and the young woman walked into the room, trailing a towel. She smiled at Sandy, ignoring me completely. "This damn city smells," she said.

"Yes," Sandy answered. Her eyes seemed to narrow a bit as she watched the athletic woman walk across the room to the bedroom door.

"God, I do love being rich," Sandy said, after a pause.

"About money," I said.

Sandy focused on me, smiling slightly. "Yes, J.D.? What's wrong? You look squirrelly."

"Well . . . ," I started, then stopped.

Sandy laughed. "After all these years we've been doing business and I've tried to throw some sugar your way, are you now trying to tell me you want to get a little profit-sharing plan going?"

"Not really." We stared at each other for a moment, then I shrugged. "Well, maybe."

"Jesus Christ, J.D., just spit it out. You're the only campaign manager I work with who doesn't demand a piece of the action. You've given me a shitload of business. You deserve a piece."

There it was. Now all I had to do was say yes. She'd been trying to give me money for years. There was no reason not to take it. It didn't have to be called a kickback, it could be a finder's fee. Or a profit-sharing arrangement. She was right. I'd never gone in for it, but this sort of stuff happened all the time in politics.

"Maybe," I finally said. "But not to me. If we did anything, I might want you to make a contribution to a little organization run by Tobias Green."

Sandy started laughing, then coughing as her cigarette smoke went in the wrong direction. "Tobias Green?" She coughed some more, and as her face strained and turned red, I thought she looked ten years older. Little lines stood out on the edges of her face that I figured were left over from face-lifts. "That poverty pimp?"

"He's a great American and civil rights hero."

"He tried to screw me at the 2000 convention."

"I'm sure he wasn't the only one."

"He comes up to me at some bullshit cocktail party and says in that deep voice of his, 'My dear, have you ever made love to a black man?' "

"What did you say?"

"I told him I'd arranged for a gang bang by a small group of Dallas Cowboys just two weeks earlier for my birthday, thank you very much."

"Good. Very good."

"Then I showed him a little Polaroid souvenir I just happened to have in my purse. We still had those things then, Polaroids. Then I told him to go to hell." Sandy smiled. "I had different tastes then."

"I see." I tried to push the image of Sandy and the football players out of my head. She was joking, wasn't she?

"You're blushing," she teased, and it annoyed me because I realized she was right.

"I'm a family-values guy, Sandy. You know that."

"Right. Just ask that little press aide of yours you're screwing."

God, this woman knew everything. That was why she was so good at her job. It was the key to her sales techniques. "Look, Tobias is helping my brother with a little independent expenditure campaign and I might be trying to arrange for some donations."

"I love your brother," she said immediately.

"You do?" I had a horrible image of Tyler and Sandy hanging out together at his club.

"What's wrong? Is this supposed to be some kind of secret? Everybody loves Paul Callahan."

"Right." That brother. What a relief she was talking about my convicted felon brother, not the other one. That was the fast slide to nowhere I was riding.

"What's going on? You embarrassed because he went to the slammer? This is Louisiana, honey, nobody gives a damn. He never bet against LSU. Now that would have been a problem."

"We sorta been out of touch for a while," I said, as if that explained it. "He's running for public service commissioner, and Tobias Green has been so moved to help his candidacy with a little independent expenditure committee since my brother is such a man of the people and champion of lower rates."

Sandy laughed. She knew all the lines. "Okay. How much cut do you want?"

I didn't say anything.

"What are you, the last Boy Scout? Jesus, J.D., it's just business."

Of course it was. Just business. I thought about all the things I had done over the years that most people would find repugnant: the nasty attack ads, the opposition research teams I'd put onto opponents to find everything possibly incriminating, lives I'd probably ruined. Not once had I ever blinked. But this was one thing I had never done: I'd never stolen, never skimmed, never diverted a dime. I'd always played the money straight down the middle.

"A hundred and twenty-five thousand."

She waved her hand dismissively. "You want me to call the home number of every delegate in town?" Sandy finally asked, moving on. "So it gets back to them here at the convention chop-chop, right?"

"And other key members of their influence circles."

"You want the delegates to hear from people they know, get an echo chamber going."

"That's it."

"I'll do a zip sort of the delegates and match it with my key opinion leaders list. You'll get the media types, mayors, Rotary Club chairmen."

"Perfect."

"You got a questionnaire?"

I handed her a piece of paper with six questions typed on it. For an instant I worried about fingerprints, but then realized that was silly—if Sandy wanted to screw me, she had plenty of ammunition without fingerprints.

"Short," she said. "I like that."

"I want maximum hits. Few hang-ups."

Sandy Morrison read from the list of questions. "'If you knew that Vice President Hilda Smith had once had an abortion, would it make you more or less likely to support her for president?'" Sandy whistled. "Nice. You know my position on abortion," she said.

"No, Sandy, I can't say that I do."

"I believe in the college rule."

"Yes?"

"Until they go away to college, a parent ought to have a right to reconsider." She continued to read. "This true?"

"Does it matter?"

"Not as long as my check clears." She smiled.

"It will."

There was always a long line in front of Galatoire's, which was just one of the reasons I hated it. The place represented just about everything I'd come to resent about New Orleans: it was old, self-congratulatory to a fault, stuck in its way for no purpose, and celebrated its dullness. This idea that you get great food in New Orleans has always been sort of a fraud concocted by gluttonous locals as an excuse to glorify the fact that they were just like everybody else: they liked to eat and did it too much. But if you hung a nice picture frame of supposed gustatory greatness around the out-of-control hunger, it made it somehow chic and high-minded, not just another bunch of folks who loved to stuff their faces. It was sort of brilliant, like the lazy turning sleeping into a much valued art. Instead of *Food & Wine* you could have *Napping*. But there weren't a half-dozen restaurants in New Orleans that could bump up against the top fifty in LA or New York or even Miami, another overheated hellhole but at least one that had a lot more vitality than New Orleans. Sure, there was better food than, say, in Jackson or Baton Rouge, but "New Orleans as a food heaven" was a lot like the city itself: better if you didn't look too close.

Jessie Fenestra, the oh-so-famous local columnist, was standing by the door to the side, chatting with the maître d'. Seeing her in person, I recognized her right away, very tall and thin, standing with a cigarette in hand, her head held at a quirky angle, as if she were always on the verge of asking a question. She wore oversized sunglasses, like Jackie O at Hyannis Port.

It was a sight I remembered well from the parking lot of our high school in Metairie. She was always surrounded by a cluster of girls, prettier than she was in a typical way, but she had a flair that clearly made her the leader. To a skinny sophomore like me, obsessed with bikes and guitars, she seemed as distant and unapproachable as a queen in a horse-drawn carriage. There were rumors about her, too, that she was "hot," a term that seemed oddly inappropriate and thus all the more appealing for this cool creature who was always so composed.

"J.D.," she said now, dropping her cigarette and grinding it under her heel, "you look like a million goddamn bucks. I knew you'd come." As if I had a choice after she'd called me and told me how good it was to hear my voice, and how proud she was of me, did you read my column on you, and, by the way, somebody tells me the FBI has been talking to you and maybe there are some problems? Could we talk? The deep, rough voice didn't match the elegant figure. She leaned down and kissed me on the cheek, roughing my hair slightly. It felt like I was meeting an affectionate aunt, not a reporter who had threatened to tell the world that some wacko at the FBI had me pegged for a cynical bomber.

She pulled me by the arm into the high-ceiling cool of Galatoire's, past the two dozen or so waiting in line, since Galatoire's made it part of their charm not to accept any reservations. "They love me here," she said by way of explanation. We settled in a corner table for four. "What's the point of being a big deal in New Orleans if you can't get a good table? I have reached the height of New Orleans ambition. I can eat at Galatoire's without waiting in line." She laughed mockingly.

"Jessie," I asked, "could you take your sunglasses off? I feel like we're in an old *Sopranos* episode."

She smiled but didn't move to take off the glasses. "It's part of my local color. It's important when you are a minor celebrity in a small town like New Orleans to cultivate eccentricity. Believe me, the glasses are the most harmless way I've come up with yet."

"I see," I said, then asked what I knew she wanted me to. "What were the other ways?"

She shrugged and pulled out a cigarette. It was a moment from a French film, Jean Seberg in *Breathless*. "The usual." She thought for a moment. "Wore a see-through gown to the Bacchus ball, dated the Saints' starting defensive tackle for a while. Black. Three hundred and forty pounds. That was after I divorced Wayne and swore I'd never wake up with another football player. I lied. Was seen all over town with a certain Hollywood actress when she was in town shooting a film. Everyone whispered that we were lovers. They were right." She took a long pull from her cigarette. "You know, the usual."

"Sounds like fun."

"It was. But then you run out of new stuff. You know this place, J.D., it's a total cul-de-sac for those of us who never got out. We're doomed to spend our lives trying to shock the same people every day. It gets old."

Food started arriving, though we had never ordered. Two martinis appeared. *My God,* I thought, *martinis. This is a town where people still drink martinis at five o'clock in the afternoon.*

"They know me," she said, by way of explanation. Then, tiredly, "Everyone knows me. I'm famous." She sighed. "Just so famous."

She took a long drink from the martini and seemed to visibly perk up. "Like you, J.D. You saw my column? My yearly wet kiss. You don't know how lucky you are. I rarely write anything nice about the living. The dead, I like the dead. This is a town that celebrates the dead, and I am the number one celebrant."

She raised her martini glass in a salute and downed it with a flourish. I had a feeling I wasn't the first one to see this little act—the martinis, the death spiel—but it still had a certain sparkle.

"Jessie," I said, looking around the restaurant, wondering how many people there knew who I was, either delegates or New Orleans friends or, worse yet, reporters. What in God's name would they think of me sitting across from this woman drinking martinis the day before the convention began? I couldn't even remember the last time I had actually sat down to a meal in a restaurant.

"You know what a tornado and a southern divorce have in common?" she asked suddenly. "Somebody's gonna lose a trailer." Another martini had appeared on the table and she took a long sip from it. "That one was the hit of the newsroom this morning. Such wits surround me."

"Jessie," I began again. "I have this distinct memory of you on the telephone telling me that you were going to write a column about me and some FBI rumors. I got a few things on my mind, but I do distinctly remember that conversation. Or tell me I made it up. That's fine. I don't really care. But let's not pretend it never happened."

When I finished, I realized people were staring at me and Jessie had a shocked and bemused look.

"Wow. You've changed," she said. "Do you shout a lot now or was that just a show?"

A few people were taking pictures of us with their phones. I slumped back in my chair. I was so used to shouting at everybody that it seemed normal. I was beginning to act like some barely domesticated animal that easily fell back into its feral ways. Jessie took a long drag of her cigarette and stared through her oversized sunglasses. "I like that. Passion. How's your brother?"

"My brother?" Which brother? I had been crazy to agree to see her. Of course she would know about Tyler. She lived in New Orleans. She was a reporter. She loved New Orleans characters. Probably used to go out with Tyler, part of his little network of wackos. Oh, this was just great.

"What's wrong?" she asked. "You know he was big pals with my husband. Football heroes together." She took a drink of her martini and I swear I could see her glow a little. "My ex-husband, that is," she clarified.

I took a long drink from the martini in front of me. It was icy and delicious. I felt lightheaded almost instantly. It made me want to drink all of it at once.

"Good, huh?" she said, catching my reaction. "It's what we do best in this town. Make and consume high-quality alcoholic beverages." She said this as if reading from a chamber of commerce brochure. "Wayne Thibodeaux went into alcohol rehab, you know."

I wondered if it was possible to get drunk from only a quarter of a martini.

"My ex. Don't tell me you don't remember Wayne Thibodeaux? God, that would kill him. It was what he was always afraid of, that people would forget him."

"I think I might be drunk," I said.

"No excuse. Wayne Thibodeaux? The football player? He played with your brother."

"Sure. I remember."

"No you don't."

"Well, I'm sorry about the rehab thing, anyway."

"Me too. If he hadn't quit drinking, we'd still be married. Drinking together was the best thing we had going for us."

She smiled broadly and took another deep sip of her martini.

"Jessie," I said evenly, or at least I thought I said it evenly, "what I'm going to do is take another sip of this drink, and then I'm going to get up and leave and go back to my sad little life of trying to get somebody elected president. Okay? But tell me first, off the record, was it Lisa Henderson who told you the FBI had called me in?"

"Lisa Henderson?"

Behind her sunglasses, it was impossible to tell if she was lying.

"A woman who doesn't like me." I paused. Was it possible that there was a human alive who didn't know who Lisa Henderson was? It was a very pleasing idea. "She's also Hilda Smith's chief of staff."

"And she's trying to screw you over? Great. I love stuff like that. How come she's after you?" She leaned forward seductively. She was good at this, getting people to tell her secrets. It was how she made her living.

Except this wasn't a secret.

"Sure. Hilda Smith hired me and fired her as campaign manager after Hilda lost Iowa. Lisa went back to the White House as chief of staff. She hates me."

"That doesn't sound so bad. I mean, being in the White House."

I shrugged. "It was humiliating, I'm sure."

"A subject you know something about," Jessie offered.

I stood up. It seemed to me that everybody in the room was watching me. This was nuts, absolutely crazy, to agree to meet this woman in a place like Galatoire's. I might as well have held a press conference.

"Well, J.D.," she said, watching me stand, calm as could be, "if you tell me there isn't a story, I believe you. It was really just an excuse to see you. Come on, I'll walk with you."

I pulled out my wallet but she waved it away. "They put it on my account," she said with gravity. "It is my one remaining perk as a writer in this town. I have an eating expense account."

When we emerged from Galatoire's, a man standing in line yelled out, "Hey, J.D., come here for a second." He stepped out of line and motioned for me. He was handsome and tanned and looked vaguely familiar. But everyone was looking vaguely familiar to me these days.

"Bobby Simmons," the man said, with some annoyance in his voice, when he realized I didn't recognize him. "Saw you in the elevator over at the Windsor Court. Talked to you about my daughter, Ricki."

I nodded. "Of course. Yeah. Great."

A short, dark-haired girl emerged from the line and held out her hand. "Ricki," she said, grasping my hand in a terrifically strong grip. "Thanks for your help." She was pretty, in a sleeveless dress with a small tiger tattoo on her biceps. I wasn't sure what I'd done to help, but I was glad I had. "Somebody from your shop called and got me that floor pass. I hope I'll see you on the floor."

"Ricki is a poli-sci major," the father chimed in. "Dean's list, Stanford." She looked embarrassed but pleased.

"Sure," I told her. "Have to show you our war room."

"I'd love that. I can't believe how you brought Hilda back after she lost Iowa. Your New Hampshire campaign was the most amazing thing I've ever seen."

Behind me, I thought I heard Jessie snort. Or maybe she was clearing her throat. "Got to run," I said. "See you on the floor."

I nodded and started walking away. Jessie fell in beside me and said, in an overly loud voice, "God, does she want to fuck you."

"I wish," I said, without thinking. Was I crazy? She was a reporter. Had I told her we were off the record? Of course we were off the record. We were talking about sex. How can sex be on the record? I had to be drunk.

"Don't worry," she said. "It was a compliment." Jessie took my arm. "So why does the FBI think you are up to something?" she asked.

"I don't think it's really the FBI. It's more like just one moron at the FBI."

"There's a difference?" She was smiling.

"Yeah, there's a difference. This was just some idiot—"

"Joey Francis," she said.

I looked at her. A woman like this—a reporter who was good—was incredibly dangerous. You never understood what she knew and didn't know, so you never knew when to lie or tell the truth. This was a disaster for somebody like me, who always skated between truth, almost truth, might be true, and downright lie. She was playing with me. She had been playing with me for days, since she wrote that article about me. That was the set-up. Draw me in. Now what did she want?

"A renowned moron." She giggled. "He's been trying to get the Kennedy assassination reopened. The Garrison connection."

"You know this guy?" No good could come from this. None.

"I know everybody connected to the dead. That's what I do. I drink, I meet people, I write about murders. Let me tell you, this Joey Francis moron must be the happiest guy in the world. We've got murders, carjackings, drive-bys, we've got gambling, a little mob, but hardly ever a real-life bomber. He's thrilled. I promise you."

"You write about murders?"

She stopped and looked at me, pushing up her sunglasses for the first time. Her eyes were large and piercingly blue.

"You haven't read anything I've written, have you."

"I read your column yesterday," I told her.

"But that's it." She sighed. "It's the New Orleans curse. I'm the Dickens of Death in this town. I write about murders. They love me. But nobody beyond the Causeway has ever heard of me. You're lucky, J.D., you escaped. How'd you do it, huh, J.D.? How'd you slip away?"

"Went to the airport." She was following me down the street. I needed to get away from her, focus on my other problems. It had been a mistake to meet her.

"And you don't miss what everybody else in this town can't live without? That New Orleans lifestyle thing. The parties. The food. The way nobody really works and that's okay?"

"I love to work. It's all I do. I don't really drink. I think the restaurants are overrated. I hate parties. It was easy." God, if only she knew. I would have ridden my bike all the way to Washington, if that's what it took to get away from the little house of horrors that was my family.

"Is that how the skinny kid into bikes and guitars took famous?"

"You think I'm famous? We lose this nomination and if I'm lucky nobody will remember me. I'm a *domestique,* that's all."

"You lost me."

"It's what they call a bike rider who will never be a star but rides his goddamn heart out so that the team star can win. That's me. I set the pace, I block, I'll crash the other guys if that helps. But that's it. At the end of the day, I'm not the one who's up there on the podium." I didn't really believe this, but it was a line I had used before with a reporter and it seemed to work. It was just offbeat enough to seem genuine, self-deprecating but believable, since it was a subtle reference to something most reporters didn't remotely understand—bike racing.

"You know why you escaped?" she said. "Because this town never knew what to do with you. Not like your brother. They loved your brother because he made Tiger Stadium rock. And they loved me, because I was the pretty girl who married the football star and gave great parties. But you—"

"I was the skinny guy on a bike. Yeah, I know. And you know what? I just don't care anymore. I really just don't give a shit." She was annoying me now. I wanted to be somewhere else.

"Maybe," she said, looking so hard at me I had to turn away. "Maybe. I'm not sure." She leaned toward me. "So did you get somebody to plant the bomb?"

"Jesus Christ." I turned and stared at her. "You don't get it. This hurts us. It helps Armstrong George. Bombs are anarchy and he's the answer to anarchy. You guys never get the real story line."

"You guys?"

"Reporters." I sighed. This was stupid. Never tell reporters how little they know, even when it's mostly true. It never pays off. Because after you tell them . . . they are still reporters.

She reached out and touched my face. I pulled back. "You're pretty," she said. "I never realized it but you're pretty."

"I think you're a little drunk."

She smiled. "You're onstage now, J.D. This is your moment. Take it. Don't be like those girls who never realized they were actually good-looking until it was too late. You're the man now. Take the spotlight and enjoy it."

Then she walked away, leaving me standing on Bourbon Street wondering what she would look like without any clothes on and annoyed at how much the notion intrigued me. Jesus, I was as bad as my old man, just with more predictable tastes.

Chapter
★
Six

"MY FELLOW AMERICANS, I come before you with a heavy heart."

The president sat behind his desk in the Oval Office, dark circles under his eyes. In the months since he had announced he was not running for reelection, any expected positive change had not occurred in the president's appearance.

"He looks like crap," said Kim Grunfeld. "The guy is broken."

We were in our war room at the Windsor Court, which felt far too nice to be a real war room.

"He's gonna screw us," Dick Shenkoph said good-naturedly.

"Why would he screw us?" asked Kim, who was smoking a small cigar. "He picked Hilda as his VP. It helps him when we win."

"He's too broken. The possibility of her success haunts him," Shenkoph said.

"What is that, some kind of quote?" Kim shot back. "You turning into some kind of poet?"

"Trust me, Grunfeld. I know more about failure than you do."

"Give her time," Eddie Basha said, then smiled at Kim.

"God, why am I always the only woman?" Kim moaned.

"We haven't noticed. Honest," Dick Shenkoph mumbled,

staring at the screen. "I had sex once in the White House, a little basement alcove near the Situation Room," he said.

"Bullshit, you've never had sex," Eddie Basha countered.

"I'm talking a long time ago," Shenkoph assured him.

I watched all this with a certain detachment, my mind somewhere between Tyler's strip club and Jessie's questions. Walking back to the Windsor Court from that aborted dinner with Jessie, I'd convinced myself that she knew all about Tyler, and if she knew about Tyler, she probably knew all about Powell Callahan and his own, well, predilections and problems. It was the only way to look at it—assume the worst. Hadn't I drummed that into every client of mine over the last fifteen years?

I knew what I'd do if I was advising a client—I'd tell 'em to get everything out in the open right away, dump it all, smother the press with information. That was the creed I'd lived by for years, and whenever a client with a problem resisted, I'd made it clear to them how much worse it would be trying to keep secrets hidden. It was so easy giving the advice. But right now, the idea of watching some reporter—say, Sandra Juarez—announce to the world in a breathless newsbreak that new revelations about the family of Vice President Hilda Smith's campaign manager, J. D. Callahan, had the Republican convention talking, just the thought of that, made me want to throw up. I knew how it would play out: "The implications for Vice President Smith's campaign are unclear, but the vice president released a statement just moments ago clarifying that J. D. Callahan has left her campaign. Let me repeat, J. D. Callahan has resigned as Vice President Smith's campaign manager. Her former campaign manager, Lisa Henderson, who has been serving as chief of staff, will return as campaign manager."

God, I would cut my wrist with a rusty cat food lid before I let that happen. Forget what it would mean for my budding television career—like flush it forever—it was the sheer, well, humiliation. I couldn't take it.

The president continued: "This violence at the Republican National Convention in New Orleans shall not dissuade us from our purpose. We will find the individual or individuals responsible for this act and bring them to justice. These have been troubling times in America and I understand that many of you are looking for reassurances that our great American values are still alive and well."

"Danger, danger, danger," Dick Shenkoph squawked. "Don't like this."

"That's straight out of Armstrong George," Kim Grunfeld muttered. "Come on, baby," she spoke urgently to the president on television. "Don't screw your own veep."

"This is not the time to turn the other cheek. There is a season for everything, and today it is the season for righteousness and justice. I believe that it is time for Congress to act to give law enforcement new tools to find crime and terrorism. I will work with Congress to ensure the passage of additional effective and powerful legislation to protect the homeland. Enough is enough. It is time for action."

"Jesus Christ," Kim Grunfeld moaned. "Son of a bitch."

"Told you," Dick Shenkoph said, smiling. "He screwed us."

"Shit, he did," Eddie Basha said, surprised. "Christ, how did you know he was going to do that?" he asked Shenkoph.

"In my experience," Shenkoph said, "weak leaders will do just about anything if they think it makes them look stronger. In my experience."

"Jesus H. Christ," Kim said. "The president of the United States might as well have just endorsed Armstrong George."

"Wasn't that bad," Eddie insisted, not very convincingly. "He didn't say he was supporting Protect the Homeland. Just new legislation. We've got to get every one of our whips on the line fast. Squash this down. Tell everybody it's not a big deal. What's our spin?"

"How about the president is a lying piece of shit who can't be trusted?" Kim Grunfeld suggested.

"What do you think, J.D.?" Eddie asked, and suddenly they were all looking at me.

"I like Kim's spin," I told them. "I can work with that."

The telephone calls first broke at the press conference to announce South Dakota delegate Bruce Dent's support for the vice president. It went down perfectly, I have to admit. A perfect little moment of duplicity, so satisfying in its treachery. The only negative was that I decided to leak it to Paul Hendricks, which let him cover himself in a bit of glory. This was troubling, in that Hendricks was not only a jerk but also a looming competitor of mine in my soon-to-be-launched television career, but it was important that the story break with somebody who had enough credibility to make it an Instant Big Deal and not anyone seen as close to me. People knew I didn't like Hendricks, so that made him a safer choice to leak. Like all leaks, it was easy: I just tipped off Hendricks to talk to a few people who had received the calls. This all had to happen fast. We were in hyper mode now, when the day was one rolling news cycle.

"Mrs. Vice President," Hendricks boomed in his best "I'm a serious reporter" voice, "there are reports circulating that Governor Armstrong George's campaign is engaged in what is known as push polling."

"Yes?" Hilda Smith answered, looking not at all bothered by the question. This was also perfect. If she seemed outraged from the start, it would have looked like she was overreacting, that the whole thing had been a set-up. For the last six months, she and Armstrong George had been beating each other's brains out with every means possible, from television ads to phone calls. What were a few more negative phone calls? "We've been down that road before," she said with a sigh.

I had counted on her reaction being genuine, since, of course, she didn't have the slightest idea what Hendricks was talking about.

"Yes, but these calls are of a particularly personal and some might say vicious nature," Hendricks continued. He had a way of raising his voice and tilting his accent when he was driving home a point that made him sound almost English. Not bad for a kid who went to Holy Cross.

Hilda Smith shrugged. Who could blame her for looking disinterested? She'd had about four hours of sleep; she'd been ambushed by the press at the hospital; the president of the United States, who had appointed her, had just all but endorsed her opponent on national television; and she had just held a press conference to express her deep, eternal gratitude for the support of a young man who had the makings of a totally repugnant human being. A few negative phone calls were not the most troubling element in her life.

When she failed to respond, Hendricks pressed on. "I have confirmed sources, Mrs. Vice President"—here he paused for dramatic effect, turning slightly so that his cameraman would catch him in his best profile—"that these calls made reference to a supposed abortion procedure you had undergone."

For a long moment, the other press members, who had been grousing restlessly at Hendricks for taking them off the juicy subject of presidential betrayal, were shocked into a rare stunned silence. Had they heard right? Did he just say *abortion procedure*? Then everyone started yelling, none louder than Sandra Juarez: "Is that true, Mrs. Vice President? Did you terminate a pregnancy through surgical means?"

Leave it to Sandra to try to take it up a notch with a juicy explanation of the meaning of abortion.

Hilda Smith stared at the press. Lisa Henderson took a protective step toward her from the side of the ballroom where we were holding the press conference. I didn't move.

"There were other charges as well, Mrs. Vice President," Hendricks out-shouted everybody. This was his story, goddamn it, and he wasn't going to let anyone hijack the moment.

The vice president seemed to stand a bit straighter, grasping the podium tightly. "I can only assume," she said finally, in a low but strong voice, "that there is no connection between these reported phone calls and Governor Armstrong George. Such actions would disqualify him, in my opinion, from leading this party and country."

With that, she turned and walked toward Lisa Henderson, who was standing by the rear exit.

"Did you have an abortion?" Sandra Juarez bellowed.

Vice President Hilda Smith turned, and for an instant her eyes seemed truly to blaze. "The next questions will have to be answered by Governor George." And then she turned and was gone, the doors leading into the back hall of the ballroom swinging behind her.

I was ecstatic.

For almost an hour, Paul Hendricks was the most important journalist in America. He had the rarest of commodities at an event in which thousands of journalists were crammed into one square mile, all covering the same thing: Paul Hendricks had a scoop.

The networks all broke into regular programming to report the phone calls. Naturally they mostly tried to seem to be reporting on the outrageous nature of politics, that such a subject could even be raised, but of course that was just an excuse to get out three words: *Hilda Smith, abortion.* Begrudgingly, Paul Hendricks of CNN was cited as the reporter who broke the story.

But within the hour, frantic reporters started confirming the story as delegates and others in their hometowns started coming forth and saying, yes, they too had received these polling questions.

The elevator ride back up to our floor was interesting. There was me, Hilda Smith and her husband, Lisa, and six Secret Service agents. Normally there would have been four agents, but that number had been expanded since the bomb went off and the threat level was raised. The agents stared ahead blankly. It was no secret that most of them would have voted for Armstrong George based on politics, but since Hilda was a decent sort of person and tended to remember their names and the names of their wives and children, they had a certain fondness for her. Plus, if she won, it would be good for their careers, since they would likely become the core detail guarding the next president. That was the most plum job for an active agent, to be at the inner circle, the "hard circle," as they called it, responsible for the protection of the president of the United States. They might have been inclined to express shock or outrage at what had just been said at the press conference, if only to offer a reassuring word or two, but their training and experience had taught them to simply try to disappear, like dinner guests when the host couple starts to argue. Be invisible.

When we got off the elevator, Lisa and I automatically followed our candidate toward her suite, but when we got to the door, she turned and said, with a strained smile, "Give us some time, okay?" *Time?* I should have shouted. *Time? We don't have any time, for Christ's sake.* But I didn't, of course, nor did Lisa. We just nodded and backed away.

When they disappeared, leaving Lisa and me staring at each other, she cut me off before I could say a word. "I need a few minutes too, okay?" And then she headed toward her room.

That left me standing in the hall, just me and the agents. It was the oddest damn thing. The whole world had exploded and nobody seemed to want to talk about it. Eddie Basha appeared and pulled me into his delegate-counting staff room. It was empty, since everyone was moving over to the convention floor, setting up shop in our trailers.

"How?" was all he said.

"What are you talking about?" I shot back.

"Right," Eddie said.

"I'm appalled that Armstrong George would do such a thing."

"Unimaginable," Eddie agreed. "Should offend all decent people everywhere."

"Particularly his squishy delegates," I said. "If the son of a bitch has any."

We laughed. "You think it will change anything?" Eddie asked.

"Hell if I know. But we need to turn out a couple dozen demonstrators at George's hotel, get some signs made up. 'No Mudslinging,' 'Apologize, Governor,' that kind of thing."

"The usual spontaneous demonstration."

I nodded. "Then do the same at the party tonight for all the delegates, the one out at that Mardi Gras place across the river. We get our people out there and make sure they get on camera. Maybe one of the George delegates gets hot and takes a swing at 'em. That would be perfect. We've got to get this bastard on the defensive."

Eddie made a few calls to his lieutenants. We were at the stage of a campaign when no one would question anything; many of the operatives Eddie and I had brought into the campaign had no previous particular loyalty to Hilda Smith, but we had been through hell together and were close to winning. Then we went back to our floor strategy for the opening session the following morning. It was something we had talked about for months, ever since it was obvious that the convention might be a real event and not a coronation. The final vote on the nominee would come on the third day. Between the opening of the convention and that vote, there would be dozens of other votes, mostly of a procedural or ceremonial nature. But it was possible to pick a vote or a series of votes and try to make them test votes, to use them to gauge how many votes you really had, to probe for weaknesses, to try to peel off a vote here, a vote there, in hopes that once delegates voted with you on one issue, they would stay on your side all the way.

"You know what the son of a bitch is going to do?" I said to Eddie. "It's what we would do."

"I don't want to hear this," Eddie groaned.

I spelled it out, making all the details painfully gory. "Push an early resolution condemning the bombing—that's a no-brainer. And tie it in with support for the president's call for new legislation with an endorsement of support for Protect the Homeland. They know that some of our people can't vote for that because they think it's fascist claptrap. Then when a bunch of Hilda Smith delegates vote against the resolution, it looks like we're defending the bombing or are too timid and pacifist Vermont to really take a hard stance against it. Just confirms that Hilda Smith is too weak to be president. Then we implode."

Eddie smiled. "That's good. Very good. So what do we do?"

I got up and stared at the chart of the delegates. Thirty-seven delegates. "We can't win that fight. So we get ahead of it. We put our own resolution out there praising the president and supporting his call for new legislation. We just don't name Protect the Homeland. But we beat them to it and get it passed with our people supporting it. They want a fight. We don't give it to them."

Eddie whistled. "Could be tough getting all our people to go with it." He thought for a minute. "But hell yeah, let's go for it. Run right into this ambush."

"You got it."

"But we'd have to keep it a secret before we moved the motion. If George's people know we're going to do it, they'll come up with a counter motion and we're screwed. We have to surprise them."

"Floor discipline. It's what we've beat into our people for weeks. We have to maintain total control on the floor."

"Good luck."

I shrugged as Ginny walked in.

"Here's your key back," she said to Eddie, tossing him a plastic card key. "Eddie and I are having mad sex," she announced at my look.

Eddie came very close to blushing. It was a shocking sight: Eddie Basha embarrassed. I wondered if it was true. And wondered how I would feel about it if it were. I didn't think I cared.

"You two look like hell," Ginny said. "Jesus. Let's go." Ginny reached out and pulled me upward. "Christ, you're soaking wet with sweat. You two in here watching porn movies or something?"

"Feeling the breath of the dragon," I said. I didn't realize how much I had been sweating. I was that excited—and nervous—about the plans I'd put in motion. It was all so desperate it might just work.

"Right. Well, you know what my old campaign manager J. D. Callahan always said? Screw fear!"

"He sounds like an asshole to me."

"But a cute one. Come on, Eddie, you're coming too."

"Catch up with you," he said, waving. "Few things to do."

We saw the long lines at the metal detectors as soon as we got close. Then the demonstrators Eddie had quickly organized. This made me feel better right away.

The party was across the river at Perkins Mardi Gras World, a building site for Mardi Gras floats. Colored lasers and floodlights spilled into the sky. The huge floats hovered in the night, looming over the crowd like grotesque gods vaguely tolerating the intrusion of humans onto their turf.

It was the big kickoff event before the convention started, sponsored by the Republican National Committee, with everyone connected to the convention invited. An elaborate system of buses had been arranged to ferry the crowds from the foot of Canal Street over the Crescent City Connection Bridge to the site, just across the river. It was probably a good idea until the NOPD, ATF, FBI, and Secret Service insisted on turning the entire party into a secure site. That meant everyone had to enter through metal detectors and everything from purses to cameras had to be scanned in the new bomb-sniffing boxes. The sniffers were made to work in the air-conditioned environment of an airport or court building, not in the swamp of New Orleans in August. The delays were massive. Hot, mostly half-drunk delegates, alternates, and reporters were spread out in an unruly mess, trying to edge their way closer to the five entrance points. Inside, the lucky ones who had gained entrance were milling about the floats, drinks in hand, listening to the Zydeco Twisters. Some were starting to dance in that awkward, stiff-jointed way that middle-aged political nerds seem to practice. The RNC had held Very Serious Meetings with both campaigns, worried that the two sides might end up in some kind of frat-party brawl, the Georges versus the Smiths. But with the shock of the bomb and the heat, everybody just seemed to want to forget about politics, if only for a couple of hours.

I spotted Sandra Juarez on the edge of the crowd. She had just finished a stand-up in front of the demonstrators and was still holding her mike, while her three-man crew collapsed, looking like sled dogs driven to exhaustion. It annoyed the hell out of me when I realized my heart was racing. Ginny took my arm and steered me away from Sandra. "Bitch," she whispered hotly in my ear. "What a goddamn bitch."

"You keep saying that," I said, laughing, or trying to laugh, amazed that just seeing Sandra could do so much to me. I broke away from Ginny and walked over toward Sandra.

"I'm sorry," she said, in a low voice, looking around to make sure nobody could hear her. This caught me by surprise.

"So you let George know that Hilda was going to the hospital?"

"No." She saw my look and reacted. "Jesus, J.D., I told you I was sorry. I didn't tell him, but you didn't give me much warning, and I had to pull a local cameraman and he sold the tip."

"Sold it?"

"A hundred bucks. Can you believe it? What a piece of shit, huh? I felt terrible. I should have called you and told you."

It struck me that Sandra was being nice. Like there was something that might be more important than the story of the moment or her career. I guess I had seen that side of her early on—I must have, to have fallen in love with her—but I hadn't let myself think about it very much.

"I've got something else for you. Really good. Big," I said. She looked at me like I was teasing her. "I'm serious."

"After I screwed the hospital up?"

I was close to her now and I could see the lines around her eyes she hid so well on camera. Ginny had moved behind her and was standing with her hands on her hips, staring so hard that I felt sure Sandra must be able to feel the glare on the back of her head.

"It's good for me, Sandra. If you break a story, no one will think in a million years I was the source," I whispered. My heart was pounding so loudly that I wondered if she could hear it.

"Why not?" she asked. "Old girlfriend, all of that. Wouldn't people think it made sense you were dishing to me?"

"No one that matters in my world," I said, "because everybody who knows me thinks I really hate you."

She blinked, her head rocking backward a touch. "I see," she said finally. "I got it. Okay."

"Good." God, it was so sweet to see her actually affected by something I said. A minor victory, but I would take it. You bet I would. "The Colorado Republican Party paid for those push poll calls attacking Hilda. A governor named Armstrong George would be the head of that state party."

"You have proof?"

"How about a copy of the script?" I handed her a folded piece of paper. "And here's the name of the phone center. Call them. Ask them who they're working for." I slipped Sandra another piece of paper with a typed number on it.

"Does Armstrong George know about it?" she asked, holding the papers in her hand, not looking down at them. She was biting. She was interested enough to worry about people seeing her reading material that was handed to her by me. That was a good sign.

"Come on, Sandra. Armstrong George invented the Colorado Republican Party. You think they would do anything without his okay?"

"But why? It seems so stupid."

"Let me tell you something about guys like George," I said fiercely. "He doesn't only want to win, he wants to crush Hilda Smith. Embarrass her. Humiliate her. Why the hell did Nixon bug the Watergate when he was forty points ahead? Armstrong George is a mean, sick fuck and you shouldn't be surprised he does mean, sick shit."

"You sound like you really believe that, J.D."

I looked around. People were watching us. "Look, I'm gonna yell at you in a second and walk off. Then you yell at me."

She blinked, confused for an instant, then understood. She nodded.

"It was a goddamn ambush!" I shouted suddenly. I watched her features tighten for a second, then I yelled louder. "Be professional." I enjoyed the look on her face for a beat more, then turned and strode off, followed by a very confused-looking Ginny.

"Oh, good, J.D. Impressive," Sandra yelled sarcastically at my back.

Turning, I spoke loud enough for anyone within thirty yards to hear. "When Hilda Smith is president, good luck on your stories, Sandra. GOOD GODDAMN LUCK!"

"Very mature, J.D. Very professional. Just stomp off. AGAIN!"

Again. This hurt. Again. God, she was good.

I took Ginny by the arm and steered her toward the gate.

"You going to tell me what that was all about?" she asked.

Before I could answer, Somerfield George was striding right toward us. He was a guy who did that—he didn't walk, he strode. Big, long strides. He had his hand out. I have fantasies about refusing to shake hands with guys like Somerfield George, but I've never done it. I shook his hand.

"Got a second?" he asked, as if we were meeting at the coffee stand at work. I just looked at him, not sure I was understanding. "To talk," he finally said, then looked at Ginny. "Just us. Sorry." He nodded at her.

"I'll just be over here by the monster with two heads," Ginny said, walking toward a float under construction.

"She really doesn't like me," Somerfield said.

"She loathes you," I said. "You're pretty much everything she hates in the world."

He nodded. "I get that a lot," he said. "Because of my dad."

"Did people like you before your dad?"

"The only time there was a 'before my dad' was when I was in the army, and yeah, I think so. I liked the army. I would have stayed."

"Why didn't you?"

He shrugged. "The family business. And I had a couple of problems." He laughed. "You going to do oppo on me now?"

I sighed. "Look, I'm pretty beat to shit and just want to have a beer and hang out and sort of try to be off the clock for an hour or so. What's up?"

He suddenly looked very serious. "Nice play with the push calls." He held up his hands before I could protest. "Nicely done. We're like two boxers beating the crap out of each other in the fifteenth round. So I have a little proposal."

"Okay?"

"What if Hilda were to run as Armstrong's VP?"

I looked at him, making sure I wasn't hallucinating out of exhaustion. "Run as your dad's veep?"

"It's the only logical way for both of us to end this and win. And winning is all that we care about, right? You and I, it's not like we're in this to save the world."

I looked around at the partygoers, all just trying to have fun. I wanted to be them. I wanted to be the guy Somerfield George had just described, the guy who only cared about winning. That's who I had been for most of my time in politics, and I was proud of not caring. But when Tyler had said I'd be happy working for Armstrong George it had shocked me, because I realized he was right, or had been right. That was somebody I didn't want to be, and somebody I wasn't going to be anymore.

"Look, Somerfield," I said, very level, without a trace of anger, "I really respect that you are trying to do what's best for your dad. Maybe it's not the easiest thing being a politician's kid, and I think I get that more than most. You've been totally loyal and stand-up and God love you for it."

"But?" Somerfield asked.

"But I really think your dad is a dangerous lunatic and I would walk through a lion's den in pork-chop panties before I did a thing to help him get near the Oval Office."

Somerfield stared at me, a little flash of anger shooting across his face. Then he smiled. "Pork-chop panties. That's good. Okay. We're cool. I just had to ask." He started to walk away, then turned around. "I always heard good things about you. Not that you give a shit, I know, but I did."

"Me? From whom?" He started to say something, then waved his hand and walked off. I looked around, wondering how many reporters had been watching. But this being a party with music and free booze, reporters had better things to do, thank God. Ginny came back over holding two beers. She held one out.

"First Sandra, then Somerfield? Busy night for the boy. You want to share with your press secretary what the hell is going on?"

"You know what I want?" I asked her. "I want for a couple of hours not to be the guy running this campaign. You can give that to me, can't you?"

My voice must have sounded so desperate that a quick look of pain shot across her face. She leaned up and kissed me quickly on the cheek. "Sure, J.D. Sure."

For the rest of the evening, we hung out on the edge of the crowd, trying to avoid everyone, drifting in and out of the darkness between the floats. We'd dance for a while in the small spaces between the floats and then Ginny would drift away and reappear with more beer, glowing in a sheen of sweat. She was small and strong and suddenly seemed like the most desirable woman on earth. Once or twice, I saw Sandra Juarez surrounded by other reporters, looking out over the party like an anthropologist at some tribal gathering. I wondered if she had called the number I'd given her yet. I would have been shocked if she hadn't called within a few minutes of me giving her the tip. That was just Sandra's way.

I felt a warm arm touch my neck and moved backward into the body. It was Ginny, I assumed, returning as she had off and on all night, but then I felt the curves of the body and realized it couldn't be her and turned as two hands twisted me around.

"You were such a cute kid," Jessie said. She still had on her over-sized sunglasses; she tilted her forehead into mine, sliding her arms around me.

"Why didn't you tell me then?" I asked, thinking that it seemed perfectly normal to be suddenly dancing with this tall woman. "You're beautiful," I said, not thinking before I said it but sure it was the absolutely right thing to say.

"You've been drinking, and you're not a drinker," she answered.

"How do you know?"

"Because I'm a drinker and I know."

She pulled away and led me by the hand around to the rear of the giant Bacchus float. "The J.D. with magical powers," she said, and then she kissed me.

"Magical?" I asked, pulling away.

"You escaped. Escaped the pleasure dome." She kissed me again. "I worshipped your father, you know."

"No." I didn't know this and didn't really care. "It doesn't matter," I said.

She pulled back. "But it does. He was magical too."

"He was a drunk," I told her. "And a monumental fuckup. Worse. You have no idea."

The sudden anger in my voice made her pull away, and she stared at me, surprised. "Well, now . . . ," she said, softly.

"You know why I escaped," I continued, knowing I shouldn't but not really caring. "Because everybody loved my father so much and it was such a joke. And Paul, he was the star. I had to, that's why." She pushed up her glasses. Her eyes caught me again, big and clear. They didn't look like a drinker's eyes.

"That's your secret," I told her. "You wear those glasses so that nobody will know that you never get drunk. You drink but never get drunk. You see everything."

"Silly boy," she said, pushing her finger against my lips. "You're all beat up, aren't you?" I pulled back but she kept her finger on my lips, sliding her finger inside to touch my tongue. "That Sandra woman, she fucked you up good, didn't she? You're angry. I love that. Nobody in New Orleans is angry anymore. Just tired." She moved her hands around my head and pulled me closer. "Angry boy," she whispered.

Two teenagers, a boy and a girl, stumbled out from behind the float a few feet away. The girl was wearing a simple black dress that had fallen down around her waist; her breasts glowed, lighter than her tan body. "Jesus," the girl cried, pulling her dress up.

"Mr. Callahan," the boy said.

I thought I might have seen him before, maybe one of our endless waves of interns.

Jessie had turned and she was looking at the two frightened teenagers.

"What's wrong?" Jessie asked. "What is it?" She squeezed my arm. Her voice was strong and clear. It was her reporter's voice and made her sound like a different person.

"There's something . . . ," the girls said.

"Maybe . . ."

"It's there."

"What?" I asked, walking toward them.

They motioned and we followed them to the end of the float. The young man pointed into the dark space between the floats and I saw it: a large bundle. I looked more closely and realized it was pieces of pipe held together.

"Goddamn it," I mumbled.

"I'll be damned. It's a fucking bomb," Jessie said, and it was hard not to believe that she sounded almost pleased.

They moved everybody outside the fence with amazing ease, given what a horror show it had been getting everyone inside. Jessie made a big stink trying to remain inside, flashing her press credentials, and had it been up to just the NOPD, they probably would have let her. They knew her and liked her, which wasn't true for those other national reporter clowns, whom they viewed with the instinctive distrust of outsiders that comes naturally to all New Orleanians. But with the Secret Service and the FBI running the show, the NOPD had the least important badges around. I saw Sandra start to complain but even she quickly gave it up. She knew enough not to fight a battle she'd lose in front of all her colleagues.

Joey Francis arrived in a helicopter, which seemed a bit much, but he looked very pleased with himself. He moved inside the fence, surrounded by a scrum of FBI agents. I watched Jessie to see if she recognized him but she didn't seem to, though maybe it was just that she was too busy talking on her phone to an editor.

"Jessie Fenestra, cub reporter," I joked.

"I called in a news story," she said with some amazement, covering the phone. "I don't think I've ever done that before." And then she said into the phone, "Oh, fuck you, Peter. I know what I'm doing. Quit laughing."

That was when, more or less, the world seemed to explode.

Parked off by itself, a bus was burning. Later the forensic pros would figure out that the bomber had entered the parked bus—the driver was enjoying the free barbecue at the party—and driven it a calculated distance. Not close enough to kill anyone but plenty close to scare the hell out of everyone.

They let the bus burn, not wanting to risk damaging evidence by dousing it with water or chemicals. More helicopters started landing within minutes of the explosion. First there were medical helicopters, but then some kind of Special Forces–looking group landed and set up a perimeter, as if expecting a full frontal assault. They looked like Martians with their night-vision goggles. I had no idea who they were or who had summoned them. These days there were all sorts of strange military units. Whoever they were, Joey Francis didn't look very happy to see them. We watched him march up and confront the man who seemed to be in charge. Anybody who arrived on a bomb scene with helicopters and guys in black jumps with exotic weapons was clearly going to outrank a humble FBI field agent, even if that guy did know a lot about bombs and had been waiting for this moment all his life.

Jessie wanted to call in another story but wasn't able to get a signal. One of the law enforcement brigades was jamming all cell signals in case the bomber tried to set off another blast with a cell phone. Somebody started yelling over a loudspeaker that everyone should leave the site, and the troops were forming columns of dazed, crying people to walk over the bridge back into town. The crowd that had looked like any other drunken New Orleans party crowd now resembled refugees from a war zone. Which is pretty much what we were.

I saw Ginny talking to a huddle of cops. She came over and hugged me. "You write nasty stuff," she said to Jessie. "If you hurt my boss I'll kill you."

"I like him," Jessie said.

Ginny looked her over but let it go. "Nobody on the staff seems to be hurt." She shrugged. "But I can't tell you it didn't scare some of our delegates into getting on the first plane tomorrow."

"Jesus Christ," Jessie gasped, "delegates? You're thinking about delegates?"

Ginny stared at her. "All I think about is delegates." On some twisted level, I was proud that Ginny had been able to shock the woman who prided herself on being beyond shockable. We started to join the crowd walking back over the river—nobody seemed eager to get inside any kind of motorized vehicle—when Francis spotted us. He strutted over.

"Who the hell are the ninja warriors?" Jessie asked, gesturing to the shock troops.

"Just some of my men," Francis said. "And nice to see you too, Jessie."

"Your men?" Jessie scoffed. "Every FBI agent I ever saw always had FBI in big letters across their field jackets or jumpsuits."

"It's a new world out there," Francis shot back. "You saw the bomb," he said flatly. "A kid and his girl told us you saw it."

"A bomb," I said. "Not the one that went off."

Francis nodded in a way that made me feel stupid. Of course we hadn't seen the bomb that went off. "Would help if you could tell us about it." He looked around. "Not here." He started to walk off toward an FBI car, then looked over his shoulder at us. "You coming?"

"Joey?" Jessie asked. He stopped and turned. "Why are you being nice?"

"He"—he pointed to me—"is an arrogant shit. But you, Jessie. I like you."

Jessie smiled. "That works."

I asked Ginny if she wanted to ride back to the Windsor Court with Francis. "I'll stay here and make sure all our people get back." She motioned me closer and whispered in my ear. "Be careful with that girl, J.D. Don't forget. She's a fucking reporter."

I nodded. "Call me when you know more."

Francis took us back to the Windsor Court, to the same command center where he and I had first met. He made us go through every minute of seeing the bomb, anything else. When he had finally had enough, it was four in the morning. I took Jessie upstairs to our floor, which was now crawling with armed Secret Service shock troops. These were the black jumpsuit guys in body armor, dripping weapons, not the regular agents in suits who looked more like very fit stockbrokers than killers. It felt like all of New Orleans was being taken over by heavily armed men in jumpsuits. For Hilda Smith, this was the worst possible scenario. She was preaching reconciliation and forgiveness and hope in a battle zone. Another bombing or two and even a Gandhi do-gooder like Lisa Henderson would be rooting for Armstrong George.

The agents wouldn't let Jessie on the floor, even with me vouching for her. She hadn't been cleared, they said, exactly what they would have said if we had been trying to enter the White House. We had never had that level of threat protection while traveling on the campaign. I'd had a Secret Service hard pin since the first day I went to work for Hilda, back in New Hampshire.

Mostly it was for the benefit of the random police forces that always backed up the Service's efforts, since the Service regulars knew everyone who was hard pinned. It was always assumed that a hard pin could bring anyone they wanted with them into a secured area, but now the agents weren't letting anyone in who hadn't been cleared. Eddie Basha saw me standing by the elevator talking to the agents. Then he saw Jessie. He shook his head and sort of shuddered.

"Can she stay here by the elevator while I just talk to Eddie?" I asked the agent. He hesitated, and then nodded.

"I'm harmless. Mostly," Jessie said, and smiled. "I'm just going to lean up against this wall and fall asleep."

"What the hell is going on?" Eddie whispered to me as soon as we were down the hall from the elevator. "What are you doing with that reporter bitch?" Eddie called any female reporter who hadn't proven herself to be totally on our side "reporter bitch." Male reporters he called "whore dogs," as in, "What does that whore dog reporter want?"

"I was with her when the bomb went off."

Eddie nodded dismissively. The idea that anyone might have been hurt seemed not to have crossed his mind. All he was thinking about was the campaign and how the bomb affected us and what we should do. I admired this, actually. "So get rid of her. Lisa has already briefed the veep. All hell is going to break loose now on that convention floor in a few hours."

"I still like our plan for tomorrow," I said. It was an instinctive response, just to get away from Eddie, which suddenly I wanted to do in the worst way. But I also thought it was the right answer.

Eddie shrugged. "It probably won't work, but I can't think

of a better one. Who the hell is doing this? This is really fucking everything up. Jesus Christ." He suddenly quivered with rage. "We had this thing going. We were going to pull this off. Who is fucking with us?"

The pure hate in his voice made one of the Secret Service agents look over at us, like a bird dog getting a scent. Jessie, slouched against the wall near the elevator, waved. She had her sunglasses back on. "I don't know. But if he keeps it up, he's going to kill somebody. Maybe a lot of people."

"Yeah, yeah, yeah. I'll cry after we win this thing."

I started to say something encouraging, but I was just too tired. Anyway, I wanted somebody to cheer me up. I didn't want to be the one who had to go around making everybody else feel good.

"Let me deal with this woman," I said, nodding abstractly in the direction of the elevators, where I assumed Jessie was waiting.

"What are you doing with her anyway?" Eddie asked.

"We went to high school together," I explained.

"Don't fuck another reporter, you understand me?" Eddie demanded. "Just don't do it."

I let it drop. "I'll be back," I said.

Jessie seemed to have reached a silent truce with the lead agent, who nodded toward her as we finally got on the elevator. When we came out of the Windsor Court, the sun was starting to come up. The Secret Service was building a perimeter around the hotel with huge city garbage trucks and there were Humvees stationed around the hotel. It was the "America Under Siege" that Armstrong George depicted as inevitable if he was not elected president.

"Jesus fucking Christ." Jessie sighed, looking around.

"I hate this city," I said. "Nothing good has ever happened to me in this goddamn town."

"I'll make you breakfast," Jessie said. "Then it will be one thing."

We walked back uptown, through the Warehouse District and the Garden District to Jessie's house. She lived on the bottom floor of a shotgun house with fourteen-foot-high ceilings and Hunter fans that looked a hundred years old. We sat in the front room, a clean, sparse space. She got us drinks and I had half of mine down before I asked her what it was.

"It's a South Dallas Martini," she said.

"A South Dallas Martini—which is?"

"Gin, silly. Straight gin."

I drank the rest and felt, almost instantly, drunk. Jessie looked at me and giggled. We were both filthy, covered in soot and dirt. She reached out and took the empty French jelly glass from my hand and I followed her to the bedroom.

Without ceremony, she took off her clothes. The bed was large and canopied and unexpectedly girlish. Her body was shocking: large-breasted and strong. "I lift," she said. "But don't tell anyone. It would ruin my image." She paused. "Are you going to just stare or take off your clothes?"

"Can I take a shower?"

"You're nervous. That's cute."

"I'm something, anyway."

"Go take a shower. I'll wait."

We woke up to a loud banging. Jessie bolted up, and when I turned around in the bed she was on her feet, nude, holding the largest handgun I'd ever seen. She held it with both hands, like on a pistol course. I started laughing.

"What the hell?" she said.

"Do you know how you look?"

"Do you know how many assholes have tried to break in here?"

"A lot, I'm sure. But not twice."

"You go to the door," she said.

"Me?"

"You be the man of the house," she mocked, waving her gun.

I pulled on pants and a shirt and stumbled to the door. Jessie had wrapped a robe around herself and stood off to the side, still holding the gun in both hands. "Christ, Jessie," I muttered.

"Police!" A large, deep voice sounded on the other side of the door.

"Bullshit," Jessie hissed, waving the gun.

"No." I sighed, recognizing the voice. "It is."

I opened the door. Walter Robinson was standing there with a sleepy-looking Paul Callahan. Walter glared at me and stepped inside. "Holy shit," he said, flinching when he saw Jessie standing there pointing the large handgun in his direction. "Don't point that thing at me!" His hand rose to his holster.

"Don't touch that damn gun!" Jessie yelled.

"For Christ's sake," Paul muttered. "Will you two calm down. Goddamn Dodge City."

Walter didn't take his eyes off the gun. "I do not like this. I hate guns."

"You're a cop, Walter. Get a life," Paul said.

"Jessie, please," I pleaded. "I am getting a serious headache—banging on the damn door, guns . . ."

"Can we make some coffee?" Paul asked.

Jessie slowly lowered her gun. " 'We'?" she asked. "Who the hell is 'we'?"

"I'll make it," Paul said. "I'd love to make it. Just point me toward the kitchen."

Walter seemed to notice Jessie, and not just her gun, for the first time. "I know you. You're Jessie Fenestra. You're famous now. You were married to a guy we played with. Wayne Thibodeaux."

She turned to me. "See?"

"Sorry about waking you up. I didn't know this was your place. Paul just said J.D. was here."

"Well," Jessie said, "that's true. And it's really sweet that you like my work and everything, and I really appreciate it, but just what the hell are you guys up to?"

Paul looked over his shoulder. "Jessie, great to see you. Been a long while."

"Jesus Christ," I said, "what happened?"

Paul and Walter looked at each other, then at Jessie. "Can we make all this off the record?" Paul asked.

"That's good," I said to Paul. "You know the drill."

Jessie burst out laughing. "You guys. You're worried about talking in front of me because I do that reporting thing. I think it's a little late for that, seeing how you already sort of broke into my house."

"They didn't really break in," I said.

"You too?" Jessie said. I held up my hands in surrender.

"You'll be cool with all this, right?" Walter said.

"I am the coolest half-naked chick currently awake with three men in her apartment in the Garden District."

Walter smiled. "How did Wayne let you go?"

"When he quit drinking, he was boring."

"I can see that," Walter agreed.

Ten minutes later we were sitting around her little retro Formica kitchen table with big mugs of coffee.

"Woodpeckers?" Walter asked, holding up the mugs. They were glazed pottery, with handles like woodpeckers.

"Shearwater Pottery," Jessie said. "On the Gulf Coast."

"He got another letter," Paul said, nodding toward Walter.

Walter reached inside the black backpack he was carrying, and from a pocket took out a sheet of yellow legal paper held in a clear plastic case. "Came from the bomber," he said.

"That's it?" Jessie asked. "That's it? Legal pad? What is this guy, a law student?"

"Could be," Walter said. "You might be on to something there."

"I think if I were a bomber and were going to send out letters, I'd at least get some nice stationery. Maybe have some kind of bomb graphic."

"Can you please just read the thing?" I asked Walter. The convention started in about four hours. I needed to be down at the Superdome in our command trailer, trying to put together our moves on the first floor vote condemning the bombings. We had our first meeting in the war room in—I looked at my watch—forty-five minutes. And here I was at Jessie's. Christ, what was it about women that made me lose my mind? And a reporter? Another goddamn reporter.

Walter ceremoniously unfolded the letter.

"This guy might as well have used Big Chief writing tablets," Jessie said. "How insulting."

Walter looked at the typed paragraph on the sheet and chuckled. "Good ol' Ignatius. If he could see what's happened to his city."

"How do you think he'd like it?" Jessie asked.

Walter thought for a moment. "I think he might enjoy just how fucked up things are. I really do." He read from the letter. "All it says is: 'The buses shall roll. America for America.' And then there's kind of a poem."

"That's it?" I asked.

Walter took a deep breath and read:

Racial pride ain't no racist hate.
Cops beat down, no it's not too late.
On the news, in the streets,
Doin' it right, still take heat.
Point a finger,
Truth don't matter,
Got a gun.
Get it done.
Whole world's gone crazy.
We're losin power but it just won't last.
Screw bodycam. Change is comin and it's comin fast.
Babies in the crib
lyin in wait.
grow up to game the system,
But it ain't too late.
Clock strikes. Time ticks.
Hold on. Don't quit.
Turn back time to when America was goin' strong.
Keep the faith. Do what's right because it's all gone wrong.
Our walk, long walk. Our fight.

Get yourself straight. Get it right.

We're losin power but it just won't last.

Screw bodycam. Change is comin and it's comin fast.

When he finished reading, Walter Robinson looked up, shrugged. "Any ideas?"

I found myself staring out the barred window of Jessie's kitchen toward Poydras Street. I played the words over in my head. There was something about them that was familiar.

"Yes?" Jessie asked me. "What?"

I reached out for the plastic-wrapped letter. There was a little Confederate flag at the bottom. And the initials C.D.

"C.D.?" I asked. "C.D.?"

"You talk to Tobias?" Paul asked, sounding sleepy. "Because I've been expecting him to call me and I haven't heard."

"Tobias?" Jessie asked. "Tobias Green?" She snorted. "He tried to fuck me at the Make-A-Wish charity fundraiser."

"Sounds like Tobias," Paul said.

"Make-A-Wish," Jessie mumbled, disbelieving. "Dying kids, for Christ's sake."

I'd realized why the words were so familiar. "Come on," I said, standing up. "We've got to go."

We drove on old Airline Highway, moving against the traffic coming into the city from Metairie.

"This twenty-four percent unemployment, it's got some advantages," Jessie said, peering out at the abandoned businesses along Airline. "One way to clean up a neighborhood."

I worked the radio for news. The most recent bomb had knocked every other story off the air. There was no mention of the abortion push polls. What had been the hottest story in America for a few hours had disappeared with the flaming bus. I figured Sandra had dropped the phone story completely to follow the bombing. The mayor had called for calm and insisted that New Orleans was as safe as any other city in America. He didn't seem to believe it himself.

"Not saying a whole hell of a lot," Walter Robinson laughed.

Just that morning a family of farmers in Sioux City, Iowa, had tried to rob the Farm Credit Bureau that foreclosed on their farm. Six people had died in the shootout, including the farmer's thirteen-year-old son, who had managed to kill two state troopers with his Ruger Mini-14 before a sniper took him out. Thirteen years old. In Sioux City.

I called Eddie. "Jesus, J.D., where the hell you been?" he yelled. "You disappeared on me! You're roaming around the lobby of the hotel at four a.m. and then you're goddamn MIA."

"I'm working on something."

"I'm looking at the feed of the nets setting up for Armstrong George. He's holding another of his press conferences at the bombing site. This is not going to be pretty, J.D. You know what this place feels like? These delegates want blood. Jesus fucking Christ, we might as well be trying to elect goddamn Gandhi as World War Three breaks out. Mrs. Goddamn Gandhi. Some are talking about leaving. Everybody is scared shitless. Where the hell are you?"

"Like I said, I'm working on something." I sighed.

"You're with people," Eddie said. "And can't talk. Right?"

"Yeah. Talk about it later. But here's what I think we should do. Get Hilda to hold a press conference a half hour earlier and release the resolution we talked about. Preempt George's presser. You've got it drafted, right?"

"Yeah, but it doesn't say anything about some lunatics blowing up a bus."

"So add a line or two. I'd do the press avail someplace neutral." I thought for a minute. "We want to tone this thing down as much as we can. Just do it downstairs at the hotel. Use a ballroom. Get on it now; we got to get the notice out."

"Why do you think I've been looking for you? Where the hell have you been?"

"I'll meet you at the convention. If you have a problem with Hilda, call me back."

"This thing you can't talk about, is it going to help us? Tell me it's going to help us."

"It's going to help us."

Eddie sighed. "That was your J.D. 'Feel better' voice, not your J.D. 'I really believe this' voice, but thanks. Got to go. Onward Christian soldiers."

"But Eddie—"

"What?"

"You're an atheist."

He hung up.

Jessie was staring at me, a faint smile on her lips. "I suppose that was off the record, too?"

I nodded.

"I'm not sure this is going to work," Jessie said. "How are we going to have a relationship if everything is off the record?"

Relationship? Relationship? Is that what we were having? I was thinking about that as we pulled in to the Body Shop parking lot. Heat waves were already rising up from the asphalt.

"This place open?" Paul asked.

"This place is always open," Walter answered.

"How do you know?" Jessie asked.

Paul laughed. "Yeah, asshole, how do you know?"

"I'm a law enforcement official," Walter said with a smile. "It's my job to know these things."

As soon as we stepped inside, it felt like we had entered a cave—cool, dark, vaguely dangerous. Two hulking men, one white, one black, were in the doorway. They wore identical blue blazers and turtlenecks emblazoned with the Body Shop logo. They nodded at Walter. "Officer," the large white one said.

"Walter," the black man said, nodding.

Jessie giggled, taking in the club: a half-dozen girls, a pair of Japanese businessmen, a couple of college students, an attractive couple in their late thirties who seemed to have ended up here after a night on Bourbon Street. Two of the dancers slowly walked over to check us out and I realized I'd seen one of them when I was here before. "Hey, big boy, good to see you back," she said, then gave Jessie a look. "This is tasty." Jessie beamed.

Their long, sequined gowns glinting in the reflected light of the mirror ball hanging from the ceiling gave them the look of forties movie stars. One was short and Asian, pretty, with high cheekbones and white teeth. Her unnaturally large breasts burst from the gown. The other was tall and blond, just a few chromosome twists from gorgeous. But her jaw was too large for her face and her teeth were oversized. There was a bit of horse somewhere in that gene pool. Not a bad-looking horse, but still.

"Hi, girls, you look fabulous," Jessie said, and seemed to mean it.

They smiled at Jessie but closed in on Walter, Paul, and me. "Lap dance?" the tall blonde asked. She drew out the words in a long Texas drawl.

I pulled Walter, who was staring appreciatively at the two women, aside.

"You know these guys?" I asked, tilting my head toward the beefy men in blazers.

"It's a small town," he said. I nudged Walter toward the two men. They looked at us with blunt, bored expressions. "We're here to see Tyler," I told them. This was met with absolutely no response at all.

"He's not here," the black man finally said. He looked at Walter Robinson. "This a friend of yours, Walter?"

Walter smiled. "Cops don't have friends who aren't cops. You guys know that." They nodded and didn't argue. "Tyler here?"

"Nope. Haven't seen him since yesterday."

"Can we just take a look in his office for a second?" I asked, standing beside Walter.

"Fuck you," the black man said evenly.

I looked at Walter. "We need to get in the office."

Walter sighed. "Okay, look, guys, you come with us, but my friend says we have to look in the office, and I think we have to look in the office. Christ, let's make this easy, okay?"

The two men looked at each other. Their necks were so large that it made it seem like their heads had been placed on top of posts. The black man seemed to be in charge. "You want to know something, Walter, I really don't give a shit. You want to look, you look. What the hell."

He led us down the same neutral hallway that I had walked down the day before. Paul and Jessie followed us. The door to Tyler's office was open. The large metal cabinet was unlocked; the gun racks inside were bare. The drawers to his desk were pulled out, empty. The large Confederate flag that had hung behind his desk was gone.

"He left," the large black man said flatly.

"Why?" I asked. Somehow I had never really expected to find Tyler, but seeing his office like this gave me a sick feeling of dread.

The black man chuckled. It was an odd sound coming from the overbuilt body. "Let's just say he didn't say. Took everything but his stereo," the black man said. "Too damn big to move."

I walked over to the metal shelves holding the sound system. The same CD player was connected. I hit play and in an instant the song I'd heard in the office the day before boomed through the speakers. This was why I wanted to come back to the club. It was loud, grating, mixed with crowd sounds. A live recording. A harsh voice wailed:

Racial pride ain't no racist hate.
Cops beat down, no it's not too late.
On the news, in the streets,
Doin' it right, still take heat.
Point a finger,
Truth don't matter,
Got a gun.
Get it done.

Whole world's gone crazy.

We're losin power but it just won't last.

Screw bodycam. Change is comin and it's comin fast.

Babies in the crib

lyin in wait.

grow up to game the system,

But it ain't too late.

Clock strikes. Time ticks.

Hold on. Don't quit.

Turn back time to when America was goin' strong.

Keep the faith. Do what's right because it's all gone wrong.

Our walk, long walk. Our fight.

Get yourself straight. Get it right.

We're losin power but it just won't last.

Screw bodycam. Change is comin and it's comin fast.

The song ended.

"Always listening to that shit," the black man said. "He loved it. You know what he called his piece-of-shit band? The Confederate Dead. He thought that name was funny as hell."

"C.D.," Jessie said. "You want to play that again?"

"Damn," the white security guard said. He was now giving Jessie a careful look. She did look great. "Worst stuff in the world."

I played it again.

"What's Tyler to you, anyway?" the black security guard asked.

"He's our brother," Paul said quietly. Then, when I glared at him, he added, "Half brother."

Chapter
★
Seven

IT TOOK ME ONLY an hour and a half to get there. It had been years since I'd made the drive, and remembering how short it was only made me feel worse about how long it had been since I'd seen Renee. *Renee.* The name had been a touch from her half-Cajun mother.

Paul hadn't argued against me going alone. He was *happy* for me to do it. We needed to find Tyler, and the best place to start was with his mother. The woman—the girl—who had been my babysitter when she was fourteen and my father had seduced her, if that was the right word.

The distance from New Orleans wasn't why I hadn't seen Renee Hutchinson in years, so many I couldn't really remember. It was the embarrassment. No, that was too easy. It's embarrassing to show up at a party in a white dinner jacket when everyone else is wearing a tux. I'd done that once to an afternoon summer wedding of some friends of Sandra's in Newport. Goddamn Yankees. In the South it would have been perfectly acceptable, complimented as a bit retro. But those Yankees thought I was a waiter and asked me to get drinks for them all afternoon. Sandra thought it was hilarious. I should have ended it then, driven back to D.C. and left her there.

It wasn't embarrassment, it was shame. A good old-fashioned, Old Testament kind of shame.

She still lived in the same shotgun cottage bought with the money quietly raised by a couple of phone calls "up north" that Tobias had made. He never told us who gave the money, but it wasn't difficult to figure out that someone with Tobias's skills could make it pretty clear why it would be a disaster if a prominent movement figure like Powell Callahan were spotlighted with transgressions that no one would defend. And that was the thing—it was transgressions, as in multiple.

Everybody in their little inner circle—Tobias and the cozy crowd who used the movement as their own fishing pond constantly restocked with attractive women—knew that my father had a thing for girls far too young. If one scandal had hit the news, odds were that other girls, women now, would come forward. It had been going on for a long time. And then there was my mother. They all loved my mother and wanted to preserve her dignity, or at least what was left of it. So it was very, very important to make sure that Renee Hutchinson had what she needed to have her baby and start a new life and not blame the great Powell Callahan. No one would have called it hush money, but of course that's what it was. Not that the girl didn't deserve the money.

Shame. Shameful. That's what I felt. But I should be used to it. I've felt that way since I was eight years old and just sensed, in that way kids have of knowing stuff, that something was really wrong. I parked in front of the small house at the end of the block. When we left the strip club, Paul, Walter, and Jessie had dropped me off at the Superdome. I'd taken one of the electric cars General Motors had lent the convention to showcase their newest model. It was a terrible imitation of a Toyota Prius, but at least it was silent, and Renee didn't hear me approach her house.

She was where I expected her to be: outside by the marsh that had come to define her life and life's work. When she and her mother and baby Tyler moved into the house, it was on the outskirts of town, by a beautiful marsh. She finished high school with a GED and commuted to LSU while her mother took care of Tyler. She fell in love with a drummer for a band that toured for a while and came back home when her mother was diagnosed with cancer. Bad cancer, ovarian, stage four. She didn't last long and that left Renee, now all of twenty, with not-a-baby-anymore Tyler. She did a little of this and a little of that until a local fertilizer plant wanted to expand near the house. It was a big, ugly thing spewing all kinds of dubious toxins, and the more enlightened locals united to block it. Four years later, the fertilizer plant was history and Renee had found her calling: she was an environmental activist. In a place like New Iberia, in the petrochemical corridor of south Louisiana, there was always a cause looking to be championed. It was against this perpetual do-goodism that Tyler, no doubt, had rebelled, fleeing to the army, his strange skinhead world, his strip club and security businesses. She had won awards and testified in Baton Rouge a dozen times, gone to D.C. to lobby Congress. It didn't hurt that she was beautiful and had a charm that I still remembered from when I was a kid.

Renee had contacted me a few times over the years for help on one cause or another. I had tried to open this door, or connect her to that person, and maybe I had helped, but there was always this awkward moment when it came time to describe how I knew Renee Hutchinson. I'd just say, "She's a friend of the family," and it always came with that rush of shame.

I was staring out the windshield of the awful toy car lost in the past when there was a tapping on the passenger window. Renee was smiling, her face sweaty, garden shears in one ungloved hand. She was still beautiful.

We sat out on her back porch overlooking the marsh and drank ice tea. "If you want sweet tea, I hope you brought it, since I don't mess with sugar," she said, with that same smile that was still so charming. And then she laughed when I pulled out a couple of packets stolen from the Windsor Court. I was planning to work around to Tyler slowly, as if I were just dropping by to see her, but of course she was too smart for that.

"What did he do?" she asked, before I could begin with my little charade. I started to protest but she just shook her head. "It's one of the busiest days of your life and you drive your cute ass out here to see Renee because you are being a good person and miss her? I love you, J.D., but that's bullshit and we both know it. You're here about Tyler. I knew that as soon as I saw you pull up in that silly car. What are you doing in that thing, anyway? It's what I'd drive."

"GM gave it to the convention to use."

"Is it really as bad as everybody says?"

"Horrible. It shakes over sixty-five."

"So what did he do?" she asked again, with a sigh.

"I don't know. I'm just trying to find him."

"He's not at that horrible club? He almost lives there."

"No. He left. Where does he live, anyway?" It just occurred to me that Walter should have tracked down where he lived. What kind of cop was he, anyway? And what did it say about me that I hadn't asked him to check?

"I saw him at the club," I said. She tilted her head when I said that, surprised. "But when I went back, he was gone." I shrugged. "I don't know where he lives or his cell."

She nodded. "What's going on, J.D.? Why in the world are you trying to reach Tyler now?"

I had thought about this on the drive and had worked out what I would say. It was along the lines of "I heard he might be in trouble and want to help." But then I thought about how terrible I'd feel if I ended up being another Callahan lying to her. So I told her everything. Every bit of it. When I finished, she got up, came back with more tea, and sat back down.

"I wanted him to do more therapy, after the accident," she said. "But he said it made him feel like a coward."

"A coward."

"The sessions were mostly combat veterans and he was just a guy who was in an accident. He said he felt like a fake soldier. 'A fucking fake soldier,' is how he put it. That club." She sort of shuddered.

We sat there for a while, listening to the marsh. I'd put my phone on vibrate and I could feel it going crazy, call after call. Renee got up and came back with an address and a telephone number. "That's the last I had," she said. "I think it's still good."

I stood up and she hugged me and I'd have given anything to have willed away all the pain my father and the world had brought down on her. "Be safe," she whispered, and kissed me lightly on the cheek. "Be safe, J.D." She felt my phone vibrating and laughed. "You better go. I bet the whole world is looking for you."

I laughed and pulled away. "I hate my life," I said, and I don't think I'd ever meant anything more.

"Sometimes we do," she said, "but it's all we've got."

On the way out, I ducked into the bathroom. It was off her bedroom and filled with pictures of Tyler: baby Tyler, grade-school Tyler, Tyler in Little League, Tyler in the junior high band, Tyler playing guitar in his first rock-and-roll band, Tyler in the military with a few of his buddies. Most of the photos were from before his accident. He had looked so handsome in his uniform. There was one of him and a bunch of buddies when they had finished basic training, laughing it up, proud as can be. I stared at the handsome, unscarred face and wondered if he had any idea then of what the future held, if maybe underneath all that exploding joy there wasn't just a trace of sadness that hinted at the knowledge that this might be his peak. I looked at the crowd with him. And then I saw him: he was three down from Tyler in a row of sweaty guys in gray T-shirts. It took me a moment to be sure, but there wasn't any doubt. It was Somerfield George. I took the picture.

I followed Ginny as we worked our way through the double levels of security toward the area of the convention floor reserved for the press and campaign trailers. Everywhere you looked there were SWAT team members, FBI, Secret Service, with more automatic weapons than an Arizona gun show. It felt like we were entering a high-tech concentration camp.

"Jesus Christ," I mumbled, looking around. "This is an Armstrong George wet dream. Forget about closing up the borders, let's just start right here at the convention."

"It gets worse inside," Ginny hissed. "They even strip-searched a couple of alternate delegates."

"Ours? They strip-searched our goddamn delegates?"

Ginny shrugged. "Alternates."

About a third of the Superdome floor had been curtained off for the press and campaign trailers. Thick cables snaked across the floor in an electronic maze. This had been one of my longtime concerns, that someone—Armstrong George or someone from the press—would drop a tap into one of the cables from the Hilda Smith trailer. I hated the idea that my cables might be running over Armstrong George's cables or CNN's cables.

Everybody thought I was crazy paranoid, and of course they were right. Right now I would have killed for convention spying to be the biggest problem I had. Instead I had one crazy brother beating up on me to extort money for his greater political good, another running a strip club, doing his skinhead thing, with maybe a little bombing on the side, an ex-girlfriend reporter who was on the loose, another reporter who I was crazy enough to sleep with and who now was learning everything about our little family house of horrors—these were real problems.

The Hilda Smith command trailer was a double-wide construction site trailer packed with radios, television monitors, and computers. Eddie Basha was sitting at a computer terminal. "Take a look," he said right away, passing me a delegate list, then resumed screaming into an iPhone. His olive skin gleamed with a slick layer of sweat even though the trailer's air conditioner was turned to morgue level.

But I was watching the image of Armstrong George on the dozen television screens packed into the trailer. He was standing in front of the entrance to Mardi Gras World. The charred bus had been hauled away. As always, his son, Somerfield, was just behind him. I stared at him, wondering: *Do you know where Tyler is? Is Tyler with you? Did you get Tyler to plant those bombs?* I turned the sound up.

"The terrible tragedy that occurred here last night is simply more evidence that the social fabric of America is tattered and torn. We cannot let the lawless few continue to rip apart the threads of decency and shared purpose that bind this great nation together. Just yesterday, the president of the United States agreed with me as he called for these criminals to pay the ultimate price."

"What a pompous asshole," Eddie said to the screen, meaning Armstrong George, then resumed his harangue into the phone. "You tell your governor that win or lose, Hilda Smith still has six months to go as the second most powerful person in this goddamn country, and there's a certain investigation by the NCAA into some very suspect recruitment practices of that shit-kicking university your governor loves so much, and if it goes the wrong way, she'll have the United States Congress looking into it and he'll be a hundred and one before his team is done being investigated. . . . Am I getting through here, Artie?"

Eddie looked up and shrugged and bore down on the phone. "Well, if you haven't heard about the investigation, that only proves how fucking serious it is. They always keep the serious stuff really quiet, and you know it. We're not talking about a slap on the wrist here, Artie. We're talking the big bullet. Death penalty. No play for years. Disband, got it? Now can we talk about these delegates?"

I wanted to reach through the television and throttle Armstrong George. What made it worse was that I knew just how reasonable and reassuring he appeared. The bombings were like star witnesses that George was putting on the stand to make his case that America needed "serious action for serious times." And if, God forbid, it turned out that my own brother was involved, it would not only kill Hilda Smith, it would also make J. D. Callahan once again the guy everybody in America could laugh at. This would make getting dumped by Sandra Juarez and walking off *Meet the Press* look like a mild social faux pas.

I tried to tell myself that it was insane to think that Tyler might have been involved with the bombings. The problem was that it did make some terrible sense. Look at the facts: Tyler had been a skinhead, a group hardly noted for their racial tolerance. He loved explosives and guns—just look at what a blown-up mess he was. He loved Armstrong George, and the son of a bitch had been friends with Somerfield George in the army—something he had never told me about. Why hadn't he told me when I saw him?

Eddie ended his call and stretched. "Where the hell you been?" he demanded. "I'm so goddamn pissed off I was hoping you did get blown up."

"NCAA?" I shot back. "That's a new one. Excellent."

Eddie allowed himself a slight smile. "What would they do if their football program went belly up? Spend all their time screwing their sisters?"

"I hope you put it to them just like that."

"It's not a time for subtlety. We've got squirrelly delegates all over the place." He pointed to the list of delegates in my hand. There were twenty-three names. "We're moving these to uncommitted."

Oh, shit. My heart started racing. Every delegate on the list had been listed as a solid Hilda Smith delegate just twelve hours earlier.

"This is death," I said simply. "Does anybody know this?"

Eddie shrugged. "I'm going by what our whips are telling us for every state. But you know how it is. Every news organization in the world is polling these delegations. Somebody's going to break a story that our people are going soft. And then . . ."

"The dam bursts. Jesus."

From the television monitor, I heard her voice: strong, level, a touch cutting. God, I knew that voice so well.

"Governor Armstrong," Sandra Juarez shouted, "can you say categorically that your campaign had nothing to do with the recent phone calls attacking Vice President Smith?"

"Yes, I can." He answered the question head-on, without a trace of defensiveness. It was a pro's response.

"Can you explain, then," Sandra Juarez continued, "why it is that the questions for the phone calls were written on stationery of your own Colorado Republican Party?"

Sandra was standing to the side of the half circle of reporters surrounding George. She was so short that she was almost covered by her colleagues. But her voice rang loud and her hand shot up, brandishing a piece of paper.

"No, I have no idea," Governor George replied, still calm.

"Are you saying that you are unaware of any connection

between your campaign and the Colorado Republican Party and these phone calls?"

"Yes."

Behind George, his aides stirred nervously. Off to the side, alone, as always, his son stared hard at Sandra, as if he might intimidate her into withdrawing the question. Good luck with that, asshole. Other reporters joined in, shouting follow-up questions. Paul Hendricks was the loudest, clearly outraged that Sandra Juarez had hijacked his story. A George press flack stepped forward, cutting off the questions. I felt a tingle of hope return. Maybe this could still work. God bless Sandra, the evil bitch.

"Here's the draft resolution," Eddie Basha said, pushing a piece of paper into my hands. The resolution read just like we had discussed, a straightforward denunciation of the bombings.

"But it's still all about defense. I hate fucking defense. All this does is maybe stop us from losing before we get started. That's it."

"We need defense," Eddie answered tiredly. "That's the point. Right now, she's our best offense." He pointed to the television, where Sandra was still working over Armstrong George. "God help us."

"This is what we do," I said, startling Eddie. "We get this resolution passed. Then we follow it up right away with another, condemning the politics of personal destruction. We draft some kind of bullshit code of political ethics and we make a motion for it to be included in the party platform."

"I like that," Eddie said immediately. "Try to pump these phone calls up into a bigger deal."

A large man in a dark suit burst into the trailer. He was overweight, with a broad, bright red face.

"Governor Kowalski," I said, holding out my hand and trying to look pleased.

The man waved a piece of paper like a sword. "This your idea of a goddamn joke, Callahan? You want me to introduce this resolution? Then what do you want? Me to get down on my knees and kiss Armstrong George's ass on national television?"

"What don't you like about it?" I asked evenly.

"Like? Like? What's to goddamn like? Are we going to fight this guy or roll over and play dead?"

I tried to explain what passed for our strategy: play defense on the first resolution, then introduce a second one about the politics of personal destruction that would make Armstrong George look bad.

The governor of Illinois's broad Polish face looked as if it were about to explode. "Well, let me tell you something, I've been running for office since you were stuffing envelopes, and you win elections by going out and kicking the other guy in the nuts, not standing around with your hands over your crotch so you won't get hurt when the other son of a bitch kicks you in the balls. You getting my message here, Callahan?"

"Governor, we think that if we can get George on the defensive on this push poll stuff, we can begin to turn this onto character and principle. Tomorrow morning, the vice president is planning a major speech that will directly challenge everything that Armstrong George stands for. We are going to clean his clock, Governor, trust me."

Lisa Henderson appeared at the door, looking annoyed as always. It was getting crowded. "Am I interrupting an important meeting, Governor?" she asked, clearly irritated that something, anything, was happening and she had not figured out how to make it about her.

"Lisa," Governor Kowalski said, "Callahan here was just telling me that the vice president plans a major speech tomorrow. It's about goddamn time."

Lisa stared at me furiously.

"And," the governor continued, "I want you to know and I want the vice president to know that I think this resolution you want me to introduce is a piece of shit. You got it? I'll do it, because I ain't running this railroad, and I'll force my people in line, because that's how we do things where I grew up, but Jesus fucking Christ, it's time we started busting some ass and quit apologizing. And this other little thing, this 'campaign code of ethics,' I guess it won't hurt, but for heaven's sake, what the fuck are we doing showing up at a gunfight with a knife?"

Lisa looked once more at me as I bent my head slightly. *Go with me on this,* I was desperately trying to plead with her. *Just go with me.*

"We appreciate your help, Governor," Lisa finally said with a sigh. "We wouldn't be here without you, and when Hilda Smith is president, we won't forget."

"You're goddamn right you won't forget, because I'll be in your face every fucking day." He laughed and left the trailer.

"What have you done this time, Callahan?" Lisa turned on me with fury. "I just saw this resolution and I think you've lost your mind. Our delegates will never go along with this. It's an endorsement of Armstrong George. And who the hell are you to think you can do this without the approval of the vice president?"

I went through the strategy once again. When Lisa heard the

idea of the campaign ethics resolution, she brightened. "Well, that I do like. These phone calls are unbelievably vicious. This is a huge issue, much bigger than anything else. I just know it. People are outraged."

Walter Robinson stuck his large head inside the trailer.

"Walter," I said, "this is Lisa Henderson. The vice president's chief of staff. Lisa, this is Walter Robinson, the New Orleans Police Department officer who has been very helpful. He liaises with the FBI."

They shook hands.

"I'm Eddie Basha," Eddie said. "Don't worry about me." He was already onto another phone call.

"I need to ask Mr. Callahan a couple of questions about the bombing last night," Walter said. "He was there, you know."

"Oh, yes, I heard he was very much there. Having a great time, I heard."

God, I thought, *she hates me. Why am I surrounded by people who hate me?*

"Mr. Callahan," Walter said formally, "could you just step out for a minute? Sorry to bother you."

Outside the trailer, Paul was waiting for us. "How'd you guys get in here, anyway?" I asked.

"I made Paul an official deputy."

I laughed.

"So what did you find out?" Walter asked. On the way back from Renee's, I had called Walter and told him to meet me at the Superdome.

All around us, people were scurrying about with the manic gleam of imminent panic. A blue curtain divided the trailers from the convention floor, where the muffled roar of a thousand people milling about mixed with the loud music pumping through the sound system. For some reason, they were playing Motown hits.

Paul walked up and pointed to a trailer marked "RNC Finance Reception."

"That's where I want to be," he said, nodding to the trailer. "I want those folks raising money for me." He looked at the bland trailer like it was an oasis in the middle of a long march through the desert.

"We're going to work out that money," I said, feeling very uncomfortable even mentioning it there. I looked around for any reporters. You didn't have to know that Walter was a cop to know he was a cop. Everything about him screamed cop. Local cop. Not a fed. How many people knew the FBI had interviewed me? Jesus, if that story got out. Now the NOPD. I'd be a goner, a total joke.

I led them to a trailer marked "Rules Committee." The Rules Committee had finished their work before the convention started and had no use for a trailer, but they still got one. Everyone always wants their own trailer.

"Jesus Christ," the man inside the trailer shouted as soon as I opened the door.

"Oh God!" the woman yelled.

The middle-aged man and woman looked up in shock. They made a comic spectacle: the man with his gray suit pants hanging around his ankles, the woman with her tailored suit pulled up, her pantyhose lowered. She was bent over one of the computer tables and the man was behind her. His already-red face exploded in color. I backed out of the trailer without saying a word and steered Walter and Paul away from the trailer entrance.

"The mayor of Cleveland and a local newswoman," I explained. "She interviewed me a couple of months ago." We walked off so the couple could scurry away.

We went back inside the trailer, which reeked of sex. It had probably been designated as the official trysting site and used by God knows how many lovers over the last few days.

"Tell me about your brother," Walter broke in, collapsing on the small couch in the back of the trailer.

"Half brother," Paul said.

"He was in the army," I started in. "Got hurt in an accident. Discharged. Drifted around. Started working as a bouncer in strip clubs. Moved into management."

"And?" Walter asked. He was looking at both of us with a level, intense gaze. He was a cop listening to a witness who was probably trying to protect a suspect. It occurred to me that Walter was likely good at this. He had been doing it for years.

Paul picked it up. "He'd been a skinhead since he was like eight years old. He was a skinhead when he went into the army and one when he got out. Those are the guys he hangs out with. Women too. There are female skinheads too, you know."

"What I don't get," Walter said, looking at Paul, "is why I've known you for over twenty years and you got this brother who's blowing himself up and running around with a bunch of Nazi types and you like never mentioned it?"

Paul answered. "He never lived with us. He lived with his mother." He paused. "They lived in New Iberia."

"Uh-huh," Walter said. "And what else?"

Paul and I looked at each other.

"What?" Walter demanded. "For Christ's sake, Paulie, you think you can lie to me? You think you can get over on me? Who is his mother, anyway?"

I sighed. "She was our babysitter."

Paul corrected me. "His babysitter," he said, pointing to me. "I was too old for one."

Walter stared for a half moment, then sort of laughed. "Oh, Jesus and Mary. He did?" We nodded. "I shouldn't laugh, but your babysitter? Christ fucking Jesus. That's something. How old was she?"

"Fourteen," I said.

Walter whistled. "Fourteen? He was a child molester."

Paul and I both winced. "Come on," Paul said. "What were you doing when you were fourteen?"

"Okay, statutory rapist, not child molester. That better?"

"Renee said she didn't have any idea where Tyler was, and I believe her. But here's something interesting. Tyler and Somerfield George were in the army together."

"You're kidding me," Paul said. "Why didn't we know this? Why didn't you know this? Like the same unit?"

I nodded.

Eddie Basha burst into the room. "Hell, J.D., you can't disappear on me. Why aren't you answering your phone?" I pulled it out. The battery was dead. Eddie looked at me in disgust, as if I had just found a decomposing animal in my pocket. He handed me a Mophie battery pack for my iPhone. He always carried extras and couldn't believe it when I didn't.

"What's up?" I asked lamely.

"We've got a full-scale revolt on our hands. Massachusetts, Rhode Island, Vermont, Wisconsin—"

"Why?" I interrupted.

"They won't go with the motion. They've drafted their own motion attacking Armstrong George as a fascist. It even has those words in the draft. 'Armstrong George has fascist tendencies.'"

"Well, that's true enough." Paul laughed. "I thought that was the point."

"They say if we introduce the other motion, they will vote against it and introduce their own. That happens, we split right down the middle. We're dead."

"Where's Governor Kowalski in all this?"

"He says it's a terrible shame, but you can tell he's loving it. He's got 'I told you so' about ten feet tall all over his face."

"Bring 'em in." I sighed.

"Who?"

"Everybody. The revolt states, the governors, superdelegates."

"J.D., we got like fifteen minutes till the gavel drops."

"So we better hurry. Let's do it in the locker room."

Eddie nodded and hurried off.

"I need Tobias," I said to my brother. "Right here, right now."

The locker room smelled of disinfectant. I stood on a bench at the end of the room, the renegade delegates and their leaders gathered around me. It was crowded. Eddie had told the leaders of the delegations that they were to come alone, but of course that didn't happen. Word had spread instantly and suddenly it was very important to a lot of people to get inside the visitors' locker room of the Superdome. The visitors' side had been assigned to our campaign; Armstrong George got the home side. This had been decided by a coin toss, and noted columnists had actually tried to dissect the latent meaning in the vice president's ending up with the visiting side.

"We don't have much time this morning," I started right in. "But I want to thank you all for coming. I'd like to begin with a few words from a man many of you know and a lifelong friend of mine and my family's: the Reverend Tobias Green."

I'd positioned Tobias at the entrance of the locker room so that everyone who entered had to pass by him. The delegates streamed into the room, spoiling for a fight, but as they encountered Tobias, a remarkable transformation occurred. First came surprise, and a few almost blurted out what almost everyone was thinking—*He's still alive?*—and then there was a sudden pleased awareness that they were in the presence of a man considered to be a genuine civil rights hero. Here was a man who had been on the balcony in Memphis when King was shot, a man attacked by Bull Connor's dogs, a man whom Robert Kennedy had called "an American hero." Naturally every delegate was wondering what in the world Tobias Green was doing at this emergency meeting in the visitors' locker room of the Superdome, but no one, not even the senators and governors who were superdelegates, asked the question. Even though Republicans, including Hilda Smith, were likely to top out at ten percent—if they were lucky—of the African American vote, Tobias was a link to a past that all but the true racist embraced. That he was willing to come and speak to Republicans, that he had shown a willingness to support a few Republicans here and there through the years, made the gathered delegates swoon in gratitude. At a Democratic convention Tobias would have been one of many prominent African Americans and civil rights leaders but here, today, he was the Republicans' star.

I helped Tobias up onto the wooden bench. He seemed to weigh about ten pounds. "Let us pray," Tobias announced in a strong, firm voice.

A few of the delegates looked at each other. Pray? What the hell for? But everyone bowed their heads, including the Jews, atheists, and Buddhists in the group, of which there were a few.

"Our Heavenly Father," Tobias began, "the source of all wisdom and goodness, guide us here this morning as we search for wisdom. Our Father, we ask for Your strength as we look within ourselves to serve You better with our actions. The road is long and we are weak. But our faith in You is eternal. In God's name, we pray. Amen."

The delegates looked up. Now what?

"My friends, my brothers and sisters, welcome to the city where we have toiled long and hard for justice. It was not long ago that the Freedom Riders were beaten in these streets, and heaven help a black man who found himself in the hands of the New Orleans police. Those of us who worked so hard for so long to bring justice for all, we are fewer and fewer every year. But as our good Lord calls us to greater glory, we pass the torch to a new generation."

The delegates started to nod as Tobias's strong voice drew them into his spell.

"Once again, these are troubled times in our great land. The heathen rage amongst us as the peddlers of hate find many buyers for the evil they sell."

"Amen, brother," murmured Tommy Blue, a Wisconsin delegate and former All-Pro cornerback with Green Bay. He was one of the few black delegates.

"Amen," Tobias echoed seamlessly. "Though there are differences amongst us here today, we are united by our desire to banish this evil and turn back the darkness." Tobias's voice began to rise in a strong, lilting cadence. "We find ourselves once again soldiers in the eternal struggle between good and evil!"

"Hallelujah!" cried Irma Levine, a real estate attorney from Boston. She was Jewish.

"Hallelujah, sister," Tobias agreed. "Though there are differences amongst us, we must now as never before join together arm in arm, just as we did so many years ago with Brother King that fateful day in Birmingham. We must walk past the dogs of hate, through the fire hoses of prejudice, never faltering, united by our love, willing to sacrifice our petty differences so that others may follow us into a brighter, more joyous day."

"Tell it, Brother Green!" shouted Mayor Henry of Burlington, Vermont. Henry was actually a former member of the Socialist Workers Party, but had made a fortune in real estate and become a Republican. He'd given more than a million dollars to Hilda through various committees.

"So I ask you, brothers and sisters, to put aside your differences and put your faith in the love that unites us! I have known this man since he was but a boy." Tobias reached out and pulled me next to him. I grabbed his arm, and it felt like a piece of kindling for a fire, hard, knotted, skinny. "When there were those in this city who would cross the street rather than walk next to a black man, his father took us into his home and surrounded us with love. When there were those who championed hate, his father stood before them and shamed them with his love for all men, regardless of race. I watched this boy grow up in a home where many a night a bright cross of fear burned in their yard. I felt for him as he endured the taunts of his fellow schoolchildren because his father was an admitted nigger lover. A proud nigger lover! Today this boy who is now a man asked me to come here and pray for us in these troubled times. But I will do more than pray, I will also beg. Beg that we may leave this room united! Let us not allow the forces of darkness to divide us! Let us join hands once again and march forth to victory! While we may question the route, let us march forth joyfully, confident that our destination will be reached!"

"We're with you, Brother Green!" Tommy Blue shouted.

"Say amen, brother!" shouted Tobias.

"Amen!" cried the delegates.

"Let me hear you say hallelujah, brothers and sisters!"

"Hallelujah!"

"Hallelujah!" Tobias echoed.

He held out his arms, his thin black hands shaking. "I can feel the love. I can feel the strength. God help those who stand in our way!"

He lowered his head, still holding his hands outstretched.

Even Governor Kowalski had tears in his eyes.

Tobias stayed in the locker room after the delegates had filed out back to the floor, any hint of a rebellion squashed. Tobias was wearing an all-access pass that I'd given him as part of our deal.

"Felt good, J.D., that it did. Still got the touch."

I had to admit that he did. His locker room performance had been like watching an aging baseball pitcher come through with 95 mph heat.

Tobias reached into his pocket and came out with several business cards with numbers scribbled on the back. He perused them in exaggerated fashion. "Phone numbers, baby," he beamed. "You didn't see them stuff them into my pocket? Let's see now"—he stared at the business cards like a gambler studying a winning hand—"I think I'll start with that blonde from Wisconsin. Do my bit for African-Scandinavian relationships. Long tradition of that, you know. Lot of brothers went to Scandinavia in the sixties." Tobias beamed.

"I'll get the money over to you later today," I told him as the floor votes started to come in. It was going to be a big procedural win for Hilda. Every delegation was delivering. "I'm sure your Truth and Justice Committee for Lower Utility Rates will put it to good use."

My cell phone rang. It was always ringing, but this was a special ring that meant the vice president was calling me.

"J.D.," she said. "I need to see you."

Chapter
★
Eight

AS SOON AS I STEPPED INTO HER SUITE, I knew it was bad. The vice president was there and her husband but the giveaway was the campaign's lawyer, Richard Gomez. He was the one who spoke first, which was a really bad sign. "Have a seat, J.D." I started to say something glib or funny to break the ice but couldn't muster the energy. Which was probably for the best.

"What can you tell us about your brother, J.D.?" Gomez asked.

"What?" I asked. I was having trouble focusing. It was strange to be in the same room with the VP and not have her say anything. We had been through so much together since New Hampshire.

"Your brother," Gomez said.

"He's running for public service commissioner here in Louisiana. What do you want to know?"

Gomez looked at the VP, as if this were a meaningful confession. "Not Paul. Your half brother, Tyler."

I sighed. Jesus fucking Christ. How the hell had it come to this? "Tyler," I said flatly. "Tyler's mother was my babysitter. He never lived with us. But he's my half brother, yes."

The three of them stared at me, and I had the pleasant sensation of knowing that I had just regained a bit of the upper hand in whatever was going on. Knowledge was power, and this they hadn't known.

The VP spoke for the first time. "Powell Callahan slept with your babysitter?" she asked, as if she had learned the pope ran a drug cartel on the side.

"Several of them, actually, at least I think so. But the only one he got pregnant was Tyler's mother. Her name is Renee Hutchinson, by the way. Lovely woman. It's just too bad she met my father. Pretty sure my mother ended up feeling the same way. They tried to make the best of it."

No one said anything for a long time. Then Gomez looked down at some notes he had on a yellow legal pad—the guy couldn't use an iPad?—and asked, "Have you seen Tyler lately?"

"Sure," I said, "which you must know, or you wouldn't be asking me. You're asking to see if I will lie about it. I saw him out at the strip club he runs on Airline Highway. Then I went back to see him early this morning, but he wasn't there."

"And why did you go back to see him?" Gomez asked.

"That's easy too," I said. "I was worried he might be involved in the bombings."

"Good lord," Hilda Smith murmured. "Then it's true?"

Which, of course, confirmed what I'd assumed when they started asking me about Tyler: someone had leaked to them. Now I just needed to find out who.

"Why didn't you notify the authorities of any suspicions?" Gomez asked, his voice taking on a harsher tone, as if he was moving in for the kill.

I frowned. "What are you talking about? I went out there with a high-ranking member of the New Orleans Police Department. Of course I notified the authorities."

This surprised them. Which told me they didn't know that much about what had happened. So I told them everything. Except about seeing Tyler's photo with Somerfield George. When I was finished, Gomez had a dazed sort of look on his face, which did please me. The whole thing was such a shit sandwich he was choking just trying to get it down.

"Well, J.D.," he finally said. "That's quite a story."

"I wish you had told me," Hilda Smith said, and sounded like she meant it. She said it like a human being who was concerned, not a politician. When you're the vice president of the United States and a hair away from being the presidential nominee of your party and a staffer has just told you how his quasi–half brother might be trying to blow up your chances to become president, that seemed like a pretty decent way to respond.

"I'm glad he didn't," Gomez said, and Hilda Smith's husband smiled. So did I. He was right. "Look, J.D., you know this is a tough one for everybody. But there's only one thing to do. We're going to have to ask you to step aside as campaign manager."

I stared at him. "Step aside," I said flatly. "Who would run the campaign?"

"Eddie Basha has agreed," the vice president said, and then it all made sense. It was Eddie who had told them about Tyler. It was Eddie who had made his move by trying to fuck me. Not trying, actually. He'd done it very nicely. I had to hand it to the guy, I'd taught him well. "We're hoping you would help him in any way you could that wasn't public."

Gomez looked at the VP sharply. It was the sort of thing he should have asked me privately, not in her presence, and she certainly shouldn't have said it. "I suppose you have a statement ready," I said.

"Yes, we do," Gomez said, and pulled out a piece of plain paper with a couple of sentences typed on it. The VP winced. Gomez's bedside manner needed some help. When you showed the patient the X-ray foretelling their death, better not to present it with, "See, those really dark spots are cancer. You can see how huge they are and how close they are to the heart. This is really incredible imaging, isn't it?"

Gomez started reading. It was a standard "For personal reasons, J. D. Callahan is taking a leave from the campaign" announcement.

"You can't do that," I said, before he was even finished.

Gomez stiffened. "Now J.D., I know this isn't easy but—"

I cut him off. "That 'personal reasons' will just create a feeding frenzy of people trying to find out the real story. It will consume the campaign. The vice president"—I nodded toward her, as if making it clear I was referring to *that* vice president—"won't be able to get any kind of message through that noise. It will kill the campaign."

"Maybe you should have thought of that before you went crazy with that brother of yours," Gomez exploded, then immediately pulled back, in that robotic, apologetic way lawyers can get when they have let slip a human moment by mistake.

"The decision's been made, J.D.," Hilda Smith said. "I'm sorry."

I nodded, then got up. "You'll put out the statement?"

"We will," Gomez said. Hilda looked a little pained when he said that, and I gave her credit for a bit of shame. "Just put it out. I won't take any press calls."

There was a long, painful silence in the room, like when the doctor has pronounced the patient dead and the family is quietly looking at the corpse. Then I turned and left the room. I knew two things I had to do: find Tyler, and destroy Eddie Basha.

Chapter
★
Nine

JOEY FRANCIS WAS WAITING FOR ME outside the VP's suite. I walked right past him, which was a dumb way to play it, but I wasn't at my best. He laughed, which really pissed me off and made me turn and face him. I was doing this all wrong but didn't seem able to stop.

"What?" I barked. Francis walked over to me and put his hand on my shoulder.

"It sucks, I know," he said.

"What?"

"Getting fired." He leaned in close to me. "You know who fucked you, right?" When I didn't say anything he whispered, "Your best boy. Eddie B. fucked you bad."

"You don't know that."

"No?" He pulled out his iPhone and showed me an email from Eddie to Lisa, all about Tyler. I had no idea how he knew, but I'd always said it was Eddie's job to know everything.

"You hacked into his email?" Francis laughed again at this, which really annoyed me. "Oh, right. Not just his. All of us. Great. How about the vice president?" He backed up, holding up his hands in mock protest.

"That would be seriously illegal."

"And hacking into other private emails isn't?"

"You ever read the fine print of the Patriot Act? When we have a terrorist threat against the safety of a vice president, I can do pretty much the fuck what I want to whomever I want. It's a beautiful thing."

I didn't know what to say. Somewhere in my head I was hearing the instructions I'd given scores of candidates: When you don't know what to say, don't say anything. I turned around and walked toward the elevator.

"We can play this two ways, J.D.," Francis said to my back. "You help us find him and all is good and glorious in the world and you might be a hero. Or you don't and I find a way to charge you as an accessory to terrorism. Maybe your brother Paul too. And your reporter friend you are way too friendly with."

I kept walking.

Jessie opened the door in a robe, holding her Glock to the side. "There's a lingerie store on Magazine that sells the gun and the robe together as a Valentine's gift for the little lady," she said, dropping the robe and putting the gun next to the bed. "It was a hot item last year. But don't worry, I bought it for myself, not gifts from a suitor. I was a virgin before I met you. Promise."

Then she pulled me down into bed.

I woke two hours later, bolting up. Jessie reached for her gun and sat up. "What?" she whispered, like we were a couple of homesteaders in old Apache territory who had heard the dog barking at the corral. I shook my head and grabbed my phone.

It had come to me when I was asleep, my brain turning over something that I couldn't quite grasp but wouldn't let go. It was two a.m., but she was awake. I knew she would be.

"What the fuck, J.D., it takes twenty-three calls for you to call me back?" Ginny was whispering but her voice still cut like a saw. "Hold on." I could hear people talking in the background and figured she was in one of our trailers at the Superdome. In a few seconds those voices grew dim and Ginny came back, louder. "I am so fucking mad at you. What the fuck? I'm supposed to work for Eddie fucking Basha?"

I had to laugh. Jessie gave me a strange look, but then maybe any look from a half-asleep nude woman holding a Glock like her favorite teddy bear might be strange. "Ginny, you are wonderful."

"Of course I'm fucking wonderful. Everybody knows that. Now where the hell are you?"

"I've got something I need you to do. Get one of the propeller heads on it." Propeller heads is what we called the brilliant kids—and they were all under twenty-five—in the research department.

"What?" She sighed. "So are you with that chick? Jesus Christ."

"I didn't say that."

"I know, but you would have told me where you were if you weren't with her. Just for the record, J.D., nobody in the whole goddamn universe has worse luck when it comes to banging reporters. Now what do you want me to do?"

"Find a boat."

When I finished explaining to Ginny and hung up, Jessie said in that half-asleep voice that was incredibly sexy, "Just for the record, you're not banging me, I'm banging you. That was smart about the boat. But I don't want to talk about it." She slid the Glock aside and pulled me closer. We were asleep in a few seconds.

Ginny called back ninety minutes later. "We've got it. I'm looking at it on Google Earth. You sure you want to go out there alone? I can go with you."

"Stay there. I'll call you. And Ginny, you're the best."

She hung up without saying anything. It was four a.m. and she was still working. She *was* the best.

"I guess I should make some coffee," Jessie said, swinging her long legs off to the side.

I didn't even try to talk Jessie into not going with me. We drank her coffee with chicory and got dressed without saying much at all. She poured the rest of the French press canister into a beat-up camouflage thermos that looked like it had spent years at deer camps. Then she dug around in a closet and came out with a short-barreled shotgun with a pistol grip. It scared the crap out of me just looking at it. Before I could ask, she said, "My mother gave it to me right after Katrina."

"Your mother?"

"She has two. One for her house and one for her car. I think it's one of the great disappointments of her life that nobody has ever tried to break into the house or jack her car. She's dying to use it." She slid the pump back and forth for emphasis, the sound as unique and chilling as a rattler.

The sun was coming up as we drove over the Causeway. "You have left the Magic Kingdom," Jessie announced when we reached the other side. For the first time in longer than I could remember, I didn't work the radio to suck down every bit of news possible. It just didn't seem important when it could all change in the next few hours, depending on what we discovered at the boat.

We found the old shrimp boat just where Ginny had said, moored at the little marina on Bayou Castine. Not fancy, but not decrepit. It looked a lot better than it had in the photo I'd seen on Renee's wall. That picture had been taken when Renee was still babysitting for me. The boat wasn't much to look at and my father hadn't paid much for it, but he had loved it. I could remember going out on it as a kid and the great pleasure my father took in docking at the fancy yacht club in New Orleans just to make fun of all his rich friends with beautiful sailboats or the big twin-engine deepwater fish killers that they kept so immaculately clean. Powell Callahan didn't have the nicest boat, but he threw the best parties, and everybody loved that old shrimp boat. After Renee "left"—it wasn't until years later that I found out what had really happened—the boat rides had ended. I hadn't thought about the boat for twenty years, until I saw that photo on the wall in Renee's house. I'd asked her about it, and she said that it had been given to her as part of the "settlement." A cousin had actually used it as a shrimp boat, not a party boat, and she and Tyler used to go out on it some. Beyond that, I'd had no idea what had happened to it.

But it was here now, refurbished and looking like the kind of place that a guy who was making a lot of money in the stripper and security business would enjoy as a weekend getaway. Yes, indeed. It still had the distinctive twin masts for holding nets, but it was freshly painted. The glimpses we could see of the cockpit showed gleaming, varnished wood that had been grayed with age and salt the last time I'd seen it, a million years ago. But it still had the same name, which was how Ginny was able to track it: *Burton's Landing*. My father had worshipped *All the King's Men*, memorizing long passages and reciting them at random, usually embarrassing moments, when the drink and his mood blended, a not infrequent occurrence. His favorite passage:

> The law is like a single-bed blanket on a double bed and three folks in the bed and a cold night. There ain't ever enough blanket to cover the case, no matter how much pulling and hauling, and somebody is always going to nigh catch pneumonia. Hell, the law is like the pants you bought last year for a growing boy, but it is always this year and the seams are popped and the shank bone's to the breeze. The law is always too short and too tight for growing humankind.

I knew Tyler drove an old Dodge Charger he had restored, but I didn't see it anywhere. "What do you think we should do?" I asked Jessie as we sat in her Mustang, looking at the boat bobbing gently at the dock.

"Simple," she said. "We see if he's here." She got out with the shotgun but stuffed it under the front seat when she saw a group of fishermen carrying ice from the little marina office to their boats. Dressed in jeans, black cowboy boots, and a white silk blouse, she already looked out of place without adding an assault weapon as an accessory. She reached inside the glove compartment and took out the Glock, jamming it in the small of her back, covered by her blouse.

I had to smile. "You look . . . fantastic," I said. She did a sort of curtsy.

When we got to the plank connecting *Burton's Landing* to the dock, I yelled, "Hey, Tyler, it's J.D." And when Jessie jabbed me in the ribs, I added, "And Jessie."

"Good to give him warning so he can set the fuse on the bomb," Jessie mumbled. "More sporting that way." Then she walked onto the boat.

It was cool and dark inside the boat's cabin, the air conditioning humming softly. It was decorated like something out of *Yachting* magazine, copies of which I'd seen lying around the private aviation terminals we used for Air Force Two (a piece-of-shit old plane, by the way, louder than a cheap tractor)—that is, except for the Confederate flag hanging on the wall. Confederate flags never made it into *Yachting*. There was a built-in flat-screen TV set into a wall of polished mahogany. A bar held expensive liquor. And framed on the wall was the same photo I'd seen at Renee's: Tyler and his army buddies, including Somerfield George. Jessie stared, transfixed.

"He was so pretty," she said, reaching out to touch him.

By the DVD player we found a stack of Confederate Dead CDs, each produced with nihilistic Hieronymus Bosch graphics. That was it: a weekend hideaway for stressed executives looking to kick back with a bit of funky luxury. Jessie pulled up the cushions in the built-in couch. "Oh boy," she said, staring down.

"What?" I figured she must have found a cache of explosives of some sort. I looked over her shoulder. A tiny woman's thong in bright red lay under the cushion. "Trophy?" Jessie asked. "Or just something the cleaning lady missed?" She started to reach for it and I slammed the cushion back down.

"No," I said, shaking my head. "Just no."

We walked back out into the bright sun. It was peaceful and brought me back to the time I'd spent on bayous and Lake Pontchartrain. Gulls swooped overhead and pelicans dove for fish. It was hard to imagine the madness of the Superdome. The entire political world, my world, would be talking about what had happened to poor J. D. Callahan and how J.D. screwed the pooch again. Everybody would be shaking their head and laughing at me, even those I'd hired and who owed me everything. How many would stand up for me? Ginny would. How many others?

"What?" Jessie asked me.

"What?"

"What are you thinking about? You had a death stare."

I shook my head, trying to clear the thoughts.

"Don't do that male asshole thing of saying everything is okay. You're not that good at it. I've had boyfriends who were total pros."

Boyfriends? Did that mean I was a boyfriend? We got into her car. "Jesus, it's hot in here," I said. And then I saw Tyler rise up from the backseat holding Jessie's shotgun.

"Jesus fuck!" Jessie yelled, turning to face Tyler. "What the hell are you doing?"

"Quit yelling," Tyler said, then he laughed. "Where'd you get this bad boy, J.D.? This is some serious shit."

"It's mine," Jessie said.

"Nice," Tyler said, then handed it to Jessie. She grabbed it and then swiveled around and tried to angle the shotgun toward Tyler.

"You stupid motherfucker! You scared the shit out of me!" she shouted.

Tyler shrugged, pushing the barrel aside. "You tell anybody else about the boat?" he asked.

"That's it?" Jessie yelled. "No apology?"

I could see Tyler looking at me through the rearview mirror. "Is she always like this?" he asked.

Jessie pumped the shotgun and aimed it at him. It didn't seem to bother him. "Tyler, what are you doing?" I asked.

He didn't say anything but got out of the car and walked toward his boat. "Is he crazy?" Jessie asked. Tyler turned and motioned for us to follow him. "He is fucking crazy," Jessie said. We got out of the car and followed him. I didn't try to convince Jessie not to bring the shotgun.

Tyler had Fox News playing silently in the background and was making coffee. One of the Fox blondes was interviewing Eddie Basha. "You're Jessie, that newspaper chick," Tyler said when we walked into the cabin. "I read your stuff. I like it. You want some coffee?"

The total normalcy of the moment was completely abnormal. Jessie looked at me. "Sure," she said. "Black."

Tyler handed her a mug of coffee. "You're hot. You ever think of dancing?"

For a second I was afraid she would throw her coffee at Tyler, but she shook her head. "I'm too shy."

He collapsed back on the bench couch, and suddenly he looked very, very tired. "I heard you got shit-canned," he said to me. I nodded.

"Oh, fuck," Jessie said softly. "Oh, fuck." She was staring at the television. They had cut from inside the Superdome to a confused scene that felt terribly familiar. It was outside a Hampton

Inn in Metairie. I knew it because the Alabama delegation was staying there and had complained that the out-of-the-way location was payback for supporting Armstrong George. Which was true. Behind it was a desolate parking lot that had once been a used-car dealership. In the middle of it sat what had once been a car, burning.

"Well, I'll be damned," Tyler said from the couch. "I'll be damned."

Jessie and I looked at him. "It's that George kid, right?" I asked. "He got you to do this."

"Somerfield?" Tyler said. "He's hopeless. Worse than hopeless." He sighed. "It's Tommy. Crazy fucking Tommy." He got up and picked up the photo from his army days. "Crazy fucking Tommy."

Tyler had a look on his face that I'd never seen before. His usual ironic smirk faded and he suddenly looked very young, scared, and sad. While the scene at the newest bombing played out silently on the television, Tyler began to talk. And he kept on talking until he had told us everything.

There had been a group of them who became pals at Fort Benning basic training. They had this skinhead thing in common, liked the same music, and loved the army for all its toys: cool guns, high explosives. They even liked some of the discipline. Somerfield George was sort of a big deal since his dad was governor of Colorado. They talked a lot about becoming mercenaries when they got out: make a big score, knock off some island, like those South African mercs. Tommy Mayfield was the craziest. It wasn't like he was some kind of southern racist, he was just an Irish Catholic mutt from Erie, Pennsylvania. But he was the only one who had a problem with blacks or Puerto Ricans. They loved the idea of the Confederacy and watched every Civil War video they could download. Tommy was always trying to egg Somerfield on about how he bet his father really didn't like those lazy scumbag minorities either, he just couldn't come out and say it, right? Somerfield would tell him he was crazy. More than anything, they loved to get high and blow up cool stuff, like old cars. That's what they were doing when Tyler got himself scorched and blown half to hell. Just high and messing around blowing up an abandoned bus out in the woods. It had been Somerfield's fault, actually. He was the one who had screwed up the detonation.

The army didn't know what to do with them after that, but they didn't want to pick a fight with a governor's son. So they just looked the other way and called it a "training accident." Afterward, while Tyler was still going through the first of a dozen operations, their little group started to fall apart. Only crazy Tommy still talked about trying to get hired as a mercenary. The rest were like kids who were playing Cowboys and Indians and one day somebody put in real bullets and arrows and scared the crap out of everybody. Somerfield got out of the military and went to work for his dad. Tyler did his strip club/ security service gig. They drifted apart, like any other group of guys who were close in the military or college and swore they'd always be close but, of course, it didn't end up that way. It never did. They still loved the same music.

"Then about six months ago, I'm at the club, and fucking Tommy Mayfield walks in. Back from the dead," Tyler said, and looked at me. "Just like you, big brother who isn't a brother. And just like you, he was all jacked up about Armstrong George. All this shit about how he could be president and we had to help him."

"Help?" I asked. "By doing what?"

Tyler held up his hand. He was going to tell this in his own time. "You think I'm batshit crazy—don't try to fucking deny it—but let me tell you, Tommy Mayfield was really batshit crazy. I play it up because it freaks people out and gives me an edge and maybe I *am* a little wacked. But he was loony tunes. Said he was trying to get in touch with Somerfield and couldn't reach him. Wanted me to help. I bought him a lap dance and told him to relax and chill out. When he left, I called Somerfield and told him Tommy was fucking crazy and out there looking for him."

"You called Somerfield?" I said. "You had his number?"

Tyler looked at me, head cocked with a flash of anger in his eyes. "A guy fucks up and blows you up, the least he can do is call back. And Somerfield isn't a bad dude. Just weak. He told me he'd look out for Tommy. That was it. I figured Tommy was off being crazy Tommy until he called me a few days before you came to see me. Told me he was going to help Armstrong. Just watch."

"Before the first bomb," I said.

"Yep."

"So what the fuck did you do?" Jessie demanded. "Just sit back and wait for it to happen?"

"Fuck you," Tyler said tiredly. "I didn't know what he'd do."

"Until he did it," I said. "Then you could have gone to the cops."

"I didn't know for sure."

"But you know now?" Jessie laughed. "Gimme a fucking break."

"It was the song. He posted it."

Tyler pulled out his phone and brought up a website: ConfederateDead.com. "It's the site we had for the band. We would post tracks and lyrics we were working with. It was linked to a Dropbox account to back everything up. Tommy posted this a couple of days ago. It was laid down at one of the gigs we played at some shitkicker club. I never liked this mix but it was the version he loved." He tapped his phone:

Racial pride ain't no racist hate.
Cops beat down, no it's not too late.
On the news, in the streets,
Doin' it right, still take heat.
Point a finger,
Truth don't matter,
Got a gun.
Get it done.
Whole world's gone crazy.
We're losin power but it just won't last.
Screw bodycam. Change is comin and it's comin fast.
Babies in the crib
lyin in wait.
grow up to game the system,
But it ain't too late.
Clock strikes. Time ticks.
Hold on. Don't quit.
Turn back time to when America was goin' strong.

Keep the faith. Do what's right because it's all gone wrong.

Our walk, long walk. Our fight.

Get yourself straight. Get it right.

We're losin power but it just won't last.

Screw bodycam. Change is comin and it's comin fast.

"Jesus Christ," Jessie yelled, grabbing Tyler's phone. "That is the worst piece of shit."

Tyler laughed but looked almost hurt. "That was our best song. Everybody loved it. 'Death Sunrise.' I love that name."

"Tyler," Jessie said, "trust me. This song is why you are in the tittie bar business and not a famous rock star."

Tyler shrugged. "This was Tommy's way of saying he was going to fuck things up. I know it was. I know Tommy. It's how he thinks. The only people who still go on this site are me, Somerfield, and Tommy. We're the only ones with the password. He's talking to us. He wants Somerfield to know he's trying to help his old man."

"That's insane," Jessie said.

"But why'd you run here?" I asked. "Why didn't you just go to the cops?"

Tyler looked at me like I was drooling. "I run a strip club. I have thugs who work for me we call 'security contractors.' I pay off cops, city officials, and every kind of inspector. I was into the big bang-bang stuff in the army and there are emails out there where we were talking shit about going mercenary. I look like a freak. My mother was a fourteen-year-old babysitter and there's no father listed on my birth certificate. You know that? 'Father unknown' is what it says. I checked."

I hadn't known that and was suddenly ashamed that I'd never checked or asked.

"You know what the fuck would happen to me if I called the cops and said, 'Hey, this old pal of mine I used to blow shit up with may be blowing up some shit around town but I don't have anything to do with it'? And say I did tell them, you think they would be any better at finding crazy Tommy than they are at stopping these bombs? You've got every kind of cop you ever heard of and a bunch you didn't know existed in town and they can't stop Tommy. So no, I didn't call the cops."

Tyler stood up and looked out the cabin window. An NOPD cruiser was driving right toward the boat. He turned around and with one quick move grabbed the shotgun from Jessie. "What the hell?" she yelled, as he spun her around and pulled out the Glock she had stuck in the back of her pants.

"Jesus," Tyler said. "You called the cops. That was really god-damn stupid." Then he relaxed and started to laugh. It was that half-crazed laugh I'd heard in the club the first time I visited him. "It's our brother," he said to me. "And that football buddy of his."

Tyler opened the door and pointed the shotgun at them.

"Goddamn it!" Walter shouted.

Tyler laughed and lowered the gun, and just as he was turning around Jessie kicked him hard in the balls. He doubled over, groaning. Jessie grabbed the shotgun and the Glock. Walter and Paul came on board and looked down into the cabin.

"Oh Christ," Paul said. "It's Annie Oakley again. Every time I see you, you've got another gun." He looked down at Tyler, who was lying on the floor, holding his crotch. "How's it hanging, bro?" He looked around the boat and whistled. "Sweet. And you never invited me? What the hell happened to family ties?"

Walter pushed Paul into the cabin and shut the door. "Shut up and listen," he said. In the distance we could hear a helicopter. "That's Joey Francis's boys. They are looking for this guy." He pointed to Tyler, who was just getting up. "And if we can find this boat, they sure as hell can."

"Jesus," Tyler moaned, then laughed that crazy laugh. "That hurt like a bastard."

Walter listened to his police radio through an earpiece. "We really should go. Now."

We hurried off the boat. I started to walk back to Jessie's car. "Hey," Walter yelled, "in here." He opened the trunk of his NOPD cruiser and motioned to Tyler and me to get in.

"Are you kidding?" Tyler asked, but then we heard the helicopter again and we both got in. It was terrible and crowded, and Tyler smelled like fear. I probably did too. I pulled out my phone and dialed Paul in the front seat.

"Where are we going?" I asked.

"Shut up," he said as we both heard sirens. In a minute the car stopped, and then I heard Joey Francis talking to Walter.

"Boat's empty," Walter said. "Just checked it out."

"Did you, now? And you brought your own reporter?"

Jessie was following in her car.

"Sure did," Walter said. "If I busted the bastard, I wanted to get all the credit."

Francis laughed. "Honest, at least. What a fucking mess."

"Yep."

"Walter, look, if you're fucking with me, just remember I can fuck you worse. Okay? And don't associate with known gambling degenerates. It's bad for the department's reputation."

"Good to see you too," Paul said.

In a minute we were moving. "Tyler," I whispered, and then I realized that he was snoring. Snoring. The guy was asleep. I tried to count back how many hours it had been since I'd been the campaign manager for the vice president of the United States. Now I was in the trunk of a cop car with my strange quasi-brother, on the run from the FBI. It had been humiliating with Sandra, but this was far worse.

The car stopped, and the trunk opened. Paul looked down at us. "Is he really asleep?" He laughed, shaking Tyler, who woke with a start. "Easy, tiger."

I crawled out of the trunk and looked around. We were parked in a small garage. Just as I was about to ask where we were, Tobias Green opened the door that led into the house. "First time I ever was glad to see a police car at my house. Come on in."

Tobias's house was a cross between a mid-seventies bachelor pad and a civil rights museum.

"Good God," Jessie said. "That's a disco ball." She jumped up and touched the silver ball. "This is like Barry White's love nest."

"Barry was here more than once," Tobias said. "I introduced him to some fine local talent."

"Is he kidding?" Jessie asked me.

Tyler was the last one to come in from the garage. When Tobias saw him he smiled and moved straight to him and wrapped him in a big hug. I could see Tyler's confused look over Tobias's bony shoulder. Tobias held Tyler at arm's length and said, "It's really good to see you, Tyler. I want you to know something. Your father was a great man. He wasn't a perfect man, but he was a great man."

Tyler looked confused, then his face softened. "Yeah, well, thanks."

"I've got an idea," I said. "This Confederate Dead site, you can post to it, right?"

Tyler nodded.

"And you think your pal Tommy is checking it?"

"Who's Tommy?" Walter asked.

"Oh God," Jessie moaned. "You have any beer?" she asked Tobias.

"A pretty girl asks for a beer in this house, she—"

"Oh Jesus fuck," Jessie said, "just get me a beer. Please."

"He's checking the site. I know he is," Tyler said.

"So you send him a message. But do it as Somerfield. Tell him he wants to meet him. Tell him that you told him what he was doing and he wants to meet."

Tyler thought for a moment. "I could do that. He'd do anything to see Somerfield." He nodded his head. "It's not stupid," he said, and pulled out his phone.

While Jessie sat at Tobias's kitchen counter drinking beer and trying to explain to Walter, Paul, and Tobias what Tyler had told us about Tommy, Tyler signed on to the Confederate Dead site. He left a message for Tommy that read, "Zolly, cavalry still rides. Bless you. Meet at Founders House to talk next raid? Mosby."

"Zolly, Mosby? Founders House?" I asked.

Tyler looked embarrassed, which was a strange thing for him. "We all took names of Confederate cavalry generals. Tommy is Felix Zollicoffer. Somerfield is John Mosby. I'm Jeb—Jeb Stuart. It's stupid, I know." He sighed. "Founders House is—"

"Beauvoir," I said. "Jeff Davis's house."

Tyler nodded. "Did you ever play Dungeons and Dragons?" he asked.

"God no."

"We had our own world like that but with the Confederacy." He thought for a moment. "Stupid."

It took half an hour for Tommy—Zolly—to reply. While we were waiting, I watched the news of the convention. It was humiliating to be reduced to getting news like a regular civilian. The convention had called a suspension for a day after the car bombing at the motel. More delegates were leaving town. I knew that Eddie would be going crazy trying to track which delegates were leaving, who the alternates were, and what it would do to our hard count. *His* hard count. The official delegate count for Vice President Hilda Smith, which now most definitely was not *our* hard count. It was another perfect Armstrong George moment. He was promising that his New Bill of Rights would protect Americans and that a strong leader would guarantee the first right: the right of personal safety. He blamed the bombing on "terrorists who threaten our democracy and are opposed to my strong stance against the criminals and illegals in our society." That he didn't have any particular evidence for this didn't seem to bother anyone.

I called Paul Hendricks on his cell. "Jesus, is this the dead man talking?" he said when he answered.

"And like a dead man, I want this OTR, good?" I knew he'd agree to off the record. He might even stick to it, though that was always a crapshoot.

"From the grave," he said. "What you got?"

I told him that I'd heard he was going to report that some of the delegates loyal to Hilda Smith were thinking about defecting to Armstrong George, and I'd been checking around and didn't think there was anything to it. Not a word of that was true, but I knew how he would play it.

"I've been working on that," he said coyly. "You really don't think there's anything to it?"

"It's bullshit," I said. "Their biggest complaint was that Eddie wasn't calling them back and stroking them enough, but I told them to give the guy a break, he was swamped."

"Got it," Hendricks said. "Don't suppose you want to give me some names of who was calling you?" I named two delegate chairmen who I knew hated Hendricks and would never talk to him. "So look, J.D., what's the story with you? All kinds of rumors going around. Why don't you give it to me and let me break it with your side of the story?"

"Let's just say I had an issue with some stuff in the campaign. So we parted ways. Complicated. But I'll make a deal. Don't do anything, and when it's time I'll give you the exclusive. Cool?"

He snapped at that like a starving man offered bread. Just like I knew he would.

Within five minutes, Paul Hendricks was reporting that he had confirmation from party chairmen loyal to Vice President Hilda Smith that they were facing defections. Among the problems was lack of response from Eddie Basha, the new acting campaign manager for the vice president. It was exactly what I knew he would do. Fuck you, Eddie Basha.

The message came in from "Zolly" asking if "Mosby" could meet tomorrow at the Founders House at the usual time. Tyler wrote back as Mosby that he would be there.

"The usual time?" I asked.

"That's nine twenty-four in the morning. When Pickett launched his charge. We used to text each other at that exact time on July Fourth every year."

"You got to be fucking kidding me," Jessie said. Tyler shrugged.

"You really think he will show?" Walter asked.

"He'll be there," Tyler said.

"You remember our deal," Walter said to me.

"What deal?" Jessie and Tyler asked together.

I waved it off. "Walter wants credit for any arrests. Don't you need to bring in some help?"

"It's called backup," Jessie said.

"Is she always such a bitch?" Tyler asked.

"Pretty much," Jessie answered.

"We're talking one crazy guy?" Walter said. "No, I think I can handle it."

Tyler asked, "What will happen to Tommy?"

"Tyler," Tobias said in his deepest voice, "he needs help. This acting out is a cry for help."

"Acting out?" Jessie said. "Acting out is when you get stoned on your class trip. This is a whole level above 'acting out.'"

Tobias looked at Jessie, smiling broadly. "You are a magnificent creature."

"Oh God," Jessie said. "Now it's the Wild Kingdom."

Chapter

★

Ten

I'D DRIVEN PAST BEAUVOIR, a big white house facing the Gulf, hundreds of times, but I'd never been inside. "This place really means something to you?" I asked Tyler when we were driving over early the next morning. It was just the two of us in Tobias's old Lincoln Continental. It drove like a boat floating on air. It took a full half turn of the steering wheel to get any response, but it was comfortable like a deep-cushioned couch.

"Can you imagine a bigger fuck-you to the government than seceding and starting your own country? That's why we love it. It's not all that slavery bullshit. It's just the balls to walk away and say you won't put up with the bullshit any longer. You spend some time in the army and that has a lot of appeal. Just the biggest screw-the-system protest in the history of the country."

"Protest? Are you out of your mind? Hundreds of thousands slaughtered?"

"Dude, you don't get it. Forty thousand fucking people die in car crashes every year driving around America. What do we say? 'As goes Detroit, so goes America.' Cars are the ultimate killing machines and we love 'em. Even this piece of shit. It's the identity."

He wasn't dumb. I had to give him that. He had Powell's and Renee's brains, and that was a powerful gene match. "Look," I said, "Paul and I, we fucked up. I fucked up, anyway. We shouldn't have disappeared on you and your mom. We should have tried to be there more."

"Oh, please," Tyler said. "Don't get sensitive on me. I hate sensitive. But thanks, okay?"

We rode in silence for a while, the Gulf to our right, Tobias's car floating along the road. Behind us were Walter and Paul in Paul's car and Jessie in her own. She had wanted to bring her car and Walter figured that the Joey Francis crowd might be tracking his cruiser. It was quite a little caravan we had going.

"You're trying," Tyler finally said. "I give you that. And it's not that I think you're a total shit. But what you have to understand, sort-of brother of mine, is that my mother and I had zero desire to have anything to do with anybody named Callahan. You got that? You disgusted us. It wasn't that you didn't come around to us; we were trying to forget that we ever knew anybody named Callahan. You were just a bunch of entitled fucks who stumbled through the world fucking things up for other people and thinking you were morally superior. And I'm not real sure that much has changed. My mom's too nice to say it and I never gave enough shits to track you down to tell you, but that you didn't realize it just sort of proves the point, right? You think you can play with people. That's what this whole politics thing is to you, right? A way to feel powerful. Master of time and space. You'll pull the strings and decide who gets to be president. Our Tommy pal is sick, no doubt about it, but you think he and you are that far apart?"

We didn't say anything else until we got a half block away from

Beauvoir. We parked at a Waffle House just off the beach. The parking lot was half filled with the usual combination of tourists and locals, some clearly coming down from all-night gambling sprees at the nearby casinos. Walter tried to take charge, but no one really took him seriously.

"So you drive," he said, pointing to Tyler, "and then we wait for your text that he's there. And then we come in."

"Do you think that Waffle House coffee is drinkable?" Jessie asked, and that's all anyone said. Tyler drove off. It was nine fifteen when Tyler left. I went inside the Waffle House with Jessie and ordered coffee. "I don't think I've ever been in one of these sober," she said. "Or when it was daylight." I thought about it and realized I hadn't either. Waffle Houses were ritual last stops after nights of partying.

"Holy fuck," she said.

"Hey, there are kids in here," said a woman sitting in a nearby booth with two young kids. Both were giggling.

Jessie dragged me outside by the arm and pointed down the street at a car. It was one of those awful electric GM things that the convention was using. "Somerfield fucking George just drove by," she said.

"What?"

Walter and Paul were sitting in Paul's car arguing over the 1999 LSU–Ole Miss game and why they had lost. When they saw us running toward Jessie's car, Walter jumped out. "What?"

"Somerfield," I yelled. "He drove past."

Ahead we could see the electric car pulling in to the mostly empty Beauvoir parking lot. "What do I do?" Jessie asked, as she drove slowly ahead.

I shrugged. "Park, I guess."

Somerfield had parked next to Tobias's car. We pulled in as far away as possible and Walter and Paul parked next to us. Then we sat there, not sure what to do. There had been no text from Tyler. I sent him a text and waited. Nothing.

I got out and walked over to Paul's car. "What do we do?"

"You sure it was Somerfield?" Paul asked.

"Jessie was. And that's a convention car."

I turned toward the brick path that led to the entrance. "I'll text you or call," I said over my shoulder. In an instant, Jessie was beside me. "No, please. Let me just do this," I said, and to my surprise, she stopped.

"Don't fuck up," she said, turning back to the car.

Inside I paid ten bucks to a middle-aged woman in a Civil War–era hoop skirt. She handed me a pamphlet, *The Confederate Summer White House.* I thought that was odd, calling the house that was used by the president of the rebellion against the White House the same name, but I suppose it made it easier for people to grasp. The house had high ceilings and hardwood floors, rebuilt after it was almost leveled during Katrina. I looked through all the rooms and found only a few French Canadian tourists. Then I started to walk out the front door to look at the Gulf and heard Tyler talking on the porch.

"Tommy, look, dude, you got to chill."

Then a high voice I didn't recognize, which I knew had to be Tommy. He sounded like he was about to cry. "You wanted me to do this. I did it for your old man. Everybody on television says it's helping him."

"Come on, Tommy, it wasn't like that," Somerfield said.

"You talked to Tommy?" Tyler asked. "You guys talked, Tommy?"

"I met him before the convention," Tommy said. "Come on, man, don't act like that."

"We met for old times' sake. He got in touch, and I didn't want to be an asshole," Somerfield said. "Tommy, look, this is serious shit."

"I was trying to help your old man. He's like us."

"You know what I think?" Tyler said, and he had that hot edge to his voice I knew so well. "I think Tommy is telling the truth and you're lying, Somer. I think Tommy did just what you wanted him to. And then you saw I posted that message and you freaked out."

"You didn't post that?" Tommy asked.

"Sure I did," Somerfield said. "I just wanted to see you and make sure you were okay."

"Gimme a break," Tyler said.

"What do you want me to do?" Tommy asked in a tired voice.

"You want to help my dad? You know what would really help, would clinch this whole deal, is if you let it out that you blew up that stuff to help Hilda Smith. Like you were helping her frame my dad."

"Oh, for Christ's sake," Tyler said. "Nobody would believe that."

"I don't think so," Tommy said, sighing. "I didn't think you'd fuck me, Somer. I really didn't. I'll leave you guys alone now."

I could hear Tommy start to walk away. "Don't do that, Tommy," Somerfield said. "Come on with me. We can talk to my dad about all of this."

"We can do that?" Tommy asked.

"He's fucking you again," Tyler said. "Jesus Christ. Don't believe anything he says."

"Call your dad," Tommy said. "Call him and put him on the phone with me."

"I can't do that now, Tommy. Come on."

I heard Tommy walking away. "I gotta go now," he said.

"Let me go with you, Tommy," Somerfield said.

I stepped out the rest of the way onto the porch. Tyler saw me, but Somerfield was walking away, his arm around Tommy. I could still hear them talking.

"I'm not stupid, Somer. But I thought you would be a stand-up guy."

"Come on, Tommy. Don't be like that."

Tommy looked at Somerfield like a lover who had just been jilted. "Is your dad going to win?" Somerfield brightened and nodded. "And you still won't have anything to do with me, right?"

"Come on, Tommy."

I went back inside while they walked around the big house to the parking lot. I called Walter on his cell phone. "Tommy's coming around with Somerfield. Don't do anything now. You don't want Somerfield to see you. Shoot some video of him with Tommy on your phone." Walter started to argue, but I hung up.

When I got back outside, Tommy and Somerfield were standing by an old Honda Accord that belonged to Tommy. Tyler walked over to me, and it seemed that his awkward, off-center walk was more pronounced than ever. "What's going on?" I said.

"Fucking Somerfield. I believe Tommy. I think he put him up to this shit. Somerfield saw what I posted and showed up here."

Somerfield turned and left Tommy standing by his car. When

he saw me standing with Tyler, he shook his head and walked over.

"What a goddamn mess," Somerfield said.

"Nice to see you," I said.

"What the hell were you doing, Somerfield?" Tyler said. "You know Tommy's a basket case. What were you fucking around with him for?"

"Truth?" He started to answer but stopped. "What are we going to do about Tommy?"

"Do?" Tyler asked.

"We need to take care of him."

"You mean hush him up," I said. I looked over Somerfield's shoulder. Tommy was still leaning against the car, staring down at his phone.

"What a mess," Somerfield said. "Look, you got fired, right?" he asked me.

I shrugged. "What's that got to do with this?"

"Can we just agree that if I can talk Tommy into getting some kind of help, we won't call in the dogs?"

Tyler looked at me. All of a sudden, I really didn't care. Seeing how pathetic and broken Tommy had looked, it was hard to argue that he should be dragged in front of the country and humiliated. Or thrown in jail. Somerfield was right. He did need help. I was running out of hate.

"Sure," I said. "Go talk to him."

We watched him walk over to talk to Tommy. From across the parking lot, Walter, Paul, and Jessie were looking at us, wondering what was going on.

"You're going soft," Tyler said.

"So are you," I said.

Tommy and Somerfield got in the car. "They going to run out on us?" I asked, not really caring.

"I doubt it. Probably just talking in the car."

Jessie Fenestra was the hottest reporter on the planet. She had the perfect scoop, not one that depended on a source, because she *was* the source, an eyewitness to the—as it was now being called everywhere—"fiery deaths" of Somerfield George and Tommy Mayfield. And she had video. Goddamn Jessie had shot it all on her iPhone. She had the two of them walking together. Then the explosion.

Most of the even quasi-legit news outlets on cable and broadcast didn't run the full video, on the pretense that the public should be spared the gruesome spectacle of two people blowing up in a ball of fire. What a joke. Online, the video damn near broke the Internet. If there had only been a little sex in it, the clip would have been the ultimate snuff film.

For a few minutes after the explosion, while waiting for the cavalcade of emergency vehicles, we had argued about what had really happened. Not that it wasn't clear that both Tommy and Somerfield were still smoldering in the heap down at the end of the parking lot, but had it been an accident, or had Tommy blown up the car on purpose?

Tyler was adamant. "Tommy was a pro. No way he would have screwed up enough to blow up his own car by accident."

But Jessie answered the question. "Look," she said, holding up her phone with the video.

"No, thanks, I saw it," Tyler said.

"Watch," she said, and then she played back the video in slow motion, freezing it just before the explosion. "There," she said, with a touch of glee that only a reporter with a scoop could muster after watching two people being blown up. We crowded around her phone as she cupped it to shade it from the bright sun. And there it was: just before the explosion, Tommy's left hand came out the window with an upraised middle finger to the sky.

"Jesus," Tyler said. "He went out with a big fuck-you."

Tyler wandered off, and I followed him. He was looking out at the Gulf, just across the beachfront highway. His usual mad glint was gone, replaced with a deep sadness. He suddenly looked a lot older. "Tommy," he said. "I really let him down. I should have done something. Anything." He shook his head. "To go out that way."

Paul walked up to us. I tried to remember when the last time was that the three of us had been together without anyone else around, and it hit me that this might have been the first time. Paul put his big arm around Tyler, and when Tyler tried to pull back, he just pulled him in closer and hugged him.

Jessie had the biggest story in the country, but that didn't mean there wasn't room for one more hot item. Before I called Paul Hendricks, I checked with Sandy Morrison and laid the track for the express train that was about to leave the station. She listened, understood immediately, and signed off with "I love you, J. D. Callahan. You are almost as evil as I am." I took it as a compliment.

Paul Hendricks assumed that I was calling about the bombing, and it took a moment to get him to focus. "Hendricks," I said, "I've got a huge scoop for you if you will just shut the fuck up and listen." He did. I explained to him how Eddie Basha had gone behind Hilda Smith's back and planted the fake push poll calls about abortion that were intended to smear her. "I thought it was crazy and didn't believe it at first," I said, then gave him Sandy Morrison's number to confirm it. "You got to keep her out of it, but on background she'll talk to you. It wasn't her idea. She's just a vendor who was hired to do it. Don't blame her."

"Is this why you left the campaign?" Hendricks asked.

"I don't want to go into that. But I know Hilda Smith doesn't know a damn thing about this. She deserves better." That last might have been a bit much coming from me, but Hendricks was already thinking how great the story would be. For him. For his career. He was only worried about one thing. "This is exclusive, right?"

Within twenty-four hours, Joey Francis was on his way to becoming famous as "the FBI agent uncovering the secrets behind the mystery bombers," as *The New York Times* put it. And right beside him, at least in most stories, was Walter Robinson, "the former football star turned New Orleans police detective who had been on the trail of the bomber when he exploded." It hadn't been really difficult to talk Joey Francis into including Walter and sharing the spotlight. "It's like this, Francis," Walter had said. "You don't have shit, and you look like the fucking idiot who couldn't find a bomber in your own backyard. Plus, you don't know a damn thing about this guy Tommy. I do. So you either look like a moron or a genius FBI go-getter, it's up to you. But the last one comes with me."

Francis stuck out his hand and said one word: "Partner."

That was right before I got the first call from Hilda Smith asking me to come back to the campaign. She was reeling from hearing the news about Eddie Basha's involvement in the abortion push polling and had just fired him. "I hear Armstrong George is withdrawing," she said. "Terrible tragedy with his son. He must have been a very disturbed soul. I need you to win the general, J.D. I can't do it without you."

I told her I'd think about it, but I knew what I wanted to do. I made one call to Ginny and asked her if she'd like to run a presidential campaign. "Fuck yes," she said. "For whom?" I told her what was going on and that I was going to get Hilda Smith to hire her. "You're not going to come back?" she asked, shocked, but before I could get the words out that I wasn't, she was already moving on in her head. "I know how to win this thing," she said. "We can kill that piece-of-shit Democrat."

"There you go. Kill 'em all and let God sort it out."

And that's how I ended up running Paul Callahan's campaign for public service commissioner. It's looking pretty good. We had a monster fundraiser at Tyler's strip club that set the record for a single event in Louisiana. Who could have guessed that a bunch of rich men would actually like the idea of having a legitimate reason to go to a strip club? What a shock. Tobias Green is the campaign chairman, and I'm pretty sure he's getting it on with our best intern from Tulane, who is quite a number. Tobias says they have a "harmonic convergence."

"I guess that means she's fun to screw," Jessie said when she heard Tobias's description. Amazon and I had both agreed to put the idea of a TV show on hold, at least until the election. Lately I've been thinking it wasn't such a good idea. Jessie got a nice six-figure advance for the inside story on "the mad bombers"

Tommy and Somerfield and was working like a fiend to finish the book. Sometimes I'd wake up at four a.m. and she'd still be out in the living room, pacing and writing. It never bothered me, and I liked hearing her sounds. I'd moved in right after the bombing, when Hilda had left town as the Republican nominee for president. We're both busy, her with the book and me with Paul's campaign, but on Sundays she likes to take me out to her favorite shooting range across the Causeway and shoot the hell out of anything she can get her hands on. I can't shoot for a damn next to her, but I'm getting better. Tyler joins us sometimes, and the two of them duel it out. Jessie beats him a lot, but Tyler tells me, when she's not listening, that he lets her win. I'm not sure I believe it.

Next Sunday we plan to drive out to see Tyler's mom. She's been a big fan of Jessie's for years and really wants to meet her. I think they might hit it off. Tyler says he's not coming, but I think he will. Jessie reminded him that they could do some shooting in his mom's backyard. And Sundays are slow at the club. Paul says he'll come. He hasn't seen Renee in years. I think it will be a nice family get-together.

For once, I really do.

A Note About the Author

Stuart Stevens is the author of six previous books, and his work has appeared in *The New York Times, The Washington Post, Esquire,* and *Outside,* among other publications. He has written extensively for television shows, including *Northern Exposure, Commander in Chief,* and *K Street.* For twenty-five years, he was the lead strategist and media consultant for some of the nation's toughest political campaigns. He attended Colorado College; Pembroke College, Oxford; Middlebury College; and UCLA film school. He is a former fellow of the American Film Institute. This is his second novel.

A Note on the Type

The text of this book was set in Sabon, a typeface designed by Jan Tschichold (1902–1974), the well-known German typographer. Designed in 1966 and based on the original designs by Claude Garamond (ca. 1480–1561), Sabon was named for the punch cutter Jacques Sabon, who brought Garamond's matrices to Frankfurt.

Composed by North Market Street Graphics,
Lancaster, Pennsylvania

Printed and bound by Berryville Graphics,
Berryville, Virginia

Designed by M. Kristen Bearse